DANCE
WITH THE
DEVILS

Also by Paul Frisby

Black Comedy

Black Tie

Identity Theft

Tartan Identity

Identity and Mr Maslow

The Dog Catcher from Keister North

Not My Circus Not My Clowns

DANCE
WITH THE
DEVILS

Paul Frisby

ASHWOOD
PUBLISHING

Copyright ©Paul Frisby 2024

All rights reserved. Apart from as permitted under Australian copyright law, no part of this book may be reproduced by any means, or used to 'train' generative artificial intelligence (AI) technologies, without the prior written permission of the author. Contact the publisher for information.

Published by Ashwood Publishing, Cradoc, Tasmania
info@ashwoodpublishing.com.au
https://ashwoodpublishing.com.au

ISBN (print) 978-0-6459137-1-2

ISBN (ebook) 978-0-6459137-6-7

This is a work of fiction. The characters, names, events and organisations in this story are fictional or are used fictitiously, and any resemblance to actual persons, businesses or organisations is entirely coincidental.

No part of this book was made using generative AI.

Set in 12/17 Minion Pro

Cover design by Susan Young. Power line image arturnichiporenko/Shutterstock; Tas devil photo Imagine Earth Photography/Shutterstock

Bible quotations contained herein are from the New Revised Standard Version Bible: Catholic Edition, copyright © 1989, 1993 National Council of the Churches of Christ in the United States of America. Used by permission. All rights reserved worldwide.

 A catalogue record for this work is available from the National Library of Australia

Chapter 1

Shit! Lachlan wrenched the wheel to the right and the Subaru leapt onto what he had hoped, correctly, was firmer ground. Some of these ruts weren't as substantial as they looked and even with an all-wheel drive, you could easily wallow and get stuck.

Lachlan Tan, MBBS (Hons) FRACGP, general practitioner and chauffeur for the day, was thankful that Omicron Medical had given him the five-year-old Forester he was driving and not a newer car. He was strongly of the belief that he was hastening it to an early grave, and it would have been a shame to do what he was doing now to one of the new ones.

Above and beyond the car's age, he did not feel as guilty about how he was treating it as he might. Needs dictated that he was driving it where he was, and in the prevailing conditions of road and weather. He had long ago learned the three rules of off-road driving: don't drive a vehicle somewhere unnecessarily if there is a safer route; don't drive a vehicle that is not capable of going where you need to go; don't drive a vehicle, however capable it is, unless you are good enough to drive it where it has to go.

He was very glad that he had not volunteered his own Tesla for the trip. The Subaru was a pool vehicle of the Omicron Medical Services company, and had no doubt carried doctors and nurses all over Tasmania as they served at the company's scattered surgeries. The synthetic grey material on the seats was marked brown and its pattern faded by exposure to ultraviolet light, and there were scratches all over the hard plastic. There was lots of hard plastic. It squeaked annoyingly and with no predictability, completely out of sympathy with the intermittent groans from the monocoque.

He had a feeling that Margaret Pursehouse, the somewhat younger nurse sitting alongside him in the front passenger seat, had feelings parallel to his own, except Margaret seemed more concerned about her own health and welfare than the potential disembowelment of the company car.

Bang! Thump. THUMP. Squeak!

Fuck. He had been forced to give the wheel another violent twist to the right, and then to the left, to avoid a large pothole, and had miscalculated. No doubt Nurse Pursehouse would be reporting on his driving skills to her friends in the company, although in his short time with Omicron he had formed the impression that she was not a mixer.

'You'd have to pay for this at Luna Park,' he quipped – partly because he felt the conditions might be showing up his limitations as a driver.

While recognising that every driver felt they were a good driver, he had been places and done things with cars and indeed heavier vehicles. He therefore felt his good opinion of his own skills was justified. His performance was not being enhanced by the diabolical quality of the road, let alone the significant weight of basic medical supplies and the tools of the general practitioner's trade, as well as their personal suitcases, which together occupied the whole of the rear of the station wagon and a roof rack that was making the thing top heavy.

I'm trying to provide some light relief, woman, and hopefully some small opportunity for personal bonding with you, my worried passenger, in the face of adversity. After all this is supposed to be something of an adventure we're sharing.

He was having trouble getting to know Nurse Pursehouse. Getting on with people was something else on which he prided himself. He fancied he was known favourably for his bedside manner. On the other hand, he recognised that many doctors who did the same were viewed by their patients as self-opinionated pains in the arse. Anyway, he had offered his passenger the opportunity to do the driving before they had set out and she had declined. She was in no position to complain that he had claimed the role of driver in a chauvinistic way or from some imagined seniority.

Lachlan Tan was sensitive to issues such as these. He should not have worried, however. Most people had trouble getting to know Margaret Pursehouse.

As a physician he was trained to be sensitive to how other people saw him. A widowed man in his late middle age, he had a lifetime's experience of the good, the bad and the ugly. Others would have probably said he had an over-developed capacity for self-criticism. He recriminated every time he made a diagnosis that turned out to be less than satisfactory, or when a treatment ended up being less than optimal. While Dr Tan was not a psychiatrist, he was a general practitioner who had been around. Experience with patients, as well as self-examination, made him aware that he knew quite a bit about guilt. Brought up in an Asian migrant family and expected to succeed, he had done so. Failure was not acceptable.

Margaret Pursehouse was obviously not in the mood to reciprocate his well-meaning attempts to lighten the atmosphere of apprehension in the car. From the occasional glance he could afford to take, Lachlan observed she was hanging on to the dashboard grab handle with her left hand with increased – well, *dedication* was a word that sprung to mind.

He also registered she was not wearing a wedding ring, which was interesting but not unusual. Nurses in their late thirties of either gender were not married for any number of reasons, and many who were of any age indeed found it easier not to wear jewellery on their hands during working hours. He did note that Nurse Pursehouse's right hand periodically grasped a silver cross she wore on a chain around her neck. He wondered, amused, whether she was anticipating an accident and having to answer to a higher authority in respect of her own guilt. It was a somewhat more significant cross than he had seen commonly around the necks of his patients. He concluded it had not been cheap.

Bonding seems to be out of the question at the moment.

'Oh fuck,' Lachlan exploded, as they came round the next corner to find a huge semitrailer plodding its way cautiously forward in front of them. If he had not been concentrating on washing off their speed without losing traction, he would have observed his passenger's disapproval of his use of the expletive.

The truck's wheels were on a wider track than theirs, and with the rain overnight and the soft ground they were on, he found he had to drive with one side of the car down in a wheel track with the opposite on the higher centre of the road, and moreover, at his now slower speed the car had lost the momentum to deal with some of the irregularities in the surface. He redoubled his concentration and put the right-hand side of the car on the high side on the basis that it was safer to give himself the better vision of what was immediately ahead. Nurse Pursehouse clutched at her cross again and her knuckles visibly whitened on the grab handle in front of her.

Overtaking was not an option. The sounder bit of the road was not that wide, and what would happen if something came the other way heavens knew – and it looked like between the two of them Nurse Pursehouse was far more likely to receive any potential communication from that direction. That was if God was a Christian of course. Lachlan was an atheist and did not have the problem of having to choose which of the many gods available was the correct one to believe in, even if he could reconcile any faith with science. *Now why would Pascal's wager spring into my mind?*

As the car slogged on, Lachlan reminded himself that what he was doing and where he was doing it was close to what he had in fact asked for. *Never ask for something, because you might get it.* This was not exactly what he had asked for, but he had wanted something new to do, something different, something less boring – and his new bosses at Omicron Medical Services had in any event not given him much chance to refuse.

Five days ago he'd been finishing up a fortnight as a locum at Devonport when the phone had rung. When he'd asked the administration manager 'Why me?' they had catalogued the criteria on which he had been selected.

'You're the new boy, you're relatively young, you're single, and you recently managed your own practice – and your CV shows you started your working life in outback Queensland, and you've been in some funny places in the Army Reserve. So, you're presumably pretty self-reliant. It's a new part-time surgery in a place called Mordbury. They're building a new power station up there and they've contracted us for medical cover. It's going to be a branch working out of Launceston, where you are based. So, unless you've caught something nasty from a patient while in Devonport, we would like you to leave next Tuesday. OK?'

Needs must when the devil drives, and they had promised him some competent help, and a patient-free day to pack the car on the Monday prior.

'Get up there, sort the place out, and have it ready to open Monday week for three or so days a week.' *No problem, no problem at all.*

Young Margaret might be competent as a nurse, but she was not a good passenger, he thought, seeing her gulp as the car tried to pull itself sideways unaided and he had to apply some firm correction. *Bugger. I hope she's not going to be sick. Vomiting patients I can cope with, vomiting nurses not. Decidedly problematical.*

Perhaps she hadn't had the sense to take a pill before they left on what was looking like a long and tedious trip. No wonder the office had strongly suggested an early start. Apparently, this was going to be par for the course for all the subsequent teams. Leave Launceston on a Monday morning; open the surgery Monday afternoon, Tuesday, Wednesday, and Thursday morning; come home on a Thursday afternoon; cover the weekend from Launceston. This first week was going to be patient free while they set things up.

Mordbury was just up the road on the map, but road maps in Tasmania were just like road maps anywhere. They didn't tell you the whole truth, and the car's GPS was even less informative. Contour lines would have helped. In the right vehicle, in the right weather, an unsealed road could be a dream run, while the same wiggling dotted red line on the map could also represent a cart track. This particular cart track led from the turn off the tarmac up a valley, which was wet and muddy. It looked on paper as if it subsequently wound around mountains, which presumably would be wet and rocky. They would have a firm surface rather than a boggy one; but the trouble with rocky mountain roads was, in his experience, that they tended to be narrow.

'Oh, shit there's another one up our arse now.'

His need for the verbalisation of his feelings was not mitigated by the perceptible stiffening of his passenger hearing his few well-chosen words.

Lachlan had checked his mirrors – there was another truck right behind them. Everyone obviously had the same idea. Get an early start in case you get stuck; and keep up your vehicle's momentum in the mud so you don't dig yourself a hole. *There is, however, such a thing as too close, much too fucking close. One misjudgement and we could be a Subaru sandwich.*

A few kilometres and some twenty minutes later the road started to rise and become firmer, which was better, except for the runnels etched into its surface where water had found its way across the direction of vehicular travel. They really tested the shock absorbers. Then there was the further not unanticipated narrowing of the track, with pinching as it switched back on itself at the end of gullies.

The little convoy in which the Subaru was embedded sped up for a bit and then slowed again. Traction was no longer much of a problem for the all-wheel drive, but the already narrow road was only just sufficient for the big trucks to negotiate – and there were starting to be a lot of bends to be negotiated. The electronics that ran the trip computer began to periodically beep their disgust at not receiving a signal. Nurse Margaret, having released her crucifix, retrieved her phone from the cup holder in which it had been parked. She looked at it in disgust. It too was seemingly intermittently losing reception; or she was looking at a larger map to see how long this torture might last.

However, she was now also showing some resolve, Lachlan reflected, with a quick glance at her profile. He liked resolve in the people he worked with.

If we do break down we'll have company. Now, if they had CB they could talk to the truckies. That would have been a bit entertaining – and he could have got that bastard behind him to drop back a bit.

It was close to an hour later when the truck in front finally gathered speed as the road became flatter and wider. Lachlan dropped the Subaru back a bit, the last thing he wanted was a broken windscreen from a flying stone, or indeed the problem of having to do an emergency stop. He was not impressed by the semi behind them not offering him the same courtesy. The chrome of the massive bull bar and radiator continued to threateningly fill his mirrors, even more so if anything with their speed quickening. *Cunt. I can assure you that if I could go faster, I fucking would.*

Margaret Pursehouse seemed to now be having less of a white-knuckle ride. She was presumably advantaged by not having a view of the threat behind them in the rear vision mirrors. At least her phone was back in the cup holder and her hand was staying off her crucifix.

They were doing sixty kilometres per hour when they passed a well-weathered sign on a no-longer-vertical wooden post on the side of the road that had once been painted white and had, in black letters, said MORDBURY; and another, a few metres further on, this time brand new and mounted on a pair of galvanised steel posts. It was endorsed with a fancy corporate logo in green and blue and said LUCIFER HOT ROCKS PTY LTD PRIVATE PROPERTY. Then suddenly they were on something that had once been a made road, in a pleasant little valley with a wide stream, which might have even been large enough to be classified as a river, running through it.

'I'm looking for a building that used to be a police station,' he said to Margaret, who almost immediately pointed across his face and shouted, 'There!'

He slowed as quickly and as much as he felt was sensible given the truck up his arse and swerved the Subaru off to the right onto the grass in front of the building, in the process extracting a blast from the air horns of the following semi.

Well, if you must be that fucking close what do you expect, dickhead!

It was a weatherboard house that had also once been a police station, if the ancient signage swinging from the eaves was anything to go by. Leaving that in place had obviously been a deliberate act of preservation. The house itself had been given a new steel roof and had been freshly painted in the corporate colours of the light green, light blue and white of Lucifer.

Extricating themselves from their seats and stretching out their stiffness, they made their way to the front door, where a very new metal sign had been screwed onto the wall. It informed them that the house was now the office of Lucifer Hot Rocks Pty Ltd Village Security, again with the corporate logo. They went in to find the interior had also been refurbished, although the old police station counter was still in place. Expecting the office to be attended, and finding it not, they simultaneously reached for the old-fashioned bell on the counter's well-worn wooden top, with Margaret demonstrating faster reflexes.

The ring elicited a gruff 'Coming!' from another room, and a tall, somewhat overweight, tanned and rather older man in a corporate uniform came out to deal with them. The badge on his bomber style jacket said Lucifer Hot Rocks Pty Ltd, and Security, and Gerry.

'I'm Gerry,' he said pointing at his badge. 'Gerry Mason. 'I know who you are, one nurse, female; one doctor, male; to be expected mid-afternoon.' He smiled. 'You're early.'

'Got an early start,' said Margaret.

'And got caught up in the convoy,' explained Lachlan. 'I'm Lachlan Tan by the way; doctor, male; and this is Margaret, nurse, female. I know, the combination is a bit archetypal. What branch of the services were you in?'

'Service Police, RAAF – it shows then?'

'You remind me a bit of my late wife. Sorry, I'll explain. She used to talk like that.'

'Late? Sorry to hear that.'

'Army nurse. Captain. Loved driving, car nut. Smashed her

old Porsche into a cow when speeding at dusk on a club trip in Queensland. No airbags, not that I think it would have helped. Died instantly by all reports. Good death.'

Lachlan suddenly realised he had sounded sadly reflective and had also run off at the mouth with too much information. This was neither the time nor the place. Why did it still stir the emotions that it did, after all he should be used to death by now? He was about to move on and was a little annoyed when Margaret cut across the conversation.

'So, what's next?' she asked.

Chapter 2

What was next was the issue of two green high-visibility vests and white helmets, followed by a short briefing on the requirement for them to be worn at all times, even in the village for the time being.

'The company is doing a rush job to get things sorted, and besides the increased traffic on the road with the drilling rig pipes being brought in, there are builders, painters and all the other trades in the village itself,' explained Gerry. 'We're even expecting the big boss tomorrow.'

He ferreted behind the counter and gave them a brochure each.

'Here you go. That's a brief intro to what's happening, and I ask that you read that tonight. There will be someone coming round from health and safety to give you a general induction tomorrow about 10 am. They'll give you a copy of the safety manual and show you the geography of the place. We start work much earlier of course but they have things to do, and no doubt you will have things to do, so we booked it in for mid-morning.'

'Fair enough. So where do we sleep?' asked Margaret, beating Lachlan to the punch.

'Well, I'll just get my vest and hat from out the back, and we'll take a short walk.'

Gerry vanished into the back room and returned wearing a vest and a helmet and carrying two umbrellas.

'I don't know if you noticed it's raining?' he asked somewhat rhetorically. 'It does that quite a bit up here when the wind is in from the northwest – or just when it seems minded to.' He smiled and handed one umbrella to Lachlan and kept one for himself. 'Follow me.'

They went out of the front door of the security office and just two houses down the street. They found themselves looking at a substantial renovated weatherboard cottage that had a very incongruous big steel-clad portable building spliced onto the side of it. With Gerry leading the way, they filed past a carport and onto the front veranda. They passed under another antique sign like the one on the former police station. This one said Dispensary. On the wall, however, was another brand-new notice, just like the one on the security building. This one identified the premises as Medical Centre.

Gerry rummaged in his pockets and found a set of keys.

'We'll get you to sign for these tomorrow, but I think you probably would appreciate the chance to unpack and get some things in order. There's a company key for the front door, that's on our key system, and an ancient one for the old dispensary inside. The third is for the internal donga door so you can lock up your medical stuff. Now the power is on, the internet is connected and if you have a play with the computers, you'll find we have a local net around the site and the village. The place has been fully redecorated and fitted out. I'm told there is one room they didn't touch when they did the renos. The house used to be the town doctor's and he also kept a small pharmacy. I suppose it's what you did or had to do in those times – the dispensary, as they called it. It's now full of bits of historic equipment they found about the place, and chemicals and stuff. They put it all in one room and left that locked up for you to deal with.'

He selected a key and opened the front door, switching the light on as he led them in. He handed the three keys to Lachlan.

'You can show yourselves around and decide who sleeps where and all that; none of my business or the company's I'm told.' His tone suggested that even so, he would personally not like to see Dr Tan and Nurse Pursehouse playing doctors and nurses.

'This is Omicron's realm once anyone from the company comes past the front door. I understand it's not Hot Rocks' business how you run the place, just our job to supply and maintain it. However, there's a company phone for each of you in chargers in the kitchen. Your own phones will work but the company ones have numbers known to everyone on site. The contact lists in them have all the company numbers you might need already loaded, and we ask that you carry them. You can make as many personal calls as you like on them … so it's now your kingdom, doctor.'

He handed over the keys to Lachlan and shook his hand, and then Margaret's.

'Oh, one more thing.'

He fished around in his pockets and produced two crumpled envelopes that turned out to be marked *Doctor* and *Nurse*.

'Instructions about how to get into the computers and a security code too for initial access. Your people will have told our people who to expect and a couple of your personal details, like your birthdates. The system will ask you to fill in your details for a match before it asks you to set your own passwords, and only then let you into the network. I think that's it. Welcome to Mordbury, people,' he said quite cheerfully and sincerely, and left them to it.

Chapter 3

As Lachlan Tan and Margaret Pursehouse were taking the keys to their new workplace, the person who had made the final decision to contract their employer and indirectly cause them to be in Mordbury, Anthony Huw Main – Anthony (never Tony) to a very few selected friends, Hughey when he wasn't around to hear, and Mr Main to most – was making himself comfortable at a dining table on the newest incarnation of the Bass Strait ferry, the latest *Spirit of Tasmania*.

People disparaged canteen style serve-yourself catering, especially after the rigours of Covid precautions, but Anthony Main appreciated the culinary efficiency it represented, and now on the new boat they did things rather well. He was enjoying a couple of glasses of Tasmanian bubbles with his seafood dinner. The system was dependable and appealed to the manager in Anthony Main's psyche. However, he knew his housekeeper would not approve.

Mrs Scott had come to him to him about two years before, the wife of a workshop employee who had died tragically young – and a woman facing a mountain of debt. He had given her a job as a cleaner, only to find that not only could she clean like no other, but she was a splendid cook. So he gave her a home too, strictly as an employee but a well-paid one. He was thankful Mrs Scott had agreed to come with him on this, the next stage in his life journey and had sent her ahead, suffering several weeks without her services.

Anthony Main was a very contented traveller in other ways. He had finally managed to arrange to cut all his ties with the Australian mainland, and in doing so trusted he had now also geographically put in his past some of the things he now recognised as being less than savoury: things he had done as a businessman, and indeed as a husband and as a parent. Gone was the chain of small car yards, and, as of today, the Jaguar/Land Rover dealership. Gone were the trials and tribulations of floor plans, overambitious and unprofessional managers, overeager sales staff, and distrusting customers. He reminded himself he had made his own contribution to the low regard in which the trade was held, but it and business generally had changed, dramatically.

The world had moved on and now so had he.

Gone were the host of little companies he had created over the years to do this here, and that there, to round robin and confuse the tax people. He had his admittedly sticky little fingers in lots of pies – but never in the drug trade, an involvement which he could readily have had. It disgusted him. In recent years he felt he had become a more mature human being and a considerably more ethical one, although he was still a businessman at heart. Moreover, his new-found morality was not confected or thrust upon him from outside. He had firstly found the need for righteousness within himself and had only then been moved to study ethics to clarify his epiphany. The little library he had assembled in his study at Perdition, the family Tasmanian home at Mordbury, was replete with religious books, books about religion, and books on ethics. Lyn, his sister-in-law, an academic who lectured on philosophy, had been an excellent if somewhat surprised sounding board for his studies. Peter, his younger brother, was so happily married to her it bordered on the astonishing.

The procession of girls, then the women to whom he had carelessly professed love before his marriage, were a bitter testament to his waste of his precious youth from the perspective of his reformed soul, not that he believed he had such a thing as a soul. Indeed, he knew only too well that if he now possessed any religious belief at all, and if it had been a Christian one, and if it was one of the branches of Christianity that still believed in a traditional hell, his afterlife would include a lengthy spell in close proximity to fire and brimstone.

He regretted his misuse of the brief time allocated to his earthly existence by genetics and circumstance. Long gone was the pretty, sexy, fun-loving girl that he had married. The party girl had quickly turned into a selfish, avaricious wife who had opportunistically divorced him; and in doing so had separated him from so much of his money in his thirties. Fortunately Edith had at least showed her true colours early enough to give him time to build his fortune again. With her went the two bitchy bloodsucking daughters he had financed through private school and then university, who didn't seem to want to talk to him once he had guaranteed their adult independence. He was, however, willing to accept that his character might have been portrayed in certain ways to them by their mother.

His younger brother, Peter, was somewhere in North America, running one more of the tourist hotels to which he had sequentially been posted by the chain for which he had worked for many years. His loyalty, ability and experience had seemingly been rewarded. Anthony had at least gotten around to sending him emails congratulating him on his promotions. An exchange of messages on their birthdays and on festive days was the general limit of their relationship. He had even missed Peter's wedding although he could have easily afforded to attend. Thanks to the personal and financial effects of his first experience with Australian family law, Anthony himself had never remarried.

He had reserved a substantial amount of cash money if not in his personal pockets, in secure bank accounts and investments. Admittedly his one remaining project had eaten up the rest of his liquidity, but he had made sure he was personally totally secure even if that were to go totally pear-shaped. Even to the well off, he was considered wealthy if not rich, and moreover principled in his dealings if not morally perfect.

Above all he now wanted to believe that the community might feel that his small contribution had been somewhat worthwhile. He might be rising fifty-nine years of age but when he looked at himself as objectively as he might he saw someone who was reasonably fit, free of encumbrances, a more than competent manager with good connections; and he was building a project that he felt was worthwhile – not just for himself, although he valued the journey, but also for the community. He had determined to die in a satisfactorily advanced old age with a reasonably clear conscience and a sense of having contributed something in the end. His last remaining company, Lucifer Hot Rocks, he had funded well. The company enjoyed investment funding from others, thanks to the support of three banks and a wealth of government subsidies.

The next morning and after a good night's sleep, it wasn't long after his breakfast that the *Spirit* began negotiating the river and its berth in Devonport. He lingered on deck to watch the manoeuvre. He thought it something of a miracle for such a big boat to turn in such a small space, and he always enjoyed seeing it done before hastening to comply with the order to go below to his vehicle and prepare to disembark. The vehicle in this case was a small present he had given himself before selling his last dealership. He had one of the new electric Range Rovers.

He had put it on as a 'demonstrator' for tax and floor plan purposes, with strict instructions that any actual demonstrating of it would be at his sole discretion. He let it be known that any salesperson putting anyone else in the driving seat, let alone allowing someone to put it in motion, should think very carefully about whether they wished to keep their job. It was all black and chrome on the outside, and cream leather with contrasting black piping on the inside. Potential customers were allowed to look at it and perhaps drool, as long as they did not drool too close to it. He firmly believed that did more for sales anyway. Tell them they can't have it and they will want it even more.

The drive off the boat was orderly and there was no delay for him at the terminal, as biosecurity did not select him for an inspection. The weather was fine, and he was in Launceston and at his desk in the compact offices of Lucifer Hot Rocks Pty Ltd and the Sheol project with no strain at all. The Range Rover was parked in the car park below, happily sucking up hydro-electricity from the Tasmanian grid and the solar panels in the garden on the building's roof.

He called a meeting with Gabriel, who ran the office there for the company with the relatively small administrative staff that it now employed in Launceston; got his mind around the status of operations at Mordbury; and, having announced he would work from there for a while, set off for what he would henceforth consider to be home. Mordbury had been a surprise when he inherited it. While the property had been in his family since it came into existence, he had never known of it in his younger days growing up in Melbourne. He felt there was a certain preordination in the circumstances that had now led him to use it for the project that would be his legacy.

He was also looking forward to the tree change. In undergoing his self-engineered transformation, Anthony Huw Main had not only gone seriously moral; he had also gone seriously green.

Chapter 4

The personal history and ambitions of Anthony Main unknown to them, Margaret and Lachlan had a prowl around the medical centre and found that it had once been a substantial (for the period) four-bedroom home with additional rooms on the front to provide for a doctor's consulting rooms. There was a small kitchen, a small lounge with a large television, and a locked room with a hatch in the wall which was obviously the old dispensary. The house was now even bigger, with a forty-foot modern transportable building attached to the side wall of the old house, accessible by a double door sufficiently wide for a hospital trolley. Turning on the bright fluorescent lights revealed it to be a treatment room with two beds, desks and cabinets, and what turned out to be a small X-ray room at the far end.

Lachlan suggested they choose a bedroom each and then unpack the car.

'We can just dump stuff in the room it's going to end up in and then see how we feel about putting it away. Personally, my priorities after we unpack are making up my bed and then having a meal and a good night's sleep.'

So, they trudged backwards and forwards to the car, with the rain making things damp and difficult. Over the next hour they pulled everything – that had taken a leisurely day to load – out of the back and off the top of the Subaru. As luck would have it the rain stopped just as they were finishing up. The sun came out briefly with a hint of a rainbow arching over the valley; but the rays, while golden, were without warmth from low on the horizon. Dusk was approaching. Wallabies were beginning to spread out, grazing on the wet green grass, and little groups of rails were scampering about as well.

'How very bucolic,' said Lachlan as he locked up the car. 'I wonder what other wildlife there is?'

'Well, I did a bit of research over the weekend,' said Margaret, 'and apparently there are Tassie devils, possums, echidna and wombats, and quite a bit of bird life in the immediate area, which was pristine native forest before the logging started but is now growing back slowly. Oh, and thanks to the prospectors before the loggers, and the loggers for whom the village was built, there is a population of feral cats and some wild dogs as well.'

'You've been studying up!'

'I found there's lots of stuff online about Lucifer Hot Rocks and the arguments about whether they should be permitted to do what they are doing up here. Apparently, they only got the project approved because the country suffered a lot of environmental degradation in the past.'

Margaret's sudden passion for the place, and indeed her loquacity, surprised Lachlan. That little speech had been more than she had said about anything so far that day; the wealth of information revealed an unexpected level of interest in the place, as well as how she might regard what was now being done to it. Lachlan had not missed the note in Margaret's voice that suggested she might have been sympathetic with the people who had tried to prevent the project from going ahead.

'OK, you can tell me more over dinner,' he said. Hopefully she was over the pain of being driven up to Mordbury by him.

The first priority was to put their rooms in some sort of order. There had been no argument about who slept where. The four rather bare repainted bedrooms all had brand-new king single beds with linen and doonas piled on them ready for making up. Presumably they could be used by staff or even patients as required. There was the smell of new carpets and curtains. Each room was provided with adequate furniture for them to unpack and not to have to live out of their suitcases.

As he put the last of his stuff away, Lachlan could hear a banging on the other side of one of his bedroom walls and went next door to find Margaret putting a picture hook into the plasterboard, using an unopened jar of marmalade as a hammer. She hung a crucifix on the hook before she noticed she had company. There was an A4 colour photograph of the current Pope in a frame on the top of the tallboy as well, Lachlan saw. *Each to their own.*

'Dinner,' said Lachlan.

They adjourned to the kitchen, where they unpacked the company's cutlery and crockery, tea towels and provisions. There was a fridge freezer, turned on in expectation of their arrival, and also a dishwasher.

'What are we going to have to eat?' asked Margaret. 'I'll leave it to you; I don't cook much.'

'Well in due course you're going to have to learn. Firstly, I am not going to play mother every day, and don't forget that we're here together by accident for this week. You'll come up with other doctors and I can't see many of them, man or woman, particularly the older ones, bending over the stove. There's Dr Giles for one …'

Margaret looked glum rather than amused.

'I think Dr Giles might be able to give you a sausage and egg on toast,' he teased. 'Oh, come on, smile a bit at least, everyone knows he's an old-school male chauvinist grouch.'

That Dr Giles was so regarded was nothing that was not general knowledge, Lachlan knew, and he thought getting chatty might help things along a bit. Margaret was bloody hard work. Probably had never shared a flat with other students.

He sorted through their provisions. 'How about stir-fry with noodles?'

'Fine,' murmured his companion, who sat down at the table and began reading the brochure that Gerry had given her.

He found a bottle of wine and unscrewed the top, offering Margaret a glass. She showed signs of refusing.

'Sorry, I just presumed you would like one after putting up with my driving.'

Self-deprecation doesn't seem to work either.

'Well, I'm not a drinker. Half a glass is my limit. But according to this brochure Mordbury is dry. No alcohol allowed.'

'I have two problems with that. Firstly, I've already brought it in; and secondly, I've already opened the bottle. Besides, you heard what the man said, what happens on these premises is Omicron business. I am currently the most senior representative of the company on site. Drink your medicine. Oh, and do your bit, put the rest of that stuff away will you?' He waved at the boxes of foodstuffs. 'If in doubt about anything except liquids, put it in the freezer.'

'I'm not totally stupid you know.'

Oops. 'Sorry, it's been a long day.'

Working tactfully around each other, they got things more organised.

Lachlan found a deep pan among the kitchen equipment, and some nondescript liquid that professed on its label to be vegetable cooking oil. There were packets of noodles, and he retrieved some frozen vegetables from the freezer section of the large fridge where

Margaret had put them away. Shrugging his shoulders, he began the process of whipping up dinner.

'I wonder why the refrigerator is so big,' Margaret said. 'If there's only going to be the one nurse and one doctor up here at any time, it's huge.'

'I suppose they've allowed for the place being snowed in. Then there's the chance that there is an accident, and we may have to feed a couple of patients and/or helpers as well as ourselves. No doubt each team coming up will need to bring more and more stuff up with them – and everyone will also have different tastes. I'll have to make a note of that along with everything else we find missing. Let me know if there's anything you think we should get the place stocked up with.'

Margaret sniffed her disapproval. Obviously cooking and catering was going to be part and parcel of the role of nurse at Mordbury.

'Put some pre-packaged frozen meals on the list then,' she said and resumed reading the Hot Rocks brochure – somewhat more intently.

'It says here,' she said, 'Mordbury was originally a grant of land to one family and clearing the forest for a farm was a condition of the grant. It was called Perdition.'

'Well, we were on the road to perdition this morning so that sounds apt,' said Lachlan, trying to make a joke as he started throwing the noodles into the main pan and making a metal-on-metal noise with a large serving spoon. He added splashes of some fish sauce he had found, and the air around the kitchen took on a distinctive oriental aroma.

'It became Mordbury as a named village a bit later when the woodcutters arrived and began getting timber.'

'It must have been hell transporting it down to Launceston over that road. It would have been pretty primitive then. In other places, like the Gordon River, they used to float it down to the mill and in the US they used flumes.'

'Well apparently they had a mill here, so they were taking milled timber out by wagon, not whole logs.'

'Makes better sense.'

'What's a flume by the way?'

'You make a channel on a slope like a waterslide out of logs and direct water down it from a river or stream. The logs then slide downhill to where you want them to go.'

'OK. Well, all the trees are protected now apparently – at least the native stuff which they almost logged out. However, there are pine and hardwood plantations between here and the north coast according to this. The trees aren't milled here anymore. The logging trucks go out to the north on temporary roads in the coupes and it's chipped and exported. Ah ha! The old mill building is still here. Apparently, Lucifer use it for equipment storage and maintenance. They say – a bit of boasting here I see – it's one of the restorations they have done on the place.'

The stir fry was quickly ready, but Lachlan couldn't find any bowls to serve it in.

'No bowls by the look of it Margaret. It will have to be plates.'

With the meal on the table in front of her on a dinner plate, he offered Margaret a top up for her glass. She shook her head.

'Not for me.'

He gave himself a second glass, having consumed the first as he cooked. He thought he detected another disparaging look on Margaret's face.

'Look,' he said. 'It's been a hard day, and we deserve to relax a bit. We aren't open for business – no patients expected – so I think I can afford to safely have a second glass. If we were on call one glass would be the order of the day.'

Margaret grunted at him – but she did seem to enjoy her meal.

Lachlan grinned back. 'You realise that since I cooked you're doing the washing up, don't you?'

They finished their dinner in silence.

Chapter 5

As Anthony Main set off for Mordbury, the employees of Omicron Medical Services were embarking on their orientation tour of the town and the worksite.

A Lucifer Hot Rocks Toyota Electrocruiser had appeared at exactly ten o'clock and the driver turned out, in the eyes of an appreciative Lachlan Tan, to be a very personable young lady. She had an enviable smooth olive-toned skin, high cheek bones, smallish bosom, and exemplary deportment: everything that would no doubt have given her a living from the catwalk had she not made the career choices she had. Even dressed in trousers and boots with a high-vis jacket ready for a day's work she looked well, very well indeed. Her makeup was simple but well done.

It was embarrassing when Margaret Pursehouse joined them.

'Oh … hello Chris,' she said. 'Fancy meeting you here.'

'Good morning,' their guide said and offered her hand to Lachlan. 'They call me Chris, but it's Christine Reynolds if you want the full name.'

There seemed to be an extra dose of assertiveness in that explanation, but she was obviously determined to be pleasant even if she was paying only cursory attention to his nurse. She followed that up with an explanatory 'Margaret and I know each other, don't we Margaret?'

'Er yes,' came the short, and perhaps a little rudely abrupt, response.

'She was my nurse when I had some surgery, in Melbourne; and she was not happy about it. Still a member of the god squad, Margaret?'

'Yes,' came an almost defiant answer to the obvious attempt to taunt her in front of her boss.

So, these two have history, do they?

'Well, we won't deal with that now, but I give you permission to tell the good doctor the full story if he wants to hear it. I presume you will get rostered up here regularly, so you had better get used to seeing me around.'

Christine Reynolds paused, perhaps recognising that she had sounded combative. The doctor had certainly noticed that she wasn't going to take any nonsense from anyone called Margaret Pursehouse.

'Alright, all aboard, high-vis and hats, and we'll take the grand tour of what the boss named the Sheol project. If either of you have questions along the way just ask them – both about your work and anything else you see about the site. I'll do my best to answer them although I'm not up to speed on the high-tech stuff. In theory I'm in charge of a pile of stuff bracketed as "workplace health and safety and environmental affairs", but all that means is that I'm a middle manager whose main job is to make it happen, hold the boss' hand and to be outward facing. I have people in my team who do detail.'

They got into the car, Lachlan occupying the front passenger seat almost by default, with Margaret determinedly pre-empting any other arrangement by sitting behind him, about as far away from their guide as she could get and still be in the same vehicle.

'You will each find a copy of the site handbook on the seats. It's for you to keep. I, or one of my people, will be doing this with each of your company's doctors and nurses when they first get rostered up here. You might let your people know that.'

'So, what are your qualifications and those of your people?' asked Lachlan, trying his hand at an icebreaking chat on what he presumed to be safe ground.

'Well believe it or not I have a primary qualification as a paramedic – but that was a while ago now. There's nothing like spending your youth around hospitals to make you want to do medical stuff. All I do with that now is give CPR training and help patch up the odd cut and scrape. I have a bachelor's in management which I hated doing, but I've made risk management my home. I have two offsiders, one in safety and one in environmental affairs, and I hired them because they both are not only highly qualified and experienced in their areas, but also not slow in coming forward. Try and cut down a tree or dig a hole around here and they both want to know!'

The road was substantially better than the one they had travelled the day before, save for every so often it ramped gently over what Lachlan presumed were stormwater drainage pipes. About a hundred metres down the road Christine carefully checked her mirrors and brought the car to a halt on the verge.

'For the next year or so you'll have to watch for trucks on this road. They'll be coming at all times of the day when there is daylight, and summer will bring daylight saving and extended hours. If you need to stop anywhere on the main drag, get your vehicle off the road. Sometimes the drivers are a bit unsympathetic to other traffic after coming up the mountain.'

'I noticed,' said Lachlan.

'Well, they understandably don't like the road up here and we identified the problem with the state government early on. However, while they have promised to fix it at a political level, at some bureaucratic level they seem to think we should do it. So, it's being held up by someone. The big boss is coming up this week, and he's going to be resident here most of the time, so he might be able to get them off their buttocks.'

'So, who is the big boss?' asked Margaret.

'Mr Main, owner, chairman of the board and managing director. Actually, the board is Mr Main, and some hangers on with relatively minor investments who do what he tells them to do. For all intents and purposes, he is Lucifer … That didn't sound too good, did it Margaret,' she said teasingly, 'having Lucifer in charge?'

I shall have to act as a referee with these two, thought Lachlan. There must be a real history there. Obviously nurses and patients could get on each other's nerves. In his limited institutional experience with longer hospitalisations there were times when nurses had to just put up with a patient they disliked while they were in their care, and be at their professional best.

There's been more to it than that with these two though. Grudges have been held, and still are being by the look of it.

'Now,' explained Christine, 'if you look down the road you can see it crosses the river and then follows it again on the other side. That's where the main village is. If you're wondering about the humps in the road, they are tunnels for the wombats, echidna and devils to use. Make good speed bumps though. Not too hard on cars but they slow those fucking trucks down. Most of the roadkill is now wallabies. Thick as bricks, wallabies, even with the excuse that the electric trucks are quiet. Turbo chooks – the rails – they're faster to get out of the way.'

'No fences?' said Lachlan.

'I suppose it does look a bit odd, but all the old rotting fences that were here have been ripped out to allow the company to mow the grass – which never seems to stop growing. It was done when the water supply was put in. We now have reticulated bore water. The houses originally had wells. After you go through the village the road goes past the old mill. Up beyond that on another little hill is the water treatment plant. That was one of the first things Mr Main put in. The road then goes through a cutting into the next valley. That's where the drilling site is, and also where the geothermal power plant is being built. We'll see that later. Now, as we go over the bridge, straight in front of you you'll see the old homestead building, overshadowed by the huge extensions done to it by Mr Main.'

A large semitrailer came up from behind them and carried on down the road to the bridge. It was carrying a huge container-sized generator. Even in the car they could hear the brakes squealing their protest as the driver slowed down to make the turn required.

'I won't stop too close to the bridge because of the trucks. Oh – in regard to Mr Main – don't be surprised if staff, when he can't hear us of course, refer to him as Hughey. It's his nickname. His middle name is Huw with a double-U, and in the good old Aussie tradition of the nickname he is God around here – sorry about that, Margaret.'

Lachlan cleared his throat loudly. Enough was enough. *I might share your views on her religiosity, but I think we should avoid what might be bullying.*

Their guide seemed to get the message. 'OK, hmm, well … as we drive along you will see that every roof with anything approaching a northern facing slope has solar panels on it.'

She pointed out of the windscreen.

'The strange bulgy stainless steel towers along the roadside are not primarily posts for the lights they support. They're vertical wind turbines. Lucifer is all about green power and right from the start Hughey wanted it to be self-supporting as much as it could be; although there were and are compromises being made on our green credentials. For example, you don't make stainless steel without some environmental compromises, or run trucks around here without causing roadkill.'

She carefully checked her mirrors before moving the car off. She followed the road which swung right and approached a very wide but ancient looking timber railed bridge.

'If you look to your left you will see an installation in the water. That's a horizontal turbine that's also producing power. We have three of them along the river.'

'How old is this bridge?' asked Margaret from the back seat, with some apprehension.

'Guess.'

'A hundred and fifty years?'

'Two.'

'Two hundred!' she exclaimed incredulously.

'No. Just two. It was designed to look like one that was here before, but it's three times the width of the original and is rated to take 250 tonnes – two laden trucks with capacity to spare. While the road we have been on is yet to be fully re-surfaced – it's ours by the way, well Hughey's – from here on the road has been done up and it's rated to take heavy vehicles. It's one of our environmental compromises.'

'So, the state government has done some work?' asked Lachlan.

'Well no. Starting from the notices that you would have seen as you came in from Lonnie, everything in the two valleys and generally to the top of the surrounding hills that's not the actual project stuff belongs to Hughey, him personally. Apparently, he inherited it from family he didn't know he had who were the descendants of the original settlers. It's not even company land. Rumour has it he's got the company paying him over the odds for allowing the project to use the site, and more for the access. It's a smart bit of business he's doing, making money for himself during the construction phase. The water treatment plant was paid for with company money, but it will be handed over to Hughey at the end of the construction I hear. He's no bloody fool when it comes to business, there is no arguing that. I think the company built the new bridge as part of the project but it's on his land of course and if everything were to go pear-shaped he would get to keep it.'

'When you say 'the company', that's the company doing the project, which is also under his control,' stated Margaret with some awe in her voice.

'Yep, Lucifer is his retirement thing apparently. Something to do now he's sold up all his interests in the motor trade and his other businesses. Probably a male mid-life crisis.'

I know all about that, thought Lachlan. *Some days I don't really want to be doing doctoring anymore.*

Christine again carefully pulled off the side of the road when the car was clear of the bridge and, looking over their shoulders, they could see a small timber building sparkling with new paint in the sunshine, at the end of a drive that must have been a hundred metres long and ended with a huge forecourt. The small timber building had a large two-storey stone and glass extension behind and above it. Oddly, given the lack of fencing in the village, there were two massive walls framing the entry to the property, seemingly built in the same stone as the building extension.

'That's Hughey's pad,' said Christine. 'It's called Perdition because that's the name the original house was given by the first settlers. Apparently, the whole property was originally called that, but at some stage someone decided that was a bit unsavoury and the property was renamed Mordbury after a village in Berkshire. It seems that the original settlers came from there. Mr Main kept the old name for the house though, just as his ancestors did. We all say that's because he was apparently something of a bastard in the motor trade and he reckons he has to pay for his sins. How you pay for your sins in a five-bedroom all ensuite luxury house with triple glazing and hot and cold running everything, a six-car garage underneath, all air conditioned and with a full-time housekeeper living in her own self-contained wing, I don't know. Why he needs to mark out his territory with those gate walls I don't know either. Apparently, they weigh tons, and the foundations go down quite deep.'

Lachlan was waiting for a comment from Margaret, but she stayed silent.

'He may have a huge ego but still he is very good to work for. I keep fit with riding horses and he lets me keep them up here for free. There's old stables and paddocks up near the old mill. My partner and I are trying to put together a stud if we can save enough money.'

'Do you do anything special with them?' asked Lachlan.

'I compete a bit in dressage. I've been riding since I was a kid and it's been a lifesaver. And,' she added with some emphasis in a somewhat theatrical lower tone, 'dressage is a gender-neutral sport.'

Margaret made a sort of snort from the back seat, and Lachlan took another look at the conformation of their driver sitting next to him, this time with a medical eye. A distinct possibility was running through his mind; a distinct possibility that might rankle with a real bible basher – as Christine put it. What's more, if young Christine was hinting so strongly with somewhat gratuitous remarks at what he thought she might be hinting at for the benefit of the new doctor, then she might be deliberately putting him on notice.

They slowly passed a number of smart renovated houses and a few yet untouched dilapidated ones, which constituted the village, then a small shop, and some new single workers' quarters where there seemed to be a lot of activity. There was what might have once been a sports ground, with its grass even now kept mowed lower than the general area, but not obviously dedicated to any particular activity, having no goal posts or other fixtures.

Christine noticed his interest. 'It's kept mowed for two reasons. Firstly, it will be good for sports if anyone does want to use it in due course, and Hughey is putting in some lights so it can be used for helicopters twenty-four seven. The single workers' quarters are, for reasons unknown but probably because they are not in the actual plant site or nobody else wants them, lumped into my responsibilities.'

There was a bit of coming and going in the village and evidence that one or two of the old but renovated houses were family homes, with cars parked in front of them and washing on the line.

'It's an old-style company town,' Christine explained. 'The little shop we just passed on the right just keeps the basics and is open a couple of hours a day. The wife of one of the engineers is running it as a personal sideline. The company is only charging her a peppercorn rent so it's worthwhile for her to supply a basic service. The company does a bus run into Lonnie once a week for a bigger shop for anyone who wants a ride in. When the power station is finished, those of us who fancy staying on are looking forward to having quite a nice little community here with the permanent staff.'

The road began to rise in front of them.

They passed a big old timber building on their left that turned out to be the old mill, which as they knew from the brochure was now used as a machinery shop. While Lachlan looked for stables and horses, Christine did not stop or slow down. Just as he thought he saw what he was looking for out of the corner of his eye, the car began entering a cutting. Then before them was another valley, and the contrast with the one they had just come from was extraordinary. They were entering what looked like a mining site crossed with an oil field, with everything that went with that, notwithstanding it was supposedly a green project. Christine pulled the car over to the side of the road again.

'There you are, Margaret,' she said. 'Our version of Dante's inferno.'

'What?'

'Dante's inferno,' Christine repeated.

'With all nine circles?' Lachlan asked jokingly.

'Of course.'

'Limbo?'

'Hughey's house, Perdition.'

'Lust?'

'Every fucking where. It's a mixed sex workforce on shifts with little houses and single men's quarters and constant bloody rain. Yes, I know that's a sexist title. We're all trying to get used to "single workers' quarters" which is the official name for the place.'

'We should probably take a note of that for professional reasons, Margaret,' said Lachlan quite seriously. 'Domiciliaries … gluttony?'

'Certainly, when we can. I keep fit with riding, and the walking I have to do in my job. Some of the older engineers have no other recreation, but the village is dry. Hughey reigns here not Augustine of Hippo.'

They both laughed, but Margaret was silent to the point of being noticeably upset, crossing her arms and staring at the view from the car window.

'Greed?'

'We're all here to make money for ourselves and of course for the company. Everyone's being paid mining rates. Then there are the contractors. They're ripping the company off on the basis of the difficulty of the access and remoteness of the site.'

'Anger?'

'Ask Margaret.'

'Behave! Heresy? No, I've already got that one covered and it sounds like you have too. Violence?'

'Look what we're doing to nature. Fortunately, as I said we are dry so no booze, and if there may be a bit of a tiff between a couple of blokes we don't let it come to that. Get sorted or get off the project is the go.'

'Fraud?'

'Don't ask me about the company, but I am certainly one.' She smiled. 'Like that, Margaret?' she asked rhetorically.

So Christine, you are a fraud by your own judgement are you?

Well, she was a most intelligent and entertaining one. If what he was thinking was correct – and he didn't have any real experience in the area – then it would be quite understandable that a religious person like Margaret might well not approve.

'Treachery?'

'No examples spring to mind but I would not be a bit surprised.'

They burst out laughing together, ignoring the silence from the back seat.

Checking again for trucks in both directions, Christine drove the car down into the valley and around a long road that circled it. She was able to point out the features of the site without them having to go into it. It certainly was a hive of activity. The contractors had even set up their own concrete-batching plant and it was particularly busy. Christine noticed Lachlan observing it.

'Concrete is another one of our necessary environmental compromises,' she explained. 'However, where we can we use waste inputs like fly ash, and materials like recycled steel and plastics in the reinforcing.'

It was past one o'clock before they were finally delivered back to the house, which was timely because it had started raining again. Lachlan decided that it was just the sort of wet afternoon that Margaret could use to finalise the arrangement of the equipment they had brought with them along the lines of generally accepted convention, while he would tackle the problem of the locked room and everything it might contain.

Chapter 6

Damian Stavropoulos had avoided the nickname of Damo, and even Stavro. He was known to his mates as Ned, which is totally illogical unless one is familiar with the Australian sense of humour and the milieu in which Ned moved. Damian was a fourth generation Australian, and he had grown a magnificent bushman's beard. So Ned, as in Ned Kelly, he was. He was the driver of the truck that had been of such concern to Dr Lachlan Tan and the safety of his company Subaru the day before. Unloaded, turned around, reloaded and struggling up the mountain again, only to be unloaded again, Ned was just about to start another return trip back down the mountain. It was planned he would do it all again tomorrow, and the day after, and the day after that.

He didn't own the truck he was driving but he was proud of it. Since he shared his time between the inside of the cabin and his family, he took a great deal of care to look after both. His devotion to the care and maintenance of the trucks he drove was in his nature but, having been noted by his employer, it was the reason that he had been entrusted with the new hydrogen-powered Kenworth. It was one of the several new trucks purchased for what would be an intensive two-year contract hauling stuff in and out of the power station site – at a very profitable price.

So far, Ned had been hauling pipes, day in day out. Lots and lots of pipes. He was told they were drilling pipes and that very soon, when his company had hauled in all the pieces for the drilling rig and then its ancillary equipment, he would be hauling in casing pipes for the holes it was going to drill, and then stainless steel production pipes for the water that was going to be pumped into, and retrieved from, the holes. He was enjoying acquiring the vernacular and being accepted as part of the whole team, and he was also enjoying being able to go home every night even if the days were long and the road difficult at times. He knew that when he was hauling production pipes into the site in due course, he would be hauling drilling pipes out. He accepted that nothing but pipes lay in his near future and contented himself with trying to haul them safely and expeditiously.

However, at this early stage in the project Ned would be carefully descending the mountain with no return load, which suited him well because he would not have to unload at the other end; and having eaten the lunch he had brought with him while his truck was unloaded, he checked the rig out as the drizzle began again.

His mood was much better than it had been on the previous day. He knew he had put unnecessary pressure on the driver of the Subaru he had been following, but the whole situation had been dictated by the ratios the Kenworth had in its gearbox, the size of the load he was carrying, and the need for him to maintain momentum on the road given the state it was in. He was hoping that the customary dryish pattern of the local climate would return soon, although everything weather-wise seemed a bit unpredictable these days.

Hopefully it's not going to be too tough today.

There was a nasty squall coming in as he scrambled into the cab, belted himself in, wound up the big engine, and checked his gauges as it ran up. They said in the promotional literature that you hardly noticed the difference, but for an experienced man like

Ned the hydrogen-powered truck felt hugely different from a diesel.

He took care to sound his horn to warn the site he was about to move off, then trundled the big rig slowly towards the cutting in the hills and the road back through Mordbury. As he descended into the village he took care, knowing that he had the right-hand turn onto the bridge to deal with. While he was not crawling along, having no load, he limited his speed so he could make the somewhat sharp turn safely on the wet tarmac.

A driver and his truck have a special bond, and to Ned the unladen truck seemed as keen as he was to get home. As he negotiated the village towards the bridge, he was a little distracted as he went through the playlists in the media centre looking for something that would reflect his good mood and keep him company as he went down the mountain. That small distraction meant that he braked just a little later than he might have when the black Range Rover came off the bridge and across his bows; not that his momentarily delayed reaction made much difference to the outcome.

The momentum of the huge truck braking on the wet road, starting its turn to the right, and the momentum of the much smaller accelerating Range Rover trying to carry straight on off the bridge in front of it combined in a way that would have delighted Mr Newton. Travelling at some speed given the conditions, and advantaged by its all-wheel drive, the colliding Range Rover nudged the prime mover to the left. It also lost traction. The laws of motion meant the trailer behind the truck tried to go straight on. There was nothing that Ned could do about it but sit in his seat and watch it all happen in slow motion. Firstly, the car was close and on his right; then the car was right in front of him where he could barely see it at all; then as the whole rig went left, the edge of the roof was below him; and finally, it vanished as his cabin rose in the air.

The truck had pushed the Range Rover sideways onto the stone wall next to the drive to Perdition. Then using the car and the remains of the stonework as a ramp it had driven onto it.

Meanwhile Anthony Main had frozen in his seat in surprise at the start of the impact, barely having time to wish he had checked to his left as he came off the bridge. His last observation was of the multiple airbags that deployed all around him in a futile attempt to offer protection. There was nothing he could have done anyway as the two vehicles, ill matched, performed their dance in compliance with the laws of motion and the theory of gravity.

Ned automatically took his foot off the throttle as things started to happen, and with no time to even think about hitting the brakes, in a reflex action used the kill switch as everything came to rest. Taking stock, he looked out of the windscreen, which was perfectly intact, and saw the quiet of the green of the countryside with the rain, now gentle, still falling. With no wipers working, raindrops were forming little rivers that ran down the glass and magnified the silence of his secluded circumstance.

He overcame his immediate surprise. He seemed totally fine when he checked his limbs, and he felt no pain. He unbelted himself. He hadn't even hit the straps overly hard. The cabin seemed undamaged, and the door opened for him as easily as if nothing had happened. On the other hand, as he opened the door the smell of hot oil fumes hit him unsuppressed by the drizzle.

Bugger, he thought weirdly in the face of the scope of destruction the collision had wrought. *The boss won't be happy.*

Then he realised there were tanks of compressed hydrogen under him. He moved quickly, finding he had to jump down from the cab onto the pile of rocks and the car beneath the cab. As he did so he felt his right ankle twist as he landed awkwardly. *Fuck that hurt.*

He continued to climb down as well as he might, wincing, and hobbled away from the wreckage as fast as he could. About thirty painful metres away he turned to survey the scene, to try to work out what had happened, and see where the car had ended up.

Even at that distance he could see that it looked like it had once been an expensive SUV, but there was nothing he could do about the car or its driver. What he could also see was a flicker of flame from the car underneath the truck. It encouraged him to move further up the road still.

That doesn't look good.

As he did so another truck was coming down the hill, and it came to a halt just as a fireball exploded behind him and he was flagging it down. He heard the *whoomph* of a fireball exploding behind him. *A BLEVE*, he thought, *boiling liquid expanding vapour explosion* – the technical term incongruously filling his thoughts as he watched its brightness reflected in the wiper-swept areas of the second truck's windscreen; and the surprise on the face of its driver.

If Anthony 'Hughey' Main had been alive after being crushed in the impact, he was definitely now on his way to meet his namesake.

Chapter 7

In its own way, going through the stuff in the dispensary was very interesting. Lachlan had started the job of going through everything, and soon Margaret had joined him, pronouncing that everything was organised to her satisfaction in the treatment room. They quickly came to a joint decision that there was nothing in the locked dispensary that posed any danger to anyone as far as its disposal went.

There was a bit of medical history that could be read into the collection, but the old equipment was corroded and bent and of no use, not even for display purposes. Nurse and doctor agreed they had both seen several museum collections of the same kind of thing in much better condition. The bottles, however, were professionally interesting for the substances that their labels disclosed they had once held. The killing of pain seemed to have been a major concern, with chloroform and ether apparently once stocked in some quantity. However, whatever had remained when the dispensary had been abandoned had long since evaporated despite the ground glass stoppers in the larger translucent bottles.

Much smaller blue bottles, identified as *laudanum* on handwritten labels and obviously for individual dispensing, now contained but a dark scum signifying that they had once held something until their corks dried and shrivelled. Other bottles and jars appeared to have once contained a variety of less potent creams, herbal medicines and home remedies, but they too had either dried out or presented no hazard from the remains of their contents, if their aged and sometimes barely legible handwritten labels were correct. There were also a couple of leather-bound notebooks that had obviously belonged to one of the previous incumbents of the practice, with all sorts of notations in a neat, but in parts blurred and faded, copperplate hand.

On closer examination the original owner of the notebooks appeared to have had a scientific bent outside of the strict confines of their medical practice. What could be easily read seemed mainly about local flora.

'The damp seems have got into these,' Lachlan remarked as he flipped through one of the books.

'But there's a lot of work gone into them,' argued Margaret. 'Someone was really interested in what they were doing.' Some of the legible descriptions of the plants seemed to be exacting, with diagrams of structures done with a skilful hand in a careful manner.

'Well, I'm certainly not suggesting that they get thrown away. We'll let the people who own them make the final decision,' Lachlan said. He retrieved one of the carboard boxes that they had previously emptied of some of the modern medications they had brought with them and put the bottles and rusty equipment into it. While he was busy doing that, Margaret was looking at the notebooks. She and Lachlan both jumped when one of the company phones rang.

'Get that will you please?' Lachlan asked as he finished up. Margaret, the two notebooks still in her hand, dutifully went and took the call in the kitchen.

He had barely had a chance to finish packing the bottles when Margaret came back in and advised him that they had an unexpected patient coming in.

Now the teachers at St Jude's had not been big on evolutionary botany, and Margaret perceived the hand of God in all of his creation. A good pass in general science at school, with a desire to serve with Christian compassion, had led her into nursing. What she had seen in the notebooks looked rather interesting to her. She went and put the notebooks on her bed and then hurried to join Lachlan in the front room to find Christine had already arrived, helping a hobbling man in high-vis through the front door. Doctor and nurse both rushed to help her get him into the treatment room and inevitably fell over each other in doing so. Margaret gave Lachlan a dirty look that made him assume his proper role while she got their patient onto one of the beds.

Christine gave a paramedic's rundown on their patient, starting with the apparent nature of the accident and ending with how he was complaining about twisting his ankle when dismounting from his crashed truck, from which he had extricated himself apparently without other injury.

'What's your name?' asked Margaret.

'Damian, Damian Stavropoulos; but they call me Ned.'

Damian, strong and loyal, mused Margaret.

Lachlan took over. 'OK Damian, my name is Dr Tan, and this lady is Margaret Pursehouse. She is a nurse. I'm sorry we don't look too medical, but we were doing other things and not expecting you. Christine here tells me you have been in a car accident, so just between us I'd like to take a good look at you and make sure that you haven't done any more damage than just twisting your ankle. Are you happy that I do that?'

'I feel fine except for the ankle, doc – that's bloody sore.' The look on his face belied anything he might have said to the contrary.

'Well, make me happy and let me have a look at the rest of you and we'll sort that ankle out as well. Are you allergic to anything?'

'Not that I know of – oh except penicillin.'

'Never had any problems with anaesthetics or painkillers?'

'Er no, but you could give me something for that fucking ankle.' He grimaced again.

'OK. Just checking before I do that. Have you seen what they call the green whistle the paramedics use on those ambulance shows? Its trade name is Penthrox. I think we'll give you one of those to use until we know exactly what damage you've done.'

He nodded at Margaret, and she went and retrieved a methoxyflurane inhaler from where she knew she had put them, and instructed their patient on how to use it as Dr Tan began his examination.

Disregarding how well the patient said he felt, Lachlan went through the process of checking him for concussion as well as other injuries. Helping him off with his shirt and allowing him to swap the hands in which he held the inhaler, he noted some bruising starting to show where the belt had held him in his seat. It wasn't nearly as bad as many he had seen. On questioning his patient, it came out that the impact his body had taken had neither been sudden nor from high speed, and there was no immediate evidence of broken ribs or internal injuries.

'How is the other driver? Was there another driver?' Lachlan asked, looking firstly at Christine and then back to his patient as he continued his examination.

'Yes,' said Christine.

'Crispy critter probably,' Ned said, and Christine confirmed it for him with a sad nod.

'Someone we knew?'

'Hughey. The boss. I think I told you he was coming today.'

'That's going to complicate life for you all.'

'I've dumped that on Gabe, the manager down at the Launceston office.'

'Fair enough.' Lachlan tried to be reassuring. 'You sound as if you've got everything under control.'

'The police are on their way up from Lonnie. I've got to sort out accommodation for two officers, and the security people are stringing up red tape and putting up cones around the site. A couple of blokes with one of our bushfire trucks are doing what they can to stop the fire spreading. I've told them to stand way back given there may be more stuff to blow. Fortunately, everything is wet and green.'

'OK,' announced Lachlan, having been working on his patient while they were talking. 'So far so good. Christine, if you will excuse us, we'll just cut the trousers off this bloke and have a good look at that leg. If you want to wait outside, I can answer any questions you might have in your role as workplace health and safety officer.'

Much to their patient's dismay, Margaret gently removed his belt and one boot and began cutting away the other and then the socks and the trousers from him. Twenty-five minutes or so later Lachlan joined Christine in the old dispensary, where she was looking through the box of bottles and old equipment he had packed.

'You can take those with you,' he said. 'There's nothing in there that needs special treatment. If you can salvage the bottles they might be of some value to a collector, or you might want to display them somewhere. Not my field of expertise. It may take a couple of goes, but warm soapy water should get the residues out of them. Just to be on the safe side whoever cleans them up, if that's what you do, should wear gloves. The glass is old and the bottles, while looking solid, may have been chipped and/or may be fragile.'

'OK.'

'As far as your patient goes, Damian will stay the night with us pending transport in the morning to Launceston. He's not bad enough for an emergency evacuation, and as it's getting late, and they probably have better things to do, I'm sure the Launceston chopper crew does not need a call from us. But I would like to keep an eye on him. We took a couple of quick X-rays, and I don't think his ankle is broken, but it's already swelling up magnificently from ligament damage. We've given him some painkillers and put the leg in a boot. I'll give him some more tablets in the morning and pack him off with one of your people by car first thing if you can arrange that, and if I think he's OK to travel. I don't think you want to be going down the mountain in a car in this weather in the dark.'

She nodded. 'Sounds good to me, can do.'

'Now, are you OK? Obviously you knew your boss and this must be a bit of a shock to the system.'

'I'm in paramedic mode.'

'OK.' Lachlan closed the door. 'So do you want to tell me what's between you and Margaret? Just so that if it's necessary I can tell Omicron she should not be sent up here again. Oh, and by the way, I can guess that Christine might once have been Christopher,' he added paternally.

Christine sighed.

'Christian actually. Well, I dropped enough hints, didn't I? Look – I know I'm a bit bitter, but I can manage it if she can't. The problem is hers not mine – I am over it, well as far as I'm ever going to get over it.'

Lachlan nodded and waited for the rest of the story to spill out.

'You're right of course. I have transitioned and it was all done in a timely and reasonably gentle manner, with my initially shocked parents agreeing, and my informed consent, the court approval required in those days, etcetera, etcetera, etcetera. Except the supposed final surgery did not go totally to plan and I had to go back for what I like to call my "touch up" job.' She smiled. 'The vaginoplasty needed some more work.'

'Cosmetic?'

'Right. Bloody Margaret was an agency nurse called in to the hospital when one of the regulars got Covid and she went off her little religious brain when she found out the nature of my surgery and started going on at me about tampering with God's creation and all of that crap.'

'Oh dear.'

'She got so religious and heavy with it I began not to cope; you know with everything else I had to deal with, and her disdain when dressing my wounds and so on. So I reported her, and I didn't see her again. From what I heard back she got disciplined. I don't know all the details, they don't tell you that, but they let me know she was banned from that hospital, and the agency dumped her I think.'

'And if you had an accident up here or have a medical appointment with us you could cope with having her look after you?'

'I think so; and I know that, if it came to the crunch, I am confident enough to ask that she not look after me without having to give any details. Hopefully she has matured a bit too.'

'I can't guarantee that, but I'll ask her how she feels and if she is happy enough, on the strength of what you've told me I don't think I need to tell Omicron. Let's face it, she won't be here permanently, just on a rotating roster. OK?'

'Fine.'

'So, what else is troubling you?'

'How's your basic psychiatry?'

'Adequate. What's up? I'll let you know if I think I'm out of my depth.'

'I have a boyfriend and he is getting serious.'

'You used the word partner before, but presumably that was more expectation than reality. You haven't told him?'

'No. But I don't want to lose him.'

'Fair enough, but I think you already know the questions you have to ask yourself.'

'Is he worth trying to keep if he can't cope with me as I am, what I am?'

'Yes, but also can you understand he may be quite challenged by the situation, depending on who he is and what he knows?'

'You mean he may be shocked.'

'Yes. My guess is that you've been keeping him at arm's length while you sort out how to manage things. He'll be a bit perplexed about that already if you have already shown each other demonstrable affection. So I would guess you've decided that you want to move on from a kiss and a cuddle?'

'Right. Well, we have a bit anyway. I just have to tell him.'

'Having sex will entail just a bit of extra preparation – but I should point out that from what I know that can be done with caring, and lovingly. And then there are the long-term expectations he may have. If you want kids then you'll have to adopt or use a surrogate; and if you use a surrogate he'll have an investment in it genetically, but you won't. That could be a big leap for a man who wants his own children, and I might add, a test for you.'

'But most of all do I care enough about him not to delay, not to string him along?'

'That's a biggy.'

'So how do I do it?'

'The best advice I think I can give you is to be prepared. Have as much information as he might need at your fingertips so you can answer the questions he may ask.'

'Fair enough.'

'Oh, and one more thing, don't be put off if he wants some time to think things through. Don't resent it. You've already made the commitment in your own mind, and you know how testing that was for you. If he hesitates, see it as a positive in the sense that he really cares to get it right – for both of you. You might want to line up someone he can talk to. You will probably know where the right resources are to be found better than me.'

'Hadn't thought of that. Bit selfish.'

'Not really. It's not something you do every day.'

They both laughed.

'OK?' He opened the door and as she moved to leave, 'Don't forget your box of bottles now, Christine.'

'Oh, right, and thanks. By the way, most people get round to calling me Chris sooner or later.'

As she picked up the box with both hands and Lachlan opened the door for her to leave he did not notice that the old water-stained notebooks were not still with the bottles. He was distracted, a little worried that he should have perhaps warned Christine that her boyfriend might be really pissed off that she had not told him earlier. *But we can't all go around wearing badges*, he told himself, and if he had done that, she might have lost her determination to do what she had to do straight away. That would have been a much bigger mistake. While he was confident in the advice he had given and the manner in which he had elicited what needed to be done, and why, that had been just a chat. From the signals that Christine herself had been sending out he knew he might see her again, as a patient. He'd better do some reading and talk to some people.

Chapter 8

Christine Reynolds was just a little busy for the rest of the afternoon. There was a road accident management plan in place and the security people and the environmental crews under her control were across what had to be done quite quickly. On the other hand, staff accommodation was in her purview, and she had to sort out two rooms in the single workers' quarters for the expected police officers, and then let security know which rooms they were. She decided that it would be easiest if she personally took Dr Tan's patient into town in the morning. Everyone else in the company would have something else to do. Gabriel rang her from Launceston. The news had reached him, and he said he would be coming up the next day. Could she see if Mrs Scott could put him up at Perdition?

Oh shit, Mrs Scott!

She went round to the home of Mrs Aziz, the only person she knew that had a close relationship with the lady. Mohammed was still at the plant, but a phone call let him know what was happening and Christine took her up to Perdition, uncomfortably cross-country as the drive to the house was blocked.

Parking in the garage under the house, which was open, they presumed to go up the internal stairs uninvited to find a teary Mrs Scott in her kitchen, sitting at the table. She looked up as they came in and burst into sobs.

'He didn't make it, did he?'

'No, he didn't,' agreed Christine. 'If it's any consolation it's unlikely that he knew much about it, if anything,' she added kindly.

'I went out to see what had happened when all the windows shook. I got halfway down the drive but couldn't go any closer … the fire …'

'I think Hughey was dead before the fire even started, Mrs Scott.'

Mrs Aziz had found the coffee machine and the capsules and was starting to make a cuppa.

'Now, Mrs Aziz has agreed to stay with you for as long as you need. If it's alright with you, Gabriel from the Launceston office will be up in the morning, and he'd like to work from here. OK?'

'Yes. Yes, yes, that's fine … what's going to happen, Christine, what's going to happen?'

'I really don't know, Mrs Scott. I really haven't a clue. The company – Hot Rocks – and the project will go on of course but who will be in charge heaven knows. Gabriel will be the best person to work through all of that. I'm sure he'll keep you in the loop as much as he can. I'm totally in the dark about Hughey's personal affairs.'

'So what do I do?'

'Just keep on doing your job, Mrs Scott. I think it's safe for me to predict that you'll be needed. Gabriel will be just the first of the people who may need your hospitality as things get sorted. There's nowhere else for them to stay. I'm sure Hughey would want you to look after Perdition as well as you always have so that things can get organised.'

Understandably, Mrs Scott was looking shattered. Christine leant towards her, concerned.

'Are you OK … as much as you can be? There's a doctor down at the surgery as of today. I can get him for you if you think he could help.'

'No, no, no, that's fine. I've got some good company' – she held

Mrs Aziz's hand – 'and I've got some pills if I need them. I'll be fine.'

'Alright. I'll get out of the way. Don't hesitate to ring me or the surgery if you need anything.'

She smiled at Mrs Aziz, who had settled down with Mrs Scott at the table, all thoughts of coffee apparently forgotten at least temporarily, and left her to it. When she got back to the car she texted a message to the surgery alerting them to Mrs Scott as a prospective patient.

I don't need another session with Margaret, and anyway the road will be blocked, wholly if not partially.

She rang Gabriel and told him that he could stay at Perdition, rang Security (as the emergency management controllers) to check if they needed anything more from her or her people, then sent a text to all of her people thanking them for their help up to that time and alerting them to the fact that the emergency plan was in operation and if Security asked them to do something, like say traffic control in the morning, they should do that if they had nothing more urgent on their plates.

As she drove away from Perdition to the single workers' quarters, retracing her cross-country route and negotiating the grazing wallabies, it was already getting dark and she could see that the flashing yellow lights of the company vehicles on the accident scene had been joined by red and blue ones. Given her 6 am start and the strange and varied events of the day, Christine was feeling very weary.

Tomorrow looks like being another big day and I am ready for some food and my bed.

She went into the quarters, hanging the company vehicle keys on the board, and then to the cafeteria. Stephen had just come off shift and was looking pretty grimy while tackling a plate of what looked like beef stew and mash.

'Is that any good?' she asked.

'It's OK, but anything would be good after the day I've had, but I hear it hasn't been great out here either. Are you OK?'

'Yea, just tired I suppose.' She sat down next to him. 'Oh fuck, I forgot the horses.'

'I've done the horses.'

'You've done the horses?'

'I've done the horses. Did them on the way over. Thought you'd be busy.'

'You lovely Stephen you.'

'I knew that.' He looked at her. 'Do you want to go to bed with me?'

'You what?' she asked, buying time. *This wasn't in the Dr Tan playbook.*

'Do you want to go to bed with me?'

'Um …'

'I've read the manuals, and the magazine articles. And I've got fed up waiting for you to initiate something.'

'What do you mean, manuals?'

He smiled. 'How to fuck the trans woman. All of that stuff. Although I have been working on the presumption that you've had the full reassignment.'

'Yes I have, but it's not that simple. And how did you know?'

'Yes it is, and a kiss and a cuddle and a grope with you is different …'

'You mean, Casanova, different from the huge number and range of sexual conquests that you can compare me to?'

'Exactly. Different from the fifty percent of women in my age cohort who live in Tasmania and that I've slept with. That's not counting the overseas ones.'

'You stopped counting those?'

'Look. I love you, you appear to love me. I'm randy and I think you are. You tell me what you want me to do and I do it – once we get over the customary embarrassment of being naked together of course. Then I tell you what I want to do and if you agree we try that.'

He put his knife and fork down.

'Come on. Since you're the boss of the people in charge of this motel your room is a bit bigger than mine and we can share a shower. You are a virgin of course.'

'Of course.' She replied without thinking. She paused and looked seriously into his eyes. 'Stephen … are you at all familiar with the concept of T,A,C,T – tact?'

'Tact. Hmm, yes well, of course it's my job isn't it? A tact switch is a push-button switch that gives you a distinct click feel when operated.'

Christine looked at him very hard.

'They can be large or small, illuminated or not, water resistant if you want. There's lots of applications. The old foot-operated dip switch in cars and trucks were tact switches …' He paused, grinning at her.

'Shit, I walked into that!'

'Am I to also presume that you have indulged in some testing that everything works? Just for technical information for the trades you understand.'

'Seems to, although they wouldn't let me choose the design,' she added cheekily.

'What?'

'It's a joke, a joke I had with the surgeons. I said I wanted to go down to Hobart and choose a design off the Wall of Vaginas at MONA.'

Stephen laughed, and in the same humorous vein asked, 'So you have everything in the way of the accessories we might need?'

'Yes.'

'OK. Back to my original question. Fancy a shower with a friend?'

He stood up and offered her his hand.

I think a shower with a friend is just what I need.

'Yes,' she replied somewhat hesitantly. 'OK.'

And as she got up from the table he slipped his arm around her waist.

'This is how rumours start,' she said.

Chapter 9

Margaret was totally fascinated by what she found in the two notebooks even before she and Dr Tan returned to Launceston. This was a whole new dimension to the wonders of nature that she had never before encountered.

Her interest, if not sufficiently stimulated by the notebooks, was magnified when she went online and discovered there was a whole branch of study called mycology, and not only that: Tasmania had some of the most interesting fungi in the world. Moreover, she discovered that the relatively unspoiled part of the state that surrounded Mordbury would have some of the most interesting subterranean mycological activity in the country.

She found and read some of the extracts from the works of the experts like Anderson and May and Plett. In fact she started to become so engrossed that Lachlan found himself relieved of her company not only for the rest of their initial stay, but also on his subsequent visits to the Mordbury surgery when she was rostered with him. What's more, she seemed to positively seek out duty at the village, and had begun what he presumed was some sort of fitness regime, going for long walks in the bush out of surgery hours. When he let his curiosity get the better of him and spoke with his fellow practitioners in Launceston, they said the same thing.

'Can't bloody keep her away from the place,' said old Dr Giles, who was something of the elder statesman of the company's practices. 'I just wish she would take her turn behind the wheel of the fucking car once in a while. That drive is getting better, but I'm not getting any younger.'

'And cook?'

'And cook, although she is starting to take a bit of an interest in the kitchen – throws a lot of stuff out though from what I can tell. Perhaps she really isn't any good at it. Once in a while you can hear the Tassie devils squabbling over the discarded fruits of her labours. I'm doing what you're doing and taking up frozen meals and sticking them in the freezer. Although, once in a while, she does put together a casserole or make some soup.'

'She's got young Connie helping her plant a herb garden you know?'

'Oh, that's what that is. I wondered who was responsible for all those plastic pots. That's young doctors for you these days. Well at least it's keeping Margaret away from me and the subject of God. I do not wish to be saved and spend an afterlife that I don't think exists bored fucking rigid, praising someone I don't believe in into eternity. And if I am wrong and do end up at the pearly gates, I shall demand to see the proprietor immediately and give him, her, or them, choose your pronoun woke or otherwise, a grilling about the human condition.'

Lachlan grunted. 'When we're in the car together she's started talking to me about the wonders of the underground world and how the trees talk to each other, how some of the mycelium on their roots here is exceptional because it can tolerate the temperatures, and how there is an untapped resource of pharmaceuticals for us to exploit for the benefit of humanity.'

'Well does she now? No doubt all part of the Lord's beneficence to his creation. Well, I can tell her about magic mushrooms if she wants a horror story.'

'You haven't …?'

'No, no no, I'm not that stupid. Alcohol and a fatty liver will get me. Although I did meet one of our erstwhile colleagues before he ended up in jail for playing about with psychotropics. By all accounts a brilliant student. He got into the drug scene at university and started making lots of money manufacturing all kinds of shit. Problem was he used it as well. He hadn't got a clue what was going on around him later in life. I think he ended in a government home – and he was one of the lucky ones. I saw a couple of girls who sent themselves totally mad with psilocybin before they died in restraint in padded cells.'

'Not nice?'

'Not nice at all. One of them tried to tear her skin off. Something about being so hot she was cooking in it. Whatever she was thinking it wasn't anything short of kaleidoscopic.'

'Oh dear.'

'One other thing,' said Doctor Giles. 'Next time you're up there a patient called Christine, er, Christine Reynolds, I think it was. Good-looking young girl, but I'm too old to be allowed to think that anymore. Anyway, she wants you to look her up. Wants to have a chat with you about something personal. Didn't want to talk to me. You been dabbling in the murky realms of the psychiatric profession, Lachlan?'

'Just GP-level stuff.'

'Well, I don't need to know, but just look her up, will you?'

'Certainly. Nice lady.'

'Watch it Lachlan. You know what they say. You can look but you can't touch.'

Chapter 10

Peter Main looked down at his plate in search of the other half of his smoked salmon sandwich only to find that he had eaten it. The empty plate was sitting on his left ready for Mrs Scott to come and take it away. He was in a navel-gazing mood, and he excused himself from actually concentrating on work for a few moments of reflection on his place in the lengthening history of Perdition.

Having Mrs Scott was one of the many things that he had inherited, somewhat reluctantly because she was a complete unknown, from his deceased brother. Mrs Scott had apparently looked after Anthony over his years in Melbourne and was a happy and willing soul, always ready to do that bit extra when it came to meetings and parties. Beyond that her background was a mystery and her interests, if she had any beyond the household, she kept to herself. She rarely took time off and never took holidays. He guessed there had been a tragedy of some kind in her life and she had been happy to become a recluse at Perdition, managing the household for Anthony.

Anyway, she seems happy enough, and we couldn't do without her.

Having Mrs Scott was a huge relief because from time to time the stresses of building Project Sheol, a geothermal power station, about which he had known bugger all when he had started doing it fifteen months before, were rather taxing. Having someone else provide him with sandwiches and coffee and freshly made meals, and generally cleaning up after him, was a sanity saver, if not a life saver. Initially he had been reluctant to take it on because he didn't really know that he wanted Perdition, even though the hotel business had nothing new to give him.

Lyn had also had enough though, telling him that she could see the hotel business was grinding him down, while frankly the whole lifestyle his job dictated was making her less than happy. Moving from city to country and country to city, even country to country, changing her own job as regularly as he changed location, was neither helpful for her career nor beneficial for their relationship. Nothing like an honest wife to make you make up your mind. Then there was what he felt was his duty to Anthony's memory.

His brother, who he had to admit had left quite an estate, had been clear in his will. Whoever inherited could have the money but had to accept the project and see it through – and preferably it was to be him.

Briginshaw and Briginshaw, Anthony's solicitors in Hobart, had their hands on the will and their staff on the phone tracking him down before the death of his brother had even become more generally known. At least Anthony had kept Gabriel at Launceston up to date when it came to his personal affairs, as well as those of the company. Peter's own mind was made up when he felt he should fight the attempt by his erstwhile sister-in-law and his nieces to grab what they believed they could while they thought the going was good.

Glad I inherited Gabriel as well.

Justice Wrench in the Supreme Court had not at all been impressed by the former Mrs Main. In his will, Anthony had been more than explicit about how he felt about how much he had already been dispossessed by his ex-wife, how much work it had taken him to recover from the divorce, and how he had generously provided for his daughters in terms of both their expensive education and lavish social upkeep.

The judge expressed himself astonished by the demands they had placed on him until they had succeeded in entrapping marriage partners of their own while avoiding any meaningful employment. While it had been somewhat overdone in a judicial environment, Phillip Briginshaw SC had, to the extent that he thought he could get away with it, lent some colour to his reading to the court of the terms of the will as written. Given the public interest and the government investment in the Lucifer Hot Rocks Sheol project, the Hobart *Mercury*, subject to what Peter imagined had been some political influence on at least one of the editorial staff, had also done nothing to discourage the judge from ensuring that his brother's will be done.

Peter took a mouthful of the iced soda water sitting next to the empty plate and, looking out of the expansive triple-glazed window, contemplated the now reconstructed wall down the end of the long drive where his brother had met his end. While it was bloody hard going at times, he still accepted the duty that Anthony had laid upon him.

Sentimental bullshit?

There was fun in learning new things though, and there were plenty of new things to learn; and moving to Mordbury and settling down had pleased Lyn immensely. She had found herself a philosophy lecturer's position in Launceston with little trouble. Whether it was a wave of foreign students, a surge in resignations, her overseas experience, her age, or just knowing someone in the right place at the right time, she had found a job, albeit at a lower level than she would have wished for. Then she too had Mrs Scott to ensure their very comfortable home was clean and tidy to come home to. It was even better than the cosseted life they had lived in the hotels. Contented wife, contented life – and they didn't have kids to worry about.

Crossing the drive near to the gate walls were two large black horses, ridden he knew by Christine Reynolds and Stephen Banbury. Employees, and they were an item from what he had heard. Besides doing dressage and driving the big horses, Christine had ambitions to breed them.

He knew this because on his table was an application from her to take over the old mill once the project had no more need for it and to set up a stud. She had done her homework and there was a sensible lease arrangement proposed, along with an outline of her business plan. She also proposed that Stephen could keep an eye on the water treatment plant. It wasn't really in his purview, but he could keep an eye on it. It was up that way and with no one from the company needing the old mill any more … *Smart bit of value-adding, that.*

Given her continuing contribution to the project, and that of her electrical engineer partner, he saw no reason to deny her what she sought. That could be announced at the next management meeting.

That reminded him, they had to arrange a meeting with the police about what they were going to do about the potential greenie protests about the new power transmission line to the north. There were apparently rumours that they wanted him to put the bloody thing underground. There were two things against that: money and money. Financially it would not have stacked up on gently undulating open country with deep soil. Going across rocky native and plantation forest land, over hill and dale, around rocky outcrops and across rivers, was out of the question.

At least they didn't have to go through a national park, and the Minister had heaved a visible sigh of relief when he had given him that news. Placing towers through the plantation leases and other

Crown land would not, presumably, be problematical, but nearer to home and quite a bit on Mordbury land they had to go through old-growth forest. It didn't matter how green the Sheol project was, how much care they took not to disturb the wildlife and generally do the work as carefully as they were, and how much it would benefit the state and the country; serious green opposition was not going to be easy to negotiate.

They might drag it on for years in the courts.

It might end up looking less than pretty in the media as well – and at this late stage in the project too. Christine had, however, given him a report that suggested they could be somewhat proactive in dealing with the issue. He liked what she had suggested; it was low cost and low risk, and even if it didn't work in regard to the transmission line, it made sense in the greater scheme of things.

Looking like you tried to do the right thing is always the best policy.

As he mulled over the problem and watched the horses pass from view, he knew that further down on the road the afternoon cavalcade of semitrailers was –just like it had been on the afternoon of his brother's death – on its journey back down the mountain. However, today the weather was fine; no doubt the drivers were appreciating the fact that he had not only finished the road through Mordbury but had also successfully put a great deal of pressure on the government to play their part in improving the road down the mountain. It wasn't perfect yet, but it was much better, and a great deal safer.

While the segments of the towers for the grid connector were coming up the mountain, what was going down was the miscellaneous detritus from the end of the drilling and construction phases of the plant itself. For all intents and purposes the next valley now held an almost complete, almost operational geothermal power station; powered by the stored heat of the earth itself. Simple enough in theory but complex in the execution, its building was what had occupied every day and often most of the nights of Peter's life since his brother's death. The experts he had employed in his team and those of the contractors had given him a not-so-short education in the science and the engineering. His own management background, and indeed the analytical skills of his wife, had enabled them to pull it all together. He had adopted the principle that he would admit to knowing nothing about the technicalities while deftly solving problems with his management skills – and, he had allowed himself to admit, his capacity to deal with the politicians. There were a lot of Greens and green-leaning independents in the parliament, and they wanted the project but didn't want it to be seen to be polluting in its construction. It was a fine line he had to tread.

Christine has done her bit there too.

Unlike the smaller plants that had not been a great success in Queensland, this one was big. Instead of just working on water being pumped underground to be super-heated, and that heat then being recovered to drive turbines, this one involved an add-on: a high pressure, super-efficient heat transfer system. It used a combination of volatile gasses to scavenge what further energy it could after the scalding steam had been through the first turbines, thus driving two more. Peter admitted he still didn't actually understand more than the basic principles involved, but then he paid other people, and paid them well, to do that for him.

My job is not to make it happen, but to set up the conditions that allow it to be made to happen.

Speaking of other people, he reflected, there was another application on his desk for accommodation in Mordbury. While it was again for someone connected with the project, it was not from one of his employees.

It had caused him to wonder whether he really wanted to continue to maintain the village as a company town and his personal fiefdom. He had imagined that the only people resident after the power station was commissioned would be the permanent staff needed for its operation, security, and routine maintenance.

However, someone called Margaret Pursehouse, a nurse with the Omicron Medical Services Group, who were providing general medical assistance for the project, said she had fallen in love with the place and wanted to lease the houses at numbers 13 and 15. She wanted to live there and set up a Christian wellness centre while she would continue to be available as a qualified nurse even after the Omicron contract ended. The submission was not very detailed, a bit amateurish really, but he liked the idea that she would be available when the intensity of the building phase of the project was over and Omicron's services were discontinued. That bit of value-adding had not escaped her either. It would have benefits when it came to retaining staff, particularly those with families. The larger hotels he had run had always had some medical backup on site, as it was a marketing point in the cities; and essential in remote areas, especially when one could get snowed in.

While he had an almost operational power station as long as something didn't break down or prove poorly designed, he also had a company that was very close to scraping the bottom of its financial barrel, and he was getting a lot of pressure from the state government, which had substantially subsidised the whole thing. It, on behalf of the taxpayers of the state, wanted to see some return on their investment, and the Minister was pressuring the company to start seeing that soon. With the transmission line problem and the commissioning of the station finally on the horizon, these minor matters were a little annoying, and this one more so as he was a bit irritated by the whole idea of a *Christian* wellness centre.

He tapped the fingers on both his hands on the desk, firstly in parallel runs then three synchronised taps.

A *Christian* wellness centre? What was different about a *Christian* wellness centre as compared to any other wellness centre? Although of course if you read your Bible – and Peter had, cover to cover several times – Christian wellness was potentially a rather disturbing and selfish interpretation of a concept. *I suppose we had better talk to the woman.*

He looked back out of the window and could just see Number 13, on the other side of the road as it gently rose on his right-hand side. The idea was not going down well with Lyn, he mused. They had talked about it. She was almost a proselytising atheist. As for himself, he didn't really care – as long as the place wasn't invaded by hordes of handclappers.

The last thing we need to be doing is battling the Christians as well as the greenies.

Decision time. The company was supposed to be having a meeting to discuss a range of problems on Friday week – so Margaret Pursehouse might as well be asked along. He would get the Lonnie office to invite her, tell her that her cause would be helped with a short but detailed and businesslike briefing note, and above all let her know that she had ten minutes of their time and no more. The coppers they would meet with before the management meeting, which could start a bit late. They would need a briefing on the logistics and construction schedule for the transmission line. Parks and Wildlife ought to be there as well. These were issues of much more moment and complexity he, well he and Lyn, had to consider.

Having your wife on the board does make things easier.

Chapter 11

The person disturbing the business thoughts of Peter Main was at that moment assisting Dr Giles at the southern end of the island that is the state of Tasmania. The administration of the local clinic they were conducting was shared between Omicron, online from Launceston, and the local council, who provided the rooms. Frontline doctoring and nursing was provided by a visiting GP and a nurse, just as it was in Mordbury.

Margaret Pursehouse found the duty less than taxing compared with the larger practices in the network because the relatively fewer patients were generally glad to see the visiting medical team, and unless it was flu season the timetable was rarely more than leisurely. Anything acutely serious the doctors immediately referred to specialist services in a large centre, in this case Hobart.

There were of course those patients with chronic conditions, and Margaret respected Dr Giles for his patience in dealing with them if nothing else, especially the elderly. Alright, he was a male chauvinist and old-fashioned with it, but his bedside manner and his empathy could not be faulted. Moreover, he professed that arthritis and a range of conditions associated with ageing were catching up with him too, and admitted he could identify with his older patients more and more.

Margaret had with her three medications she was working on. One was a little powder she had developed from what appeared to be a species of *Ascocoryne*. It had been sketched in detail in one of the notebooks found at the Mordbury dispensary, and the sketch and written description had been annotated as a potential tonic. She had taken to walking around Mordbury, and she had found the mushroom. The notebook had suggested that it should be processed by drying and then crushing it to a powder. She had followed the directions and processed a batch and had then tried it out on Dr Giles a couple of weeks ago. About half a teaspoonful in a cup of tea seemed to be the right dose, and the old doctor had seemed quite reinvigorated the next day.

Given its effects on Dr Giles, she had tried it herself one day when she was feeling down and out of energy. It also worked well for her too, although she had had some strange dreams that night. Sex had never figured largely in her life, let alone in her dreams, and she had been quite shocked when she had woken the following morning to recall where her subconscious mind had been. She was not totally naïve in such matters but bondage? Really? Where had that come from?

She had christened it *Ascocoryne antidefessus*, and kept a little stock on hand with the other things she had discovered. When she was working with him she continued to dose Dr Giles to apparent good effect, and had decided to try it on a couple of the elderly patients they were seeing that day to see if it helped them too. If she could do good by rediscovering these things provided by God for man to use – well, it was her duty to relieve suffering. She had something that looked like it was going to work out as a great calming tincture too, and some cream that contained herbal agents that seemed to be good for skin conditions.

Dr Giles never called her Margaret, always Nurse Pursehouse, even when they were the only people present. Just at the moment he had Mrs Spencer in with him, and he had been seeing Mrs Spencer for at least twenty minutes. He would be probably seeing her for a bit longer yet. Mrs Spencer was elderly and was dying, but she was doing it incredibly slowly and seemed to be unable to decide which of her many diseases or ailments to die from. A true survivor, she had twice overcome Covid on top of all her other difficulties, large and small. No doubt one day the visiting medical team would no longer find Mrs Spencer in need of a consultation, but the way things were going that day seemed a long way off. The woman's resilience amazed them all, but for Margaret she was a prime example of the strength that belief in the Lord could bring. She and Mrs Spencer liked each other. They were both devout Christians even if Mrs Spencer was an Anglican and not a communicant in the true faith.

Margaret was alone in the treatment room for the time being. She had redone the dressing for Mr Pratt, whose leg ulcer was healing nicely, and now she was spending her time working on one of the Mordbury notebooks, rewriting it more legibly in a school workbook. Having deciphered other sections, she now felt able to substantially fill in the gaps where the notes were damaged. She was working out to the best of her ability what had been lost, by looking at how the rest of the books had been written and by following the sense of the wording. However, in many instances that lacked anything else to guide her, she was putting down what seemed sensible. The project had become something of a mission in healing for Margaret – the duty of a nurse and a true Christian.

While Mrs Spencer was having her unexpectedly long consultation and Margaret was hard at work on her private project, the patients were banking up. Mr Joules, who always made an appointment and always expected to be seen at the exact time set down for it, was being the obnoxious pig he often was. Grandstanding, he was playing the salesman, trying to draw the rest of the waiting room into supporting his argument that the system was broken, and it was clear that the problems were down to the incompetence of the people involved in running it, especially those who were there at that particular minute.

Given that everyone in the waiting room had some sort of malady and was not feeling well, Mr Joules was decidedly unpopular. Even the young council clerk behind the desk had found a lot of paperwork to do. The man intimidated her. Now Margaret was privy to the practice notes not only on him but also those on his long-suffering wife. She knew the poor woman had been the subject to bullying and a couple of quite serious assaults that the doctors had attributed to him. She felt the council clerk had every right to feel intimidated.

Mr Joules was huge, corpulent, and a manual worker whose dirty high-vis wardrobe bulged with both muscles and fat. Presumably all he needed was a fresh set of prescriptions for the blood pressure medication he had to take, yet he was carrying on as if a little delay was a major problem threatening the future of the world. She observed him through the crack between the hinges on the half-open door to the treatment room. As she watched he got out of the plastic chair that his enormous rear end had been swamping and lumbered across the room to approach the young girl at the counter again. He banged his right fist down on the countertop and commanded her attention and then spoke his mind. Margaret could not hear the detail, but whatever he said had obviously not been nice. He returned to his seat, leaving the girl crying and searching everywhere for the box of tissues that was usually kept on the desk.

This cannot continue. Margaret thought of that other tincture she'd brought along – she hadn't personally tested it on another person before, but it might be just the thing to try on Mr Joules to calm him down and make him more amenable. It was of the ones in the

Mordbury notebooks where the notes had been badly affected by damp and the ink had faded, so she'd had to fill in a great many gaps. But she was fairly sure it was intended to be used as a calmative.

So, she went over to the man and meekly apologised for his having to wait.

'Look, I am sorry for the delay, Mr Joules,' she said, 'but some patients do have bigger problems and the doctors do like to make sure they cover everything they need to.'

Reclaimed some ground there.

'Why don't I get you a cup of tea?' she asked. 'What do you take?'

That took some of the wind out your pompous sails.

'White and three sugars … please.'

'Well, just stay there and I'll be right back with one of those for you.'

With Mr Joules calmed a little and satisfied with her servile act, Margaret went to the kitchenette and made the tea. In the absence of other instructions in the notebook, she had crushed the fungus and diluted the fluid she had produced with alcohol to make an extract. She found the bottle in her bag and slipped two drops into the cup. Since she was experimenting, she would normally have used just one drop, but she decided on two in Mr Joules' case. He was a big man after all. In what she felt was an abundance of caution she decided three might be excessive.

Two should calm him down. It might do nothing. It will be interesting to see.

🐈

Margaret had not bothered to think about what other medication Mr Joules might be taking, or whether he had visited the pub for lunch. She blithely proffered the cardboard cup to him in the waiting room and his giant short-fingered hands enveloped it, grime engrained in their cracking skin. Leaving him to it while she answered Dr Giles's call for her to come into the consultation room, she hadn't even had a chance to close the door behind her when there was a sigh and a thud, followed by a call of 'Oh!' from the girl at the desk.

Mr Joules was slumped on the floor. The dregs from his cup were spilled on the carpet.

Chaos of course ensued, with Dr Giles sending for this and for that while he worked on the body. In fact, his ability to get down on the floor and valiantly deal with his patient displayed an energy and flexibility everyone present felt was beyond the doctor's mature years.

They reflected as they watched him using CPR on the big mound of flesh on the floor that he did look very well for his age. An example to us all, they felt. Must be following his own advice, they observed.

His energy had surprised Dr Giles himself. 'A one and a two and a three and a four and a five and a six, twenty-four to go before the breath. And bugger the ribs.'

I haven't been able to do this sort of thing in years.

While he refused to take statins, as he agreed with the opinion and indeed recent research that they were pretty useless and the side effects were unpleasant if not dangerous, he too was on the usual blood pressure medication, diuretic and anti-inflammatories just like many of his overweight mature-aged patients with arthritic joints. His now sedentary profession as a locum GP did not lend itself to much exercise.

'Twenty-six, and twenty-seven, got the defibrillator, nurse? Good, a breath and we'll try the machine.'

He called it after a suspenseful quarter of an hour, and only two applications of the defibrillator. Jump starting, as he called it, wasn't going to work. The man was dead, and he had done what he reasonably could, and moreover had been seen to make an effort. He was happy to pack everything up and walk away.

The consensus of those present, and subsequently among workmates, family and the community when they heard what had taken place, was that Derek Joules was not a man who would be missed. Dr Giles had not only demonstrated an admirable medical dedication but had been more committed to the revival of Mr Joules than generally they themselves might have been, and that had therefore been a further credit to him for a man not only of his age but also as someone who would have been aware of his patient's character. The episode enhanced his reputation.

So, while the earthly presence of Mr Joules lay under a treatment room blanket on the floor, awaiting the arrival of the police, Dr Giles quickly and quite cheerfully saw the remaining waiting patients and then closed the surgery for the day. Two remarkably unconcerned police officers duly arrived and wrote down what Dr Giles, the clerk and Margaret had to tell them. By the time they had done that, the Geeveston ambulance, in lieu of a mortuary ambulance, had arrived. All present were needed to assist the paramedic firstly to roll the dead weight of the corpse onto a backboard, and then to lift it and transfer it onto the ambulance trolley.

Margaret crossed herself as the body was loaded and the doors closed upon it. She was shocked about what had happened and wondered if it was down to her, even if she had acted with the best of motives. Dr Giles informed the paramedic and the police that he would see to the death certificate, and took it upon himself to relieve the officers of the duty of visiting Mrs Joules and advising her of the passing of her husband. *And tormentor*, thought Margaret, making sure the paper cup from the tea Mr Joules had drunk was washed three times and then disposed of in the garbage. She said a short prayer and crossed herself again.

A gift from the Creator, she reflected, even if she had been a little generous in handling His largesse. She would need to dilute the extract before she could use it again. The world would not miss Derek Joules, she told herself.

It's all worth it for the greater good.

While she did feel some guilt, she rationalised that her motives had been good. She almost managed to completely absolve herself of any guilt in his passing, never mind that he had departed with the assistance of a cup of adulterated tea she had made for him.

He might have been going to die anyway. It was coincidence probably.

It was a generally unknown variant of *Amanita* in that tincture. The person who had discovered it and described it so well in his now faded, water-stained notebook had christened it *Amanita mordburyia*. It was small and not very prominent, and very picky about the time it chose to bloom. Margaret had found it quite readily with the help of the notebook – just as she had found other fungi on her working visits to the Mordbury valleys where she was now wont to stroll around after surgery.

It was a shame the notebook had been particularly damp at the bottom of the relevant page and therefore uninformative about dosage. If Margaret had been the beneficiary of all the original writings about the fungus in the notebook and not so hell-bent on her new career as a healer, she would have known that the original author had only commended the use of the fungus in formulating a sedative for horses. He had written at length about its potency. The smallest amount was immediately fatal for the Tasmanian devils he had baited to test it on. The rudimentary post-mortem examinations he had made of them suggested that their hearts had just stopped.

Despite her best efforts, by the following Saturday and after much reflection, Margaret had some greater guilt about what she had done. After all she had been trained in guilt ever since she was a small child.

Contrary to her custom of monthly attendance, she made a special visit to church and waited her turn for the confessional. She always felt so much better about life after letting everything out, and usually most of the things she confessed to were so minor as to warrant a commensurate penance. Like many penitents she always put as light as possible an interpretation on her sinful thoughts and acts, because while she wanted to let God know that she recognised her faults, she saw no reason to let his representative get too intimate with her life. Anyway, these days God, according to his unworthy priests, didn't seem to want you to spell things out at length. Presumably he knew the details anyway and, in his omniscience, only wanted your acknowledgement of the errors of your ways.

So, as she took her place in the short queue in the austere surroundings of the confessional area, rehearsing the familiar litany, she thought through how she was going to put things. She had not been early enough to see who the priest on duty was for the day, but had been hoping it was not one who knew her well. She always found a rehearsal of the words gave her confidence. Margaret was a practised penitent and always put the worst offence at the bottom of the list, hoping it would be less noticed.

The confessional became free, and she gave it a couple of seconds before rising from her pew and entering.

Here we go.

'In the name of the Father, and of the Son, and of the Holy Spirit. Amen.'

'May God, who has enlightened every heart, help you to know your sins and trust in his mercy.'

It was a voice she did not know, and it was an accent she could not place. He sounded like an older man, however.

'Bless me, Father, for I have sinned. It has been a week since my last confession. These are my sins:

'I have thought ill of others, particularly those who do not believe, and while I have prayed for them, I feel I may have treated them more harshly in word and deed than I should have. As the commandment says, I should not be the judge of others.

'I have wanted some of the things that other people have, and as the commandment says, I should not covet the property of others.

'I made a mistake that seriously affected someone, and as the commandment says, I should always treat others in the same way I would hope they would treat me.

'I am sorry for these and all of my sins.'

The priest was indeed of some age and commensurate experience. He immediately recognised that he was dealing with a regular penitent, but something told him that on this occasion, by her tone of voice and contrary to the simplicity of her words, she was more than usually worried. He decided to probe a little and see if she understood that being judgemental was not appropriate.

'My daughter, as believers we all wish that others would follow us in the true faith – although you should understand that the best path is to encourage belief in others through the manner of your conduct of your own life as an example. What is your occupation?'

'I am a nurse, Father.'

'So, you are engaged in trying to do God's work and relieve the pain of the sick.'

'I try to do that, Father.'

'Most worthy. The Bible tells us that healing the infirm was important to Jesus in his ministry. Now, in relation to your mistake. Was it at work?'

'It was while I was at work, Father.'

'And the person concerned. Do you think they are a good person?'

'Well, no, Father, the person was not very nice. I'm not the only one who thinks so,' she hurriedly added as a justification.

'Hmm … Well, it is not of course for us to judge. Given what else you have told me, can you honestly say that you did not act deliberately against this person with malice but that you made a genuine error?'

'Yes, Father. The problem occurred because I went too far in the hope of helping him and in doing so, helping some of the people to whom he was causing distress. It all went wrong, and I am so sorry.'

There was indeed something she wasn't telling him, the priest decided, but on the other hand she seemed to know that she had sinned and was genuinely sorry. He might, however, not just issue the usual type of penance. He bet himself that this penitent was the type who might be talking to God quite frequently, and she needed something more than five Hail Marys to remind her of her contrition.

'My daughter, do you pray?'

'Yes, Father, every morning when I get up and sometimes at night.'

'Do you say the rosary?'

'Er – rarely, Father.'

You mean you don't. Alright, let's be a bit old-fashioned.

'Yes, well … well, remembering that God knows the truth about what has happened, what you did and why, and will recognise your genuine contrition, I will assign you the following penance. When you pray this week you will say the rosary on the appointed days, and as you do, remember to remind yourself that one should not rush to judgement. You must say it in full. Do you understand?'

'Yes, Father.'

'Then say the Prayer of the Penitent, and say it from your heart.'

'My God, I am sorry for my sins with all my heart. In choosing to do wrong and failing to do good, I have sinned against you whom I should love above all things. I firmly intend, with your help, to do penance, to sin no more, and to avoid whatever leads me to sin. Our Saviour Jesus Christ suffered and died for us. In his name, my God, have mercy.'

'May our Lord and God, Jesus Christ, through the grace and mercies of his love for humankind, forgive you all your transgressions. And I, an unworthy priest, by his power given me, forgive and absolve you from all your sins, in the name of the Father and of the Son and of the Holy Spirit. Amen. Now give thanks to the Lord, for he is good.'

'His mercy endures forever.'

'The Lord has freed you from your sins. Go in peace.'

Margaret felt a great deal better as she left the church, although she felt the old priest had gone a bit over the top. The full rosary was a bit unexpected. It was so long since she had said it, let alone as prescribed in the weekly calendar, but she would do what she had been instructed.

I shall have to look it up.

Chapter 12

Margaret emailed in her further submission applying for her Christian Wellness Centre lease on the Tuesday before the management meeting.

She had been surprised when she received an immediate reply advising her that the meeting would be held at Perdition starting at 11 am the following Friday, and that if she would like to attend, she would be welcome to talk to the submission and answer questions. She had expected the meeting to be held at the company offices in Launceston, but on reflection she understood that most of the management who would be attending the meeting, and indeed Mr and Mrs Main, were based on site. She therefore was forced to take leave for the day. Fortunately, she was rostered at the larger Launceston practice, so it was possible for it to be granted at that short notice.

She determined she would not be late and, having arrived at the bottom of the driveway somewhat prematurely before half past ten, she had to decide whether to wait or go up to the house. Wondering if turning up early would be considered bad manners or be impolite, as Mr and Mrs Main might not be prepared for business matters before the time the meeting was to start, she decided to risk it. Sitting alone in the car at the bottom of the drive, loitering, was about as embarrassing as things could get.

However, as she got closer to the house, she found that there were several vehicles already parked on the forecourt. Checking them as she decided where to park, she was somewhat apprehensive to see that one of them was a police SUV, another was a Parks and Wildlife car, a third was a dual cab utility with a Lucifer company logo, and there was a fourth which was unmarked. As she got out of her car, two more company vehicles arrived to park next to her.

The occupants of those cars asked if she was there for the meeting. When she said yes, they escorted her into the house through the front door of the original colonial building – it was, she noted, immaculately restored – and thence up a short flight of stairs into the new and grand extension. She found herself in a long open-plan room that almost ran the length of the house. It featured a table that could accommodate double the customary six diners, and a lounge area with very expensive-looking sofas and chairs that could easily seat the same number. There was a massive television screen on the wall at that end of the room.

Set up for business, the dining area had a sideboard with urns, coffee and tea, a range of plates, cups and saucers and light refreshments; and surrounding that were uniformed police and wildlife rangers, as well as a couple of civilians. They were putting down their used cups and plates and shaking hands and being farewelled by Mr Main, whom she knew by sight, and a woman she thought was probably his wife. Neither of them had needed medical care from the Omicron surgery, at least never while she was on the roster at Mordbury. A woman she did know as a patient was Mrs Scott, problem depression and the onset of menopause, who had appeared from the rear of the house and started clearing up the sideboard. Margaret did not count her as a friend.

The person she presumed was Mrs Main called the meeting to order even while Mrs Scott was working, and those who had been helping her clear up sat themselves around the table. Margaret, with no one to tell her what to do, found a vacant chair for herself.

It was some distance from the middle where Mr and Mrs Main sat next to each other. She had only just sat down when the person she had presumed to be Mrs Main caught her eye and asked quite abruptly, 'And who are you?'

Blunt to the point of discourtesy.

The rest of the table turned to look at her while she spluttered out a response. 'I'm Margaret Pursehouse,' she said, and added 'the nurse' for further explanation. 'I was invited.'

'Oh, OK. You can stay because there is nothing too contentious going to be discussed, but we won't be getting to your business until later on. As you would have seen we had an earlier meeting and some of those around the table need to leave as soon as they may. Just to let you know the rules, we expect people to speak their minds and there is nothing said at these meetings that is stupid. Everybody is stupid most of the time anyway, so any suggestion anyone has about any subject is welcome on the chance that it's brilliant. Mr Main and I are not top-down people. On the other hand, while people here take this for granted, we don't talk about what is said outside the meeting. Have you got that?'

'Er, yes,' replied Margaret. The Mains might not see themselves as top-down people but there was an authority in Mrs Main's voice – she was now certain the lady was Mrs Main.

'Good. By the way, we don't take minutes of these meetings as such, we just digitally record them for posterity.' She waved her hand at two flat microphones on the table and got down to the courtesies. 'Well, Chris who handles our environmental stuff is known to you I believe; I'm Mrs Main and the rest are the various members of the management team from both here and Launceston that are helping us make this work. I'm not going to go round the table. You'll probably pick up what they do from what they have to say. Right, let's get on.'

While she had been speaking, every person at the table except Margaret had produced a laptop and was studying what was on their screen.

The practice meetings are nothing like this. I suppose I should have brought at least a pen and paper.

'Item one,' Mrs Main said. 'Greenie protests and the transmission line.'

There was an audible groan from around the table.

'The meeting we just had with the powers that be was pretty good. We know that they will probably be actively protesting but with any more difficulties that are created it will all likely be happening at the northern end on the government plantation land. As you are all aware, the powers that be had a chance to get a feel for what could happen when the contractors began clearing at that end. I suppose the TV stations got their money's worth, but of course this end is Main land and we can at least limit media access if necessary. If people want to tramp through the bush, there is not much we can do about it. I suppose if they do, they will be greenies, so they won't upset the devils, the wombats and the platypoi. The power station is reasonably secure of course and I can't see any protesters wandering off into the bush or indeed the plantations if they have any sense at all.'

'They'll need a good sense of direction or a map and compass if they do,' came a comment from down the table, which caused a few others to snigger.

Somebody else murmured, 'I think it's platypuses.' They were ignored.

Mr Main picked up from where his wife had left off.

'Now as you can see, Chris has come up with an idea that might make things a bit easier if anything will. I for one can do without any unnecessary publicity. So, for those who haven't read her report, this is what we are thinking. The police have given us a list of half a dozen names of the people who might lead any protests. On the basis that we will invite them and anyone else we think ought to come, within reason, to visit us here at Mordbury and let them have an inspection at the plant. Free tea and biscuits and all the good green messages we can put together in a talk and a tour. A bit of an embarrassed mea culpa about the not-so-green things you have to do when you build a 165-meg power station, and what was done to mitigate even those. As we all know, the amount of tree planting and landscaping that has been done makes things look pretty good if you come in from this side. The roofing is almost finished, and the mounting of the solar panels is keeping up with that, so our green credentials in both theory and practice are probably as good as they can be.'

A male voice came from down Margaret's side of the table. 'It's just that I can't do much to make bloody commercial power station transformers, a switching yard and a transmission easement and towers look anything other than what they are.'

'No, you can't, Barry,' affirmed Mrs Main, 'and we are not fucking going to ask you to try to do that. I know it's late in the piece, and to give Chris the credit she deserves, what she has done previously liaising with some of these people has kept the protests to almost zero to date. It's the transmission line that's the problem. Although I can't see why anyone would think you can build a power station and not have one. The idea is that we show the greenies what a great job we've done in building an environmentally brilliant geothermal commercial power plant on land that was already environmentally compromised by the settlers who cut down all the trees; and not only have we gone as green as we could in doing that, but we have put a hell of lot of the trees back too, even if they aren't very big yet.'

'And the hope is?' asked Barry.

'And the fucking hope is, as Chris points out in her report, that at least some of the people who are pissed off that we have had to chop down some more virgin forest to send the power to where it is needed, come to see where the environmental balance is. You can't expect them not to have a bigger agenda but at least they might be neutral about what we are trying to achieve.'

'I don't know who has noticed with how busy we have been, but we have also managed to do something about the "Oh Jesus Christ!" thing that everyone always does the first time they go into the valley,' Christine said.

Margaret was not impressed by this blasphemous statement, particularly coming from her old antagonist, but no one else at the table turned a hair. She was in a minority of one. While she had not been into the other valley since her induction morning, she did remember how astonished she was with what she had seen after they had left the green and bucolic scenery of the first valley.

Christine continued. 'No doubt the truckies are not thrilled, but we waited as long as we reasonably could. For those with their minds on other things who may not have noticed, last week we finished the new kink in the approach road and put in a big hummock with a double row of some rather expensive semi-mature trees on it. So, as you come over the rise you have to turn left for about fifty metres before you do a U-turn and see the plant. It's not four hectares of power station in your face anymore, and of course the completion of the roof and the sections of timber walling that's been put up break up the industrial look too.'

'OK,' said Mrs Main, 'anyone got any objection to hosting a by-invitation inspection of the Sheol project by the green revolution?'

There was no more comment.

Peter Main took over. 'Right. Chris, put the wheels in motion, will you? Pick a day – soon. Everyone else, I know the pressure is on. Sorry about the pun, but please, do what Chris needs to have you do to make it work,' he ordered. 'Don't forget to invite some friendly media, Chris. You can limit the number by explaining the limits on the number of people we can cope with on an inspection.'

'Now, Mohammed,' said Mrs Main. 'Next item. What's this about ambient heat in the buildings?'

Mrs Main seems to act as chairperson while Mr Main pronounces the decisions, or do they sort of work as a single unit?

A rather swarthy man sitting next to Margaret on her left cleared his throat.

'Lyn, guys. It's something we didn't really think about; but with the roof on we are trapping more heat from the plant, and it's got to go somewhere.'

So, Mrs Main gets called by her Christian name by the management team.

Interesting, thought Margaret, given what she had seen of and heard from the woman so far. She did not think that Lyn Main was quite happy for that to be the case, watching her manner.

'As I say in my report,' the man said, 'we don't yet know how much we're going to have to deal with until we have everything fully up and running. We can try to calculate the efficiency of the secondary heat exchange and what heat will escape, but while the modelling is good enough to tell us we have a problem, we don't really know what the actual figure will be. Notwithstanding the insulation on both the water and the gas circulation systems being the best we can economically do, we will have waste heat and it looks as if we may have quite a bit of it. If we didn't have seventy percent of the plant underground or roofed then we would have an ugly plant which would be hard to work on given the vagaries of the climate, and lose a couple of hectares of solar panels, and the heat would just get taken away in the wind – which would not exactly fit our environmentally correct ethos – but it would work.'

'So, what do you want to do?' asked Mr Main. 'And remember it's got to be cheap because we are running out of dollars like I don't believe.'

'Well, as I explain in Appendix Two of my report, the only really good idea that my people have come up with is to construct some sand batteries and get someone else to pay for the privilege of putting up some greenhouses and growing vegies with the stored heat. As everyone knows, we don't have a shortage of water …'

There was the hint of mirth around the table.

'I know it's a bit imaginative, but if we can recover the capital cost pretty quickly and make it cost-neutral for us in the longer term, well actually the medium term, well … Peter, I would like everyone to look at the idea and get back to us with why it won't work and/or any better ideas. I'd like Launceston to do some figures on it because, while we can build it readily enough, the economics are not our area of expertise – and I don't know what the potential is for someone to be interested in doing it and paying us for the heat etcetera etcetera, so someone needs to have a look at the market.'

Lyn Main adopted her chairperson role and looked for further comment, sweeping her eyes around the table. 'Right,' she said. 'Gabriel, get a couple of bean counters onto that and give us a full report the meeting after next, will you?'

Margaret thought she heard a half-stifled sigh from the other end of the table.

Whoever you are, Gabriel, you're feeling a bit overloaded.

Peter Main took up the running. 'OK we do that. Moving on. Gabriel, while we're talking money and while your own report to the meeting is pretty clear, is there anything you want to add to it?'

'Not much to say really. To be blunt, stop fucking spending money unnecessarily, you people. We always knew the project plan was, shall we say, ambitious, and that the budget was an approximation with a lot of guesses about unknowns; but basically I don't think the banks will lend us any more, and I know the government is getting antsy about their investment. Until we are pushing water down the hole, or should I say holes, and electrons down the wires – what you see in the financial report is all you're likely to get.'

Mr Main came to his manager's support. 'I asked Gabriel to be blunt, people, but I had expected not quite that blunt.' He raised his eyebrows in the man's direction. 'But we're nearing the end of the project and every dollar we overspent before is money we don't have now,' he said. 'We have bought lots of stuff and it's sitting there on the site or in the ground. There's over fifteen kilometres of the best Korean stainless steel piping of various diameters with custom made pressure joints for a start, and that did not come cheaply I can tell you. When my brother signed the original contracts for that they were rise and fall, and while I don't think he ever expected a fall, he did not budget sufficiently for the rise. Our mate Vladimir and events in the Middle East saw to that. Then there's the other contractors. Even the trucking contract had a clause in it around fuel prices. Very wise if you are the contractor, but it made things a bit open ended for us. Now we saved a bit by offering accommodation on site, but that required us to hire Omicron because we couldn't get agreement without onsite medical cover. We got longer days with a fitter workforce and less absenteeism, but using Omicron and other things to do that was unforeseen. No daily travel but the cost of renovating houses, putting in the single workers' accommodation, even the shop and weekly shopping run added to the wrong side of the ledger.'

'OK, Peter,' butted in his wife, the only one who really could. 'People, there's enough money to finish the project, but only just, if we don't get any more surprises. I guess in six months or so we'll be selling power and paying bugger all to produce it. For those of you staying on to run the place that will be rewarding; for those of you who see the project through and move on, you will have something huge to add to your CVs as well as knowing you've done something worthwhile. Now what's next?'

The meeting moved on to more minor matters, matters that involved the management of the project and the testing and commissioning of the plant.

Margaret had never previously been aware of what it took to manage an enterprise as large as the one Lucifer Hot Rocks was engaged upon, and while she was annoyed that they had not gotten to dealing with her request as yet, she was fascinated to see what had to go on behind the scenes to make things work. There was obviously a detailed commissioning plan behind it all and, while she did not have access to it because she neither had a computer nor was part of the company, everyone involved was talking to it, and indeed changes to it were being proposed and accepted or rejected.

What also surprised her was that, while it was clear that Mr and Mrs Main were in charge, everyone felt able to have their say. They even had the confidence to get up from the table and get themselves a coffee and a snack while the meeting was still in progress. By two o'clock she began to see why. Her tummy was grumbling. It had been an early start, and she always ate a simple breakfast. She was just about to tempt fate by doing the same when Mr Main wrapped up other items and came to hers.

'Now, Ms Pursehouse – Margaret,' he said. 'Sorry about keeping you waiting, but the agenda just got bigger in the last couple of days, and we should probably have asked you to come later. Anyway, your project. My wife and I are not unsympathetic to what you want to do. Is there anything you want to add to your written request?'

'No, I don't think so, Mr Main.'

She paused, distracted by Mohammed and a couple of other people quietly packing up their computers and discreetly getting up from the table.

'I didn't know whether you wanted to have other activities in the village when the construction had been finished, but I have grown very fond of it while I have been attending with Omicron and also feel I can do something worthwhile given my background and skills.'

'Alright, apart from Gabriel who has already had a word in my ear, does anyone else at the table have anything they want to say?'

There was silence around the table. If anyone did have anything to say they had probably had enough of the meeting anyway and had other things on their minds. For most of them the matter was somewhat irrelevant.

'Alright, Margaret, we will approve your application to set up a wellness centre, as you call it. Planning permission is not a problem, we've double-checked that. There will however be some conditions to that approval, and I want you to liaise with Gabriel in Launceston to sort them out. He's our administration manager. Principally they are the following. You will incorporate the business, obtain appropriate insurances, choose something non-religious for the name of the centre – my wife and I are both atheists and while we appreciate your motivation, and respect your right to your beliefs, even if they seem irrational to us, we do not intend to promote them. You will need to agree a lease for the premises and also to enter into a contract with us with a range of provisions including things like your being subject to our security requirements, cooperating with our maintenance people, respecting and having your guests respect the fact that you will be operating on my private property, etcetera etcetera. Can you do that?'

Margaret was dazed by the amount of stuff she had to get her head around, but having heard what had gone on in the rest of the meeting she had begun to see that the Mains were in business and knew what they were doing.

I've got a lot to learn about being a business person.

'I think so,' she replied. 'I suppose I should get a solicitor to sort this out.'

'That sounds like a good idea,' said Mrs Main, not unkindly. 'It may seem a big expense, but it will be quicker and more simple for you, as I don't think you have done anything like this before. Between us, it will make things easier for us if you do too. The one thing you will have to come up with straightway though is how you want to structure the lease. You haven't put anything in your application about that, but Gabriel has come up with some ideas about making that relatively simple for you and you need to talk to him about the options. OK?'

'Er, OK.'

'Gabriel,' asked Mr Main, 'is there anything you want to add?'

'No, Peter, except that I've written out the options we discussed for Ms Pursehouse and can give her those to consider before she leaves today. If we get onto things quickly, Ms Pursehouse can be visible, if not up and running, by the time our guests come and see us for the environmentalists' open day. I think we can get Ms Pursehouse off to a good start.'

That sounded good.

'Alright, Margaret,' said Mr Main. 'Please talk to Gabriel before you go.'

With no more said by anyone he closed the meeting, thanking everyone for their attendance. If she had thought there would be a chance for friendly conversation afterwards, Margaret found herself disappointed. All the other participants in the meeting left quickly and without ceremony to deal with their own responsibilities. That included Mr and Mrs Main. The man called Gabriel approached her.

'Let me walk you out.'

They went to their cars, and he said, 'Call me, or get your solicitor to, as soon as you can when you've looked at the options and you've got your incorporation organised, and we'll finalise the contract and a lease.' He gave her an envelope which she later found contained his business card and a sheet of paper with the company's rough proposal outlined on it.

That was it. Nothing more. She got into her car somewhat stunned. It hadn't been unfriendly, they had agreed to what she had wanted (on their terms), but she had found the process well … brutally businesslike. She had to ask herself '*what did I expect?*'

What Margaret hadn't realised was that to some extent the whole meeting, while necessary for the functioning of the Hot Rocks business and mainly concerned with that, had been tweaked to make sure she did exactly what the company wanted. They could have dealt with her at the start of the meeting, but they had quite deliberately made her wait. For people like Peter and Lyn Main, and Gabriel, turning Margaret's ambitions to their advantage was second nature. While she felt treated well enough, she had been convinced that she was a very minor cog in the main machine. She had been rushed into lots of decisions to which she felt she should have had time to give more consideration. Peter and Lyn had noted she had not even had the confidence to get herself a cup of coffee.

By the time Gabriel had managed her ambition, and her rather naïve firm of suburban solicitors, through the issues in three days flat, she had gotten agreement to a business name compromise. Gabriel had suggested Vision Wellness Centre and she had compromised with calling it just Vision but putting what she wanted as an addendum to the name. So it would be VISION (Christian

Wellness Centre), and she had been gratified that he would arrange for the erection of signage for her as well. The signage was no great expense for the company, of course, and it wanted consistency in that regard so there was no generosity involved – if she had realised it. Whether she wanted it or not there was not going to be a cross on the sign. Gabriel had his own agenda, and he needed Margaret in a good mood to achieve it.

She had agreed to all her clients travelling from and to Mordbury in the Lucifer Hot Rocks company bus with either she or they paying a fare. It was put to her that Mr and Mrs Main had the right to know who was coming and going, and also not to have lots of strange vehicles on what was actually their rural retreat. She submitted to the company auditing her revenues as 'the structure of the lease allows for a smaller lease fee and if you do well only then will you have to pay us commission just like a shop in a shopping centre'. The company retained right of access to ensure maintenance of the houses 'in exchange for a smaller bond'; and a limited one plus two plus two contract. 'So, if your business does not go well, you are not stuck with breaking a long lease.'

So, on behalf of his employers Gabriel had made sure that Hot Rocks could know who was coming and going, the ambiance of the village was preserved, and the business signage was simple and in the company colours. The company would get its cut if the business went well in due course, had an excuse for unrestricted access to monitor what went on, and could get rid of Margaret at short notice if it desired for the meanest of reasons and the minimum of compensation.

It was clear that the company would have to continue to run a bus service to Launceston and back for its staff and their resident families, and he now had a potential revenue stream that would hopefully subsidise that too. Moreover, Ms Pursehouse would be available to give medical help to the extent that she could. Above and beyond any practical advantages this might give, it would certainly give added confidence to staff and their families who would be considering living on site into the future.

He was a happy administrator, content that he had her stitched up nicely. Lyn and Peter might notice the name on the sign and perhaps grumble, but if they did it was a minor compromise and there was too much happening for it to matter in the greater scheme of things.

Job well done.

Chapter 13

Much to Peter and Lyn Main's annoyance, it took six weeks to set up the environmental activists' tour of what was now the Hot Rocks Power Station.

Technically, after years of planning and construction, it was nearing completion, and the Minister had been pleased to recognise it by approving the name they had asked for to replace the Sheol project. Asking for it might have been a bit premature, since no power could yet be sent to the grid, but it showed progress had been achieved, and Lyn and Peter knew that progress demonstrably achieved gave the Minister a warm feeling about the government's investment. It also gave him the opportunity for a media release, and if he wanted it, a photo opportunity. It took the political pressure off.

The tour, now known within the company as Greenies' Day, had not been as simple to organise as they had hoped. While they did not blame Christine for the delays since many of the causes were outside her control, not only had work on the transmission line started before the tour could be held, but the protests were already gaining some momentum, at least in the media. They had already produced negative publicity, and negative publicity was something Peter and Lyn had hoped to avoid. It put the political pressure back on.

Construction on the foundations of the first two towers had begun at the Mordbury end of the route, and some steelwork was already growing out of the ground. Their admittedly raw prominence was publicly unobserved due to the privacy of the site. It would have been better if no towers had been erected before Greenies' Day, but the project schedule could not be subject to interruption, or indeed the extra expense a delay would have incurred. Towers were also being erected at the other end of the line, but despite their industrial ugliness the principal trouble came from the clearance of the easement.

As Peter said in a moment of frustration: 'The problem is that you can't fucking hide two D10s ripping out everything in as straight a course as can be environmentally managed across hill and bloody dale, through plantation and fucking native forest. When they say it's a scar on the landscape, they are right. A necessary fucking scar it may be, but it's not pretty!'

The staff who witnessed his explosion had been somewhat taken aback. Those who had known his brother might have expected it from Hughey, but not of Peter. They knew he was running a project which had demanded technical details outside his knowledge, but in all the time they had known him he had taken advice, and his management skills had allowed things to be progressed as best they might. Now with the end in sight he seemed to be showing signs of the accumulated stress.

There had even been the problem of some drone flights spying on their activities and the pictures taken ending up on the web. The Civil Aviation Safety Authority said they would only do something about drones piloted over Crown land if Lucifer Hot Rocks would pay for the overtime. Which they could not afford to do. No one was going to try to make a guess in advance where the pilots were going to base themselves, and then sit around waiting and hoping that they had picked the right spot, and that they were there at the right time, and on the right day. They had better things to do.

Lyn dealt with the airborne spying activity over their own home and the village environs by the simple expedient of having the security team shoot the drones down when they came over their private property. No complaints could legally be made, or were, even though three of the machines met an unholy end. They were also holey in the sense that even at the limits of its range, 12-gauge shot does nasty things to low-flying drones.

There were certainly no complaints from the Lucifer security officers, who had enjoyed themselves immensely for a couple of days until whoever had been using the drones over Main property decided to cut their losses. The remains of the machines that fell from the sky indicated they were not cheap toys, but something more expensive. However, Peter and Lyn recognised that using even that level of violence to make the point about privacy for person and project might only have generated more ill will had anyone gone public.

Earlier, flying of drones over the power plant under construction was something they had just put up with. There were no secrets to be revealed. The company had been completely open about the technology it was using, and it was in use elsewhere anyway. They were in fact promoting it along with their other environmentally correct credentials, and so was the government. Moreover, there was nothing to see after the roofs went on the turbine and generator halls. It was generally felt that if someone wanted to watch rows of solar cells being installed, a plantation of vanadium redox flow batteries being established, or landscaping being done, day after day come rain, hail or shine, then good luck to them.

The biggest problem in organising Greenies' Day had been finding a date which suited the tour group they had wanted to assemble; and then, when a date had been finalised, making sure Mordbury and the project site were looking their best. A side issue was that commissioning of the plant was well advanced, and although everything was going well, indeed much better than expected, safety was going to be more of a concern than usual. Something going wrong with the testing in front of their guests, which included media, could just not be allowed to happen. It made everyone on site just a little nervous.

Chapter 14

Greenies' Day did not start well. It was absolutely pouring down in torrents when the company bus, driven by Christine and with Lyn as hostess, left Mordbury for town; and it was still raining, if not quite as hard as in the hills, when their guests boarded the bus in Launceston.

It was Lyn who had decided who would escort the tour. Obviously both she and Peter had to be the hosts. Christine was not only behind all the arrangements but could deal with environmental questions, so she was an obvious choice as well. She added Stephen to the team. He was young, personable, one of the engineers who was at this stage intending to stay on after the plant was commissioned, and he could probably deal with anything technical that might be asked even if it wasn't actually within his immediate scope of expertise.

Everyone hoped the weather would not be too unkind to them.

As Christine negotiated the road up to Mordbury, Lyn Main turned on the charm and recited the scripted welcome she and Peter had spent hours editing. Fortunately, the project team had done what they had been asked. While Christine could see only one or two vehicles behind her in her mirrors, once they were off the main road and on the road to Mordbury itself there was no traffic coming the other way. While the road was much improved from the early days of the project, and the Electrocoaster had two motors providing drive on both front and rear wheels, she had not wanted anything heavy coming down the mountains at her in the rain.

Mercifully, having to concentrate on her driving saved her from having to listen to Lyn Main giving their passengers a summary of the history of the project, telling stories about Hughey Main and describing the accident in which he was killed, and the general ethos for the project that he had set when he had begun it in the first place. Not only had Christine lived it but she had heard it all before, and she had given similar speeches to so many inductees that it was all rather boring for her now. What's more, concentrating on her driving was taking her mind off what could go wrong.

I am not at my best this morning.

As the bus climbed the rain began to clear, and knowing how well the entry into Mordbury could look with the change in the weather, she slowed as they passed the company's sign and pulled over as planned to the left of the road for everyone to enjoy the scene. The cars behind her passed them by. Her passengers de-bussed to take in the view, which was the epitome of bucolic splendour. Everything was sparkling from the recent shower. As they looked down the road an echidna wandered carelessly across what would have been their path.

Lyn Main sidled up to her with a smile on her face and whispered in her ear.

'Cheer up. The rain's stopped. "'Twas brillig, and the slithy toves did gyre and gimble in the wabe" – as they say.'

'The what?'

'"All mimsy were the borogroves" – it looks lovely doesn't it? Margaret Pursehouse has been using her connections with the powers above for our benefit I see!'

Not funny, Lyn! Margaret fucking Pursehouse was the last person she wanted to be reminded of given that the day was to be, at least partially, a significant test of what she had spent her working life doing for the last four years. Anyway Johnny Depp sucked all of the original joy out of that poem – and the bloody echidna should have been using one of the tunnels under the road as well!

She did, however, manage a somewhat grim smile in return, concentrating more on whether or not the two television crews were getting the appropriate shots with the appropriate people in front of their lenses enjoying the scenery. She made sure they filmed the echidna and then the tawny frogmouth perched statuesquely in a nearby tree, its camouflaged presence unnoticed until she pointed it out.

She knew the frogmouth would not move for two reasons. Firstly that's what tawny frogmouths normally do – sit on gum tree branches, immobile in the face of any potential threat, pretending to be the stump of a broken tree branch. Secondly this particular bird was roadkill – well eagle kill more probably – that she had come across and had taken the trouble to have eviscerated and stuffed.

My own dead parrot sketch – but strictly speaking the deceased parrot in question is not actually a parrot.

It had taken her two somewhat difficult and dangerous hours in breach of all her own health and safety guidelines to get it secured up there in the tree the previous afternoon. She had done it on her own because she realised if anyone else had been in the know, her contriving to have the bird in the right place at the right time through devious means would probably have been leaked. There were plenty of frogmouths on the property, but she could not think of any other way of making sure one would roost in the right tree at the right time.

Christine gave their visitors enough time to see what she wanted them to see, and before anything unexpected could go wrong she marshalled them back onto the bus and they resumed their journey.

Warning signs to caution drivers about wallabies, roos, echidnas, devils, rails and wombats were newly and evenly spaced along the left-hand side of the road. There was no roadkill evident for the day, nor should there have been. Her team had been told to make sure there was none.

Her immediate destination was Perdition, where morning tea was to be served, booklets were to be given out, and key staff were going to be available to answer preliminary questions. As she drove, she vaguely heard Lyn Main speaking about the vertical wind generators, the water turbines and the tree planting she had been responsible for, to further inform their passengers of their green credentials.

Yeah, yeah. Heard it all before.

Chapter 15

While their visitors were in Perdition, Christine took the opportunity to plug the bus in for a quick power boost in the garage under the house. The ceiling was high enough, and the car accommodation large enough, stretching the full length and width of the house extension above it. Stephen was upstairs with them, and he could hold the Mains' hands for a while.

Anthony Main, fascinated by cars all his life, had kept his private collection there and had installed a hoist so he could fiddle with them – not that he had ever had any opportunity, that pleasure having been denied him by his not looking to his left and crossing in front of a moving semitrailer. The company-owned four-wheel drive used by Peter and Lyn Main was there, but they had also kept two of the cars from Hughey's collection.

Lyn loved her Citroen DS and sometimes used it as a daily driver; while Peter shared his brother's taste for British cars and had kept his Rolls-Royce Silver Cloud. Mrs Scott's Kia was tucked away in the corner next to Lyn and Peter's Skoda, which Lyn favoured for going to work in Launceston especially when the weather was bad.

A rather eclectic mix.

Having put the bus on charge, Christine put a company high-visibility jacket, helmet, and safety notes on every seat. There would be more than required but no one was going to have the excuse that there was not one on their seat, and no one was going to be allowed to go further on the tour without proper personal protective equipment and a safety briefing. Especially not today, she reminded herself. They might only be going into safer areas but today the engineers were by an unfortunate coincidence running the plant to two-thirds capacity for the first time. The power generated was going to be stored in the massive batteries that heretofore had only received a trickle from the solar arrays.

She then wandered upstairs and listened to the end of Peter Main's talk and circulated among the guests as she was required to do – to find out who was who and what their principal interest in the project might be. The guest list had been expanded from the half-dozen she had first suggested, and Lyn and Peter had invited people she did not know. Her first targets, however, were the media people; they all seemed happy enough. Peter had apparently made it clear that nothing they would see might not be photographed. There were to be no secrets – company policy.

There were several local people she knew from her own ongoing outreach activities for Hot Rocks, and she presumed they all would not only be happy enough but would also be providing information and supportive opinions to other guests. Some of the others that had been invited she recognised from pictures she had seen of them on environmental websites. Making up the numbers was Gerry from Security in civilian clothes. He had snuck into the crowd and was trying to pretend to be environmentally friendly in jeans, woolly pullover, and a green puffer jacket that had seen better days.

Well one never knows I suppose, she mused. Having a security officer on board could not hurt. It was like having air marshals in civvies on planes. She bet that was Lyn Main's idea. If she thought herself a bit clever with the frogmouth, she knew that Lyn had at least one more deception planned that would more than match her own effort. *Devious lady.*

Eventually she found herself talking to a woman she didn't know or recognise who was on her own, drinking, with deliberation, a cup of what looked like tea. She was conducting a careful examination of the other people in the room.

'Dreadful, isn't it?' Christine said with a nod in the direction of the cup.

'It's not that bad. It's wet and warm and not without a certain charm. I'm just looking at who is here and trying to sort out the agendas. There are the energy freaks, who want to see a pollution-free modern geothermal power plant in all its glory; the carbon-neutral freaks who want to see how many resources have been chewed up and how much pollution has been caused in the building of your modern geothermal power plant; the land freaks who want to see how much destruction you have wrought on the country given that it was well on the way to recovering from previous depredations; and the nature freaks who want to see how much native flora and fauna is being destroyed in the name of the evil of power generation. And then there is that lonely man over there in the pullover who I presume is one of yours. He looks like security to me.'

Christine laughed. 'You don't miss much. Yes, he is. One just never knows. And which category do you fit into, may I be so rude as to ask?'

She didn't recognise the name on the woman's name tag, and had expected her to put out her hand for her to shake and give her credentials. It didn't quite happen that way. The woman simply returned her cup to its saucer.

'I'd like to think that I am in the rational group that realise that society needs electricity, and this may be one of the safest and ecologically most sound ways to provide it. I'm not, of course.'

'What?'

'Rational.'

'Oh that. Who is? What's your problem?' Christine was wondering what new set of potential environmental concerns she might have to design a response for.

'Well, I fully realise that from now on there is no coal being burned, no gas being burned, no birds being chopped up by massive turbine blades and all that sort of thing to produce your power; but I am concerned about how much energy has been consumed and how much carbon has been produced in just building the place. Oh, I know you are replacing energy derived from fossil fuel and all that, and the plant has a projected minimum sixty-year lifespan, but looking at what has been made public to date, it's a massive investment in both financial and environmental terms.'

'I can answer some of those questions, at least without the technical detail, the actual numbers – but you can get those from the company if you want to ask for them. Some of them are in the brochure you got earlier.'

'So, tell me. The place looks gorgeous, the river turbines and vertical rotors are clever and cool, but this is just the warmup, isn't it?'

'Yes. We go over into the next valley and it's a bit full-on industrial in parts – though not like a coal-fired station with an open pit next to it. It's well … well, just big; and about two-thirds of it is below what is now ground level while the rest of it has to be rudely out of doors for safety and maintenance reasons.'

'As someone in your parliament with red hair once said – please explain.'

Christine noticed that while the woman spoke perfect English, she had a European accent that she could not pin down. 'OK. Well, this used to be old-growth forest, and then in the colonial days it became a farm and some trees got cut down. The timber was so good it became a timber cutting operation with its own mill, making good money with what we now think of as native timbers. Then it became a farm again when that became too hard. Left behind for farming were two valleys of green grass with a river running through them draining the surrounding hills. The valley that the plant is now in did not drain well and it had a lake in it which accumulated biomass over the decades after clearing, and it became a bit of a swamp. Hot Rocks dug all the crud out to get to firm ground and built a power station in the hole – a big hole. The crud was used to landscape around it and raise the sides of the valley a bit.'

The lady's face wrinkled in confusion. 'I'm not familiar with the word *crud*.'

'Sorry about that, Aussie slang. It means everything from dried mud to anything nasty and smelly. What was there would probably have ended up as peat after several centuries, but it was mainly just a smelly bog. We separated some of the really good soil out and used it for landscaping, and replaced a lot of trees that might have been here before the woodcutting started. We dug a tunnel that now drains excess water into this valley and the river more effectively. If it really rains hard some water will go north into the forest and the pine plantations. Just like it used to.'

'So, how many trees?'

'I've planted twenty-two thousand so far, and that's just trees. I've lost count of how many understorey plants we've put in.'

'You?'

'Well, me and my team.'

'So, you count that as a carbon offset?'

'I suppose we do, but it's all about the ethics of the company. Hot Rocks did not have to do that,' stated Christine, staying on message.

'And what about everything else? I bet you used a lot of concrete and steel.'

'Yes, but a lot less than you might imagine, and we are willing to admit to where we've had to do what we've had to do.'

'Like what?'

'Well, you'll see when we go inside the plant, a lot of what might have been previously done with structural steel is all laminated plantation timber. Great engineered spans of it. Where it could be, the concrete we had to use, for want of a better material, is reinforced with recycled plastics and not steel. The roads are all made with recycled glass and plastic. All those kinds of things.'

'And what about the real environmental downsides?'

'There are several, but I suppose the two biggies are the piping, and the energy taken to get stuff here and to build the place. While some of the trucks were hydrogen powered, we did use a lot of fossil fuels doing that, and the piping is substantially stainless steel, and most of that came from Korea – although there is some Australian I understand. I suppose the offset for that is that at end of life it can be recycled, as can all the copper and iron in the generating plant. And of course, we don't consume anything but the stored energy underground to produce power. And we're making sure we extract as much of that energy for our investment as we can.'

'I shall observe with interest.'

So what is your interest?

'May I ask what group you are with?'

'I am not with a group, as you call it, although as I said I do notice that there are a number of environmentally concerned people here today. I'm a freelance journalist. I specialise in the IEA.'

'I'm sorry, I'm not familiar with that.'

'Hmm. I'm sure your boss is. The International Energy Agency – the United Nations. I'm just a journalist you understand, not a heavyweight from the IEA. Several things you have done, are doing here, are a bit novel. I shall be writing about them.'

'Well, it's been lovely talking to you, but I have to get the bus ready to leave. I'm back in the driver's seat. Please excuse me.'

'Of course. I look forward to the tour.'

Christine mumbled to herself as she went looking for Peter. *He could have told me who he had invited.*

Chapter 16

Having found Peter, Christine got her charges rounded up with his help. When she took him to task, he explained he had met the journo at some international conference at one of the upmarket hotels he had managed. He had the decency to apologise and added that he was now going to do the tour of the power plant.

'Change of plans, Chris. Lyn's already had enough. By the way, did you spot the couple from the Australian National Office of the Global Sustainability Trust?'

'Yes,' she replied. 'At least I know Francis Pratt. I know quite a few in the Tasmanian branch. I've been talking to them on and off from the start. He's been up here before, right at the start – but I haven't seen anyone else.'

'The woman in the very handsome naturally dyed tartan skirt and the grey woollen coat; leather boots; keeping her distance but not too far away from him. Dressed very sustainably if I may say so.'

'Never seen her before that I can recall.'

'Very clever lady. Catherine Wheelwright. Lots of degrees but not published much at all. She's in charge of their Canberra office.'

'Lobbyist?'

'I think she would probably title herself something more like an *ambassador for the environment*.'

'Don't know about the boots though?'

'Sustainable; we've been wrapping ourselves in animal skins for millennia. Keep an eye on her. She doesn't run anything but the ANGST office, but if she used her connections to suggest something to anyone with a more, shall we say *operational* view, it would probably be taken up.'

'Who suggested we invite her?'

'I sent an invitation to their Canberra office as a matter of courtesy, protecting my back. We don't want anyone to feel they were deliberately left out, do we? I'm a bit surprised that they decided to send someone, and someone a lot higher up in the pecking order than your mate Francis.'

Having got everyone on the bus, Peter introduced himself and instructed them all on the safety aspects of the tour. He requested they put on their high-vis gear before they moved off. That necessitated everyone having to stand up in the confines of the bus with the attendant chaos and surprising good humour. There was one more serious matter Peter had to raise, however – and that was the problem of pacemakers and other electronic medical devices.

'Be aware, everyone, that we will not be going anywhere near what we know is a danger area for any of you who may have a pacemaker. However, this is a power plant and because for all intents and purposes the plant will be in operation when we go in, just make sure you stay with the group and don't wander off. Likewise, when we go through the area where the battery storages are, we will not stop. You will be safe enough on the bus. You may see people wandering about looking at meters. It's not for radioactivity or anything like that. We are just checking where any electrical fields are as we wind up the clockwork.'

With that warning advice given, he sat down in the left front seat and directed Christine with a wave of his hand to drive off. She thought she could detect a deal of tension in his manner. If one knew him, as she did, he was showing the pressure he was under to get the plant operational; no doubt that was at least partly why Lyn had bailed and passed the tour over to him. No one wanted any embarrassing mistakes made.

They went down the drive and through the village, past the new Vision (Christian Wellness Centre) and the old mill, to the entry to the second valley. When they reached the crest of the hill Christine had to stop the bus at the newly installed security bollards that were obstructing the road. She pulled up next to a communications box on a post and, after an exchange with the duty security officer on the other end of the connection, the metre-high bollards sank slowly into the ground. As the bus proceeded, the passengers with access to the view from the rear window saw them magically rise again from the surface of the road. There was the odd murmur about the security.

Christine herself glanced in her mirrors to see that the bollards had indeed worked properly, metaphorically wiping her brow.

We won't tell you that they tend to get stuck on occasion. Yes, we do have security.

The bus then turned left at the banking that blocked the view of the valley and then right, back onto what had been the original road. There were a few gasps and then a lot of chatter as the plant came into view. Out in the open on their left were the well heads, surrounded by a large area of gravel. Wrapped in thick layers of insulation, pipes led from the well heads to the plant. They were decorated in green and red and equipped with pressure control devices and large valves. They were surrounded by the typical industrial chain link fence with barbed wire on the top. CCTV cameras were in evidence if one looked, and Peter noticed that some on the bus did.

Peter asked Christine to stop the bus.

'This is where the water is sent under the ground and where it comes back up super-heated,' he announced. 'It's uncovered, unlike the rest of the plant, because if there is any part of the power plant we think we may need to get to with really big machinery, this is it. The fencing also keeps the wildlife away,' he added jokingly. 'The red pipes are very, very, very hot and could easily cook you a wallaby or wombat supper.'

He got a bit of a titter for the joke but not the full-bodied laughter he had hoped for. With a shrug, he directed Christine to drive on. Tension was really starting to show in his face.

Fifty or so metres on, the bus was swallowed up as it slowed down and entered what seemed like a huge underground mine entrance, but turned out to be a substantial pavilion, its roof supported by massive, laminated timber piers curving from the vertical to the horizontal. The guest reaction was bigger this time, with several gasps from their passengers. It was impressive, especially as instead of the usual working light levels, Lyn had ordered that everything be turned on at peak brightness.

It's not as if the power is going to cost us anything.

The phrase *hall of the mountain kings* sprang into Christine's mind. Glancing to her left, she could see a little smile on Peter's face. She understood his satisfaction. She too still felt a bit of the wow factor here, and they had both played a part in making it all happen.

Christine parked the bus adjacent to the entry to the main access corridor that split the two similar pavilions that housed the generators. Barry Kidd, Mohammed and her Stephen were waiting for them to assist with the tourist guide duties, and to answer any engineering questions. They took the passengers into the plant proper with Peter, while Christine stayed on the bus. Half an hour later they all came back out, and she started what she was fully aware was the going to be the immediately most contentious part of the trip.

She took the opportunity to listen to her passengers as they got on the bus and heard some grumbling about the fact that, while they had been able to see the control room and the tops of the generators, they had not been permitted to go to the floor below and see all the piping, the turbines and the heat exchangers. Some of them seemed to think that the excuse of the plant being tested at capacity and that the area on the floor below was somewhat inherently more dangerous, was not good enough.

For fuck's sake! Christine took the party out the other end of the hall, past the workshops, and the fire trucks, and all the other support facilities that were housed under the curve of the huge roof. She stopped the bus and pointed out the offices where she and the people like her worked, hoping to introduce some lightness into the proceedings, but without much success.

Turning left as they exited the hall at the other end, the next part of the road took them through the battery farm and thence to the opposite side of the facility, on the northern side of the valley. Peter kept up a commentary over the PA with a special reference to the vanadium redox flow batteries designed for grid-scale energy storage, rattling off technical detail she knew he had memorised but did not understand about their role in balancing continuity of supply in the face of changing demand.

Chris had read up on it too and was giggling to herself, firstly because he sounded so authoritative, and secondly because Lyn Main had done the trick that rivalled Christine's stuffed frogmouth in a tree. Playing her part in Lyn's deception, Christine slowed the bus down to let everyone get a close look at two people, a man and a woman, both in crisp and smart military style clothing, leading two German Shepherds as if on patrol. Peter turned in his seat and called out to the passengers.

'Walkies,' he announced to make sure no one missed the dogs, and then he made no further comment, turning away from the passengers and looking through the windscreen.

A picture worth a thousand words. Don't come here without an invitation.

Christine wondered what he would have said if anyone had asked for further information: if he would admit to the fact that they were two bushwalking friends of Lyn's from the university who had been given a day out, and presumably a good lunch along with some free outdoor clothing, for the privilege of walking their ageing pound-rescued German Shepherds in the right place at an opportune time. Chris had met the dogs once or twice when she had been summoned to Perdition. She knew that the worst thing they would do was to try to park their substantial and somewhat arthritic bodies in the same lounge chair you were sitting in and to snuggle you into incapacity, negotiating for a bit of spare space with a lick and a consequential wet ear.

It was a short distance from the battery park to the start of the transmission line easement, and Christine was pleased to see that with the cooling of the early afternoon, the visibility was decreasing. While the easement was a blight on the landscape and very new and raw, she felt it did not look too bad. The fact that its service road had to wind left and right to safely traverse the landscape, and mitigate against erosion, helped. While there were now three skeletal towers under construction leading the eye off to the north, and huge piles of tower components stacked neatly ready for use, if you had to have a transmission line easement – and they did have to have one – it was not the worst she had ever seen.

Everyone took the opportunity to take a spell off the bus and the cameras came out. Of course the questions flew quick and fast.

With the mitigation of any environmental potential protest being the principal reasons for the tour, Peter enlisted Christine's help to answer them.

Yes, they had cut down some native forest, but they had done so with state government permission and supervision, and they had tried to choose a route that avoided the oldest of the remaining trees. Christine confirmed that she and her environmental people had been active participants in the selection of the best route. It had not just been left to the engineers and the bean counters.

She advised that her team had already planted thousands more replacement trees than the government permit required for remediation and offset, and they were still planting; the majority of the route took a line through forest that had been logged in the past, and thence through plantation forest that had long since been established.

Yes, progress was going well, with towers also being erected from the other end of the easement, Peter advised. Cable was being stored at the other end because there was easier road access and better storage facilities. Yes, contractors were being used for the construction of the line; yes, they were a Tasmanian firm. No, while it looked as if they had a lot left to do, a number of towers were already in place, and they should shortly be rigging the line and there were only a couple of kilometres of easement left to be cleared. Yes, the cost of the connection was being shared as part of the government's participation in the project. No, he was not hiding it, nor was the government – Lucifer Hot Rocks was a private company but a copy of the construction cost reports was available to anybody who contacted the Launceston office.

It went on and on, and the questions started to drift into other areas. Peter started to look very tired. Christine was able to spell him for a while by launching into a little speech on the health and safety record of the building of the plant – there had only been three serious injuries, one being the death of Peter's brother, the previous owner of Mordbury, in a road collision.

That elicited what Peter tried to make the last question, and it came from the overseas journalist.

'Why here, Mr Main, why here? The plant is impressive, and you have obviously been as careful as you can with the environment, but why here?'

'A combination of factors,' Peter answered. 'Firstly, my family owned the land. Secondly, my late brother, who had accumulated quite a bit of money from various enterprises, wanted to do something to leave a socially positive legacy. Thirdly, while other sites around here might have been able to provide access to the same underground heat source, this one was relatively close to existing infrastructure, and apart from minor concerns, building it was not going to be hugely destructive. If there were any Indigenous sacred sites on the land before colonial times, regrettably they had long been destroyed. Other potential sites that have been historically identified are for example under pristine forest or indeed a national park.'

Francis Pratt interjected. 'But Tasmania doesn't need the power, with the wind and hydro we already have.'

'True,' replied Peter with a sigh. *Francis fucking Pratt you know the answer to that one.* All the fool was doing was trying to get himself onto the evening news.

'But the rest of Australia does, and Tasmania needs money for other things like hospitals, housing, and roads. This green power, with the other surplus generated in the state, will go across Bass Strait to keep the wheels turning and the lights on across the mainland grid – beside supporting our own needs. It works when the sun stops shining and the wind stops blowing.'

Francis Pratt looked grudgingly satisfied and did not follow the matter up, even though Peter paused to give him ample opportunity before indicating that everyone should get back on the bus.

As Christine loaded her passengers, counting them as they boarded, Gerry kept his eyes open for stragglers and at the same time answered a call on his mobile phone. Christine watched as he went over to where Peter was standing and the two conferred. Gerry was looking a little satisfied with himself while Peter Main's face remained stern but calm. She knew him better than that. He was very angry.

That looks deep and meaningful. I wonder what that's all about.

Gerry was second-last on the bus. Peter paused to gaze over the surrounding woodland and take some deep breaths before taking up the rear.

'Chris,' he said as he sat down next to her, 'stop in the main hall will you please, there's something I want to pick up.'

They drove back the way they had come, and Christine stopped as she had been instructed. One of the security staff in his customary uniform, and Lyn's doggy friends in their camo clothing, were obviously waiting for them, so she pulled up next to them. Peter got out and collected something from the security man and got straight back on the bus. He addressed their passengers, not on the PA but standing at the front facing back down the aisle, his head bowed to avoid hitting the ceiling.

'I have something unexpected to tell you all before we go back to the house and send you on your way. Isaac Forrest, I have something of yours. Would you hold up your hand so I can see who and where you are please?'

Looking in her central driving mirror, Christine saw a hand go up and then Peter's back blocked her view as he went down the aisle. He came back to the front of the bus and made an announcement.

'I have just given Mr Forrest back something he left at Perdition earlier on. It's a book that was not on my bookshelves when you arrived this morning. It's actually quite a sophisticated bugging device in the form of a hardbound book. I've also given Mr Forrest a data stick with a copy of the footage of him planting the book on the shelves in my study, or at least entering the study in a rather suspicious manner. The study is adjacent to the main living/dining room where the rest of us were chatting over morning tea. That open plan space is actually the only room in the inside of my house with cameras, although the house does have cameras outside. One of those inside cameras covers the door into the study. Of course, we have security surveillance over the plant and my security staff are going over the recordings now to see if Mr Forrest has left anything else anywhere else. It will be a bit tedious but we do have facial recognition software so it will be a little easier for our people to follow your travels, Mr Forrest.'

There was a stunned silence on the bus as Peter flopped wearily back in his seat next to Christine and indicated to her that she should move off.

Fuck he's angry.

The silence continued until they arrived back at Perdition. As everyone got off the bus Gerry and Peter approached Mr Forrest. Peter tapped him on the shoulder and quietly said to him, 'You are not welcome on my land Mr Forrest, ever. Please don't come back.'

'Think you're smart don't you,' said Forrest, 'embarrassing me in front of everyone.'

'I don't think you deserve anyone's trust.'

Forrest seemed to move closer to Peter, and Gerry immediately moved well into what he might have considered his personal space.

'I wouldn't, cunt. Get any closer and I'll drop you,' he said. 'Just get back into the fucking bus and sit down where I can see you.'

As Forrest moved away from them, Christine saw Peter raising his eyebrows. Gerry's blunt response had been a bit strong to her mind as well. Gerry, seeing their astonishment, remarked, 'Sometimes the less subtle approach is the most effective.'

Christine took that on board, and observed Peter shrug his shoulders and go to say goodbye to the rest of their guests, while Gerry stood with her and watched Forrest get into the bus. Clearly, Peter had had enough for the day and would not be taking the trip into town with the guests and back again. Christine thought that it was something he should have done. It had been a long day for her too, and for that matter for Gerry.

Well, we can talk to each other. The passengers can talk among themselves.

Chapter 17

Having delegated accompanying his company's guests back to Launceston, Peter discovered Mrs Scott had cooked lamb shanks for dinner. He told her how grateful he was, after what had been for him a very stressful day. He opened a bottle of wine and offered her a glass, which she accepted. She told him his wife had already eaten and had gone to bed.

'Just a couple of biscuits. She said she had a migraine and wanted an early night.'

I can understand that.

All sorts of things could have gone wrong, and they hadn't. What had gone wrong had come as something of a surprise. He thanked Mrs Scott profusely, which he felt was the least he could do since she had not only fulfilled her normal duties but had also catered for the morning tea, looked after the dog owners, and tidied the place up so it looked like it had all never happened.

The privilege of ownership meant that while Mordbury was officially dry, Perdition wasn't. After the wine with his meal he drank a couple of whiskies to relax by and then, finding his brain still churning over the events of the day, he took a tablet to make himself sleep. He was therefore not feeling the best the following morning.

He knew it was a bad habit to wash down medication with alcohol, and he knew it made him feel groggy the next morning, besides the potential detrimental effects on his liver if he did it regularly. On the other hand, he also knew that it made the tablets work immediately he put his head on the pillow. His wife seemed to have no problem sleeping, although she did complain that he snored more than usual when the pills and the alcohol combined to knock him out. That meant she had been kept awake by him, and that made him feel rather guilty all over again.

Despite the fog in his brain, the weather was turning out sunny and mild, with no rain in the immediate forecast. After seeing Lyn off to Launceston, he decided to give himself the day off. As the boss he felt he had the right to do that. Lyn at least had the diversion of her work, while he was always on call at Perdition – and it wasn't just being on call. The fact that the project was five minutes away had led his people to believe he could be summoned to the site whenever they felt the need for an instant decision, whatever else he might have been trying to do. To an extent he had to admit that his readiness to do so when he first inherited the project had been a mistake.

I made a rod for my own back.

He put on some favourite older clothes, some well-used comfortable hiking boots and his backpack, and set off into the bush. He went down the drive, past the comparatively raw-looking wall that replaced the one where his brother had died, and across the bridge. He headed roughly northwest along a path he knew well. On his right was a stream, just a trickle this morning, that he knew could become a significant watercourse after rain. He was familiar with the path – his chance to get away. Wherever he went in the valleys and their immediate surrounds he was always contactable by phone. Provisioned by Mrs Scott, he would grab his fossicking kit and spend the day in nature, wasting his time looking for gold and sapphires. Most of the time he came home with nothing save a bit more perspective on life, but occasionally it wasn't a waste of time in a prospecting sense. Sometimes a little stone or a bit of colour in the riddles of his pan gave an extra point to the exercise.

It was something he had started in Canada. When he ran hotels in the city he had to make do with parks. However, he had developed the habit more when he had been in charge of the kinds of hotels that made the front of postcards because they were huge and palatial, or huge and ruggedly outdoorsy, surrounded by pine trees and snow. He found he liked the Australian bush just as he had liked the pine forests of North America. There though, he had been more careful about where he went given the size of some of the wildlife. While the Australian bush had its hazards, the bitey wildlife was smaller. Moreover, in Tasmania the weather tended to be milder, even in snow season. *It does seem to rain a lot but.*

After a thirty-minute leisurely walk he was well into the trees and came to a pond with a bank of gravel just upstream of it. He had previously fossicked here and had found some sapphires, although gold, if it was in there somewhere, had yet to show up.

I wonder if my forebears did this? He imagined himself as a Main family pioneer as he sorted himself out. He laughed to himself when he put on his wetsuit gloves with the index finger and thumb tips removed. In the old days they would have gotten their hands frozen with the work, their stoicism and diligence in sometimes appalling conditions the only way to a livelihood.

He spread out a square metre of light canvas on the grass and began digging in the gravel, putting scoops onto the canvas in preparation for panning, and chucking off the larger stones as he went. When he thought he had shovelled enough he made a small fire and boiled a billy.

Standing there with a warm cup of tea in his hands and gazing around the trees to see if anything moved, he felt he was starting to unwind and was putting some perspective on the previous day. The forest, in his experience, was never completely still and never completely quiet, except perhaps when there was a storm approaching. Otherwise, there was always a slight breeze, and beside the trees growing and moving with it, he fancied he could hear the faint sounds of the world they protected going about its daily business. Somewhere, and possibly quite near, there would be animals of all shapes and sizes. Some would be active now in the day while others, like the devils, would be sleeping after their dawn patrols. They would be rested and ready to come out in the evening to catch what could be caught, and to scavenge what needed to be cleaned up, and throw themselves under the wheels of any late-night road traffic.

Peter had just decided to get back to work when he heard the distinct and intrusive sound of someone else, not on the path he had followed but coming from the west. As he stood there watching, Margaret Pursehouse came into the clearing. She was dressed in new and rather fashionable bushwalking clothing and new hiking boots of the same brand as his. She seemed as surprised to see him as he was to see her.

'Ms Pursehouse.'

'Mr Main. Good morning. At least I think it still is morning.'

'I think you're right. You've caught me having some time to myself.'

'I'm sorry, I didn't mean to disturb you. I'm just passing through on my way home. I thought I remembered there was a path somewhere here.'

'You don't want to go off wandering about the place, you know. It's not hard to get lost.'

'I know my way about pretty well by now, and even if I didn't have a compass in my pocket I could always just walk downhill. You're bound to come across a stream if you do that and the streams all flow into the river and that will always get you home.'

'Very good bushwalking skills, but having you lost is not something I want to have to concern myself with. What are you up to anyway?' he asked more kindly. 'You can't be bush bashing like that when there are plenty of easier ways of taking the air.'

'Oh, I've been collecting. You probably didn't know but I have this hobby, natural medicines you find in the bush.'

'Really, and are there a lot of useful plants around here?'

'Oh yes. There are some great fungi too. Of course, you have to be careful with what you collect and how you prepare it, but I find it all fascinating. And you, Mr Main, what are you doing out here?'

Peter recognised she might be a little apprehensive about finding herself out in the bush alone with him, so he set out to be reassuring, even though she was disturbing the time he had appropriated for his own recreation.

'I think you had better start calling me Peter. Mr Main is rather formal.' He made a sweeping gesture pointing out his kit. 'Well, I come out when I need to relax, I do a bit of panning. Sometimes I find a bit of gold, sometimes the odd sapphire, and of course the bush is just the place to get away from things. Yesterday was a bit stressful and it was a long day. So, I thought, bugger it, I'll get away on my own for a bit. Would you like a cup of tea? I have plenty.'

'You think ahead.'

'Well actually my housekeeper, Mrs Scott, thinks ahead for me.'

'That's very kind. Well, since I've already spoiled your solitude, I'll accept. I carry a water bottle and a snack, but I've been out longer than I planned and a cup of something warm would be welcome. I heard you had visitors yesterday.'

'It's a very, very small village, Margaret, isn't it? Yes, well, we are aware that the construction of the transmission line from the power plant to the coast is causing some people to be upset and Chris, as you know if you were listening at the meeting you were at, came up with the idea of showing some key people around to see if we could get the word out that we are not evil destroyers of the environment. Although it's now a bit late in the piece with the plant almost ready for commissioning. I suppose Chris has done a good job with the PR to date and we have had the advantage of the privacy up here to get on with things without too much bother.'

He had started making the tea while he told the story, rinsing the mug he had used with some tea from the billy before filling it again for his guest.

'Only one mug. Neither Mrs Scott nor I expected me to be entertaining.'

'If it's too much trouble …'

'No, not at all – plenty of tea and stuff.'

'And how did it go? Yesterday.'

'Milk, sugar, yes … no?' he asked, thankful his gloves protected his hands as he offered the handle on the hot mug to his guest.

'Sugar would be good.'

He found a sachet and gave it to her. 'Everything seemed to go quite well, that is except that some bastard decided to try and bug my office.'

'What?'

'Yes, some bloke decided to plant a mike and a camera with a little transmitter in a book in my office. Clever little gadget. All too easy these days I'm afraid. I didn't bloody anticipate that, and I am fucking pissed off.'

He saw her frown at his language.

'Sorry Margaret, but I am more than just ordinarily upset. I don't know what he expected to get with his little spy set-up or indeed where he and anybody with him were going to monitor it from, although our security people are doing some checks around the place while we speak. They tell me however that it could have its own relay close by, or they could even have hacked my home Wi-Fi, heaven help us. We don't have any real secrets, but I suppose they may have some action planned and wanted to overhear how we might be going to deal with it.'

'I can see why you must be a bit stressed.'

'Ah, the psychologist's' approach. Empathise. Did they train you to say that to the patient, Margaret?'

He was teasing her, and he could see she knew it.

'I suppose they did, but I wasn't being a nurse. You're running a big business with lots of problems, and then someone tries to spy on you …'

'And all sorts of things happen in my study, besides business phone calls and meetings with my staff.'

Margaret looked at him, rather puzzled.

'Well, I talk with people about people and I'm sure they don't want their confidences spread about. Then my wife and I relax in there. Its cosy and full of books, and rather friendly when the weather is worse than usual … between you and me, Nurse Margaret, my wife and I are sometimes, shall we say, intimate in the study.'

'Oh, right.' Margaret hadn't bargained for that admission, but she had been a nurse long enough to know more than a little about what people did in their private lives however distasteful it was. After all, Peter and Lyn Main were married. In a way she was a little jealous. She had spent her adult life avoiding all temptations of that type in trepidation that her own weakness might lead her to fall into accepting what she considered to be the greatest temptation of all.

Peter's phone rang.

Saved by the bell. Deliberately or not, she was getting me to talk a little too much.

'Excuse me Margaret, someone wants something from me,' he said, patting his pockets to find which one he had put his phone into. Finding it, he stabbed at the face, answering its persistent ringing with an annoyed 'Yes?'

He listened for a while standing where he was and then started pacing up and down as he spoke. Margaret could hear every word he said including *trespass*, and *police*, and *media*; and a comment that he made that seemed to be an attempt at a joke, 'a chicken has come home to roost'. He then went on about someone having a phone with a camera and telling someone to 'keep everyone away'.

He terminated the call and announced, 'I shall have to pack up and go back to work I'm afraid, Margaret. Thank you for the chance to chat though.'

'No, thank you for the tea. May I ask what has happened?'

'You may, and it explains a lot.' Jaw clenched, he picked up one side of the canvas allowing the stones to roll off, and then shook it out with a snap. 'While my people and I were congratulating ourselves on our openness yesterday and debugging my office, at least two people were tramping through the bush onto my land. Very early this morning, before the transmission line riggers got there, they had set up home for one of their number up the top of a half-completed transmission tower. Well, halfway up a half-completed transmission tower if you understand what I'm trying to say.'

'What are you going to do?'

'My inclination is to do nothing except cut off media access to my land. He or she can stay up there until they starve or freeze, and we will work on other towers until they get sick of it.'

That didn't go down too well. Too harsh perhaps.

'But I need to get back and check out exactly what is happening. Don't look so worried. I'm sure whoever is doing the tower climbing has made adequate arrangements for their own comfort … and there's no value for me or the project in not making sure they are OK.'

Peter relieved Margaret of the now empty tea mug and began

shoving the pan and canvas roughly back into his backpack. 'Do you want to walk back with me or are you staying out for a bit longer?'

She hesitated, slightly intimidated, but made her mind up on the basis, having made friends to a certain extent with him, that an opportunity to get to be friendly with one's landlord was never something one should avoid, particularly if one used it to push one's own message.

'Yes, OK. I'll take the opportunity to tell you all the news about the wellness centre on the way back'.

Chapter 18

While Peter was planning his strategy on the track back to Mordbury and Perdition, he was only half listening as Margaret explained enthusiastically what she so far achieved and what she was planning for her wellness centre. He did note that she said she was still working part-time for Omicron. She eventually got onto the subject of the notebooks they had found when she and Lachlan Tan had first occupied the medical centre on behalf of that company, many months before; and her enthusiasm for her subject started to take Peter's interest. She told Peter how she had been copying out the books – filling in the gaps where the original writing was unreadable, photocopying the drawings – and had been searching out and collecting the fungi described in the notebooks. He gave her his undivided attention when she said she had started to experiment with processing the ones she had collected into useful natural remedies.

'I'm not going to have to explain to the authorities why I have a drug lab on my property am I?' he asked.

'No, no, no,' she reassured him. 'Did you know that beneath our feet there is a whole world of fungi that allows the trees to take up nutrients, and indeed talk to one another? They say there could be over a quarter of a million different fungi in Australia.'

'Really? Well, I am not unaware of what fungi's role is in the greater scheme of things. I can't say it's been something that I've been overly interested in. I do know that at one of the hotels I managed in Canada, the eco guides were always going on about it to the guests.'

'That's interesting. Did you know that it would seem some of the Australian fungi have a better tolerance for heat, whereas those in pine forests don't?'

'Really?'

'Oh yes, there's lots of research that's already been done, and more being done on it now.'

'You seem fascinated by it?'

'I think it's just another wonderful part of God's creation. All science does is find out just how magnificent the whole thing is.'

'Perhaps we might have an argument about that. For me it's a clear indication that evolution works. So, these potions you have been making. Are they any good; and what's more to the point, are any of them dangerous?'

'Well, I think we all know that you shouldn't pick and eat just anything that looks like a mushroom. We all get taught how dangerous some fungi are as kids, don't we? To get things right you need to be an expert, and that's where the notebooks come in. Whoever was their author did lots and lots of work on what did what. I am learning a lot.'

'And what have you produced that's useful so far?'

'Well, the best one I have is one that calms you down. It's very potent and I have to dilute it a great deal to make it safe.'

'And how do you test these potions of yours?'

'Cats.'

'Cats?'

'Cats, and rabbits,' affirmed Margaret, having learned from her initial experience on a human patient. 'I trap them myself or get them from friends who trap them around the city. Just one or two at a time. It's a public service getting rid of cats you know.'

'Very ecologically sound, although I would have thought that they were part of God's glorious creation too.'

'Well, we are told that God gave man dominion over the animals so don't try and tease me there. Besides, it's the fault of us humans that they were brought here in the first place and then allowed to go loose and go feral as well. I think I'm sort of helping to make good our mistake.'

'You won't find too many around here. Christine and her people have done a good job in clearing up the ones the devils don't get as kittens.'

'Yes, well, that is as may be, but around Launceston they are very bad in places. I don't have any trouble getting them.'

Peter was wondering whether the RSPCA would approve of what this woman was doing, but just for the moment he had other things to worry about. Whether or not she had got the appropriate licences and was using the appropriate procedures was not high on his personal list of priorities. Besides, he happened to agree with her views on cat control. It was something he had personally made sure Christine had in their pest management plan when he initially arrived at Mordbury. Nevertheless, he felt that he should issue Margaret a caution.

'Well, I won't delve further now but I don't want you getting me, or the company, into any sort of trouble, Margaret—' Before he could finish what he was saying his phone rang. 'Oh bugger,' he exclaimed, 'they can't leave you alone.'

He found it again in his pocket and answered the caller.

'You are kidding?' Margaret heard him say. 'OK. I'll be back at the house in about ten minutes. Unless someone's borrowed it there should be my ute there – you might check on that for me with Mrs Scott?'

'Problems?'

'Our green campaigning friend in the tower appears to have a decent-sized solar collector and enough power to support a live streaming service. Apparently, we are now featuring internationally as criminal destroyers of hectares of remnant Tasmanian old-growth forest.'

'Are you?'

'No, it's a very misleading and somewhat defamatory accusation too. I can't see the government being too happy about that given the investment they have put into this project; and needless to say, I am personally rather pissed off. We are doing some damage, but we're doing our best not only to keep it to a minimum but also to replant and fix up some of the depredations that went on in the past.'

'But this is what you wanted to do isn't it, and you knew there would be problems?'

'Yes … and no. Let me explain. I can walk and talk. This whole project had nothing to do with me when it was started. My brother wanted to do this as his legacy. When he got killed, he left it to me and there were two things that drove me to pick up where he left off. Well, three actually. Firstly, I accepted the trust he evidently placed in me. I could not betray my brother and let it fall into the hands of my nieces, whose hands, incidentally, he did not want the place to fall into. Secondly, I wanted to be my own boss and had had enough of hotels and demanding, whingeing tourists and what I had been doing for years. It was getting repetitious and admittedly I was bored, although I did once in a while meet some interesting people. Thirdly, Lyn had her heart set on it, and as you have seen she loves being on the board. I just wish she wasn't working in Launceston all the time when she could take some of the burden here with day-to-day stuff – like greenies up half-finished transmission towers dirtying our name and reputation.'

They parted ways as they got over the bridge and Peter reflected as he walked up the drive to Perdition.

Note to self. Those notebooks she was going on about probably belong to me. I need to take that up with her at a later date.

Chapter 19

Angelique Deloraine considered herself a leader in her cause, and indeed had impressed many with the strength of her commitment and the application of her obviously significant intelligence to the saving of the planet. The financial wherewithal of her parents, one a teacher and the other an economist working for a New York environmental think tank, had been a contributing factor to both her success in life and her activism.

She had been in the forefront of the intellectual aspects of environmental protest, and in the frontline of a respectable number of physical protests as well. She was consequently approved of by the people from whom she wished to have approval. Moreover, those to whom it mattered, while considering her a bit overintellectual about the whole thing, accepted that she had been in the right places in the frontline at the right times. She had a name that was internationally recognised among the environmental cognoscenti. Thanks to being arrested in fashionably peaceful ways in various countries in the media spotlight, her face was sometimes publicly recognised, not just remembered on police data bases.

Good schools and a Bachelor of Science from the Université de Montréal had set her up with a basic qualification. Naturally imbued with sporting ability and better than average looks, she had spent her time and more of her parents' money trying to find herself, working in ski resorts in Europe, climbing mountains in the

USA, and as an eco-guide at tourist resorts. While neither of them would have remembered it, she had once worked for Peter Main, well at least with Peter as her General Manager, for the same resort management company in Canada. Their paths had momentarily crossed at the Rocky Peaks Hotel.

At twenty-six years of age she had found herself. She had decided that she had to start to take life seriously and was now studying for a master's degree in sustainable forestry at the very university where Lyn Main lectured. Neither of them would have remembered each other either. The one ethics lecture of Lyn's that Angelique had attended had been, for her, embarrassingly basic, while the assignment required of her in relation to the ethical issues in sustainable forestry had been easy enough given her international perspective. It had earned her good marks because you don't become a significant ecological activist without knowing a great deal about economics, notwithstanding what your father did for a living and the way the financial world operates.

The discomfort of her position at the top of a half-built transmission line tower in northeastern Tasmania, she accepted. She had prepared for it. What she had not anticipated was that the people who were supposed to be helping her maintain her position had, at least temporarily, quit the scene. They had gone to join others at the northern end of the transmission line's course, where they would be on public land with easy access, in the full glare of publicity, making their cause known. No doubt some of them would get themselves arrested over the next few days. She had been expecting a regular supply run in the dead of night for the time her protest continued. She did not fancy having to live on stale bread and muesli bars for as long as her protest lasted, although she had a good supply. Hopefully that part of the plan would be fulfilled.

However, Angelique was also annoyed. The protest about the

transmission line was late – late in the sense that it was to have occurred just under six months earlier. The reason for it being late was down to a lack of decision-making in the group.

She had to admit that stopping the construction of the line or even changing its route significantly was now impossible, when previously it had been a possible if improbable outcome. It was hard to convince anyone, especially a party or parties with a large financial investment, that they should divert such a line through developed land or even underground: the cost of doing so was, she well knew, hugely more expensive. She also accepted that a geothermal power station was one of the better ways to generate electricity, that electricity was needed, and generally Lucifer Hot Rocks Proprietary Limited had not been total environmental vandals in the pursuit of their plans.

Angelique had decided that on her part she did not want to be in a push and shove with well-trained police, looking damp and miserable and a bit pathetic in the media for what was a lost cause. She had decided to do something more emblematic, and dramatic in its own way. However late the protest was, she had committed to playing her part in it and was determined to follow through on that commitment for the sake of public awareness if nothing else. She had agreed to do what she could, and she kept her promises. What she could do was climb a structure and suffer the inconveniences and indignities of staying up it for a significant time while making appropriate noises on the internet about what she was doing and why. Even if what she was doing would not change this project, it might well influence decisions about later ones.

She and two companions had hiked into the site the easy way: up the easement being cleared for the transmission line. Fabian and Elizabeth carried an aluminium plank and consumables for her to survive for a somewhat spartan week, while she carried her ropes, her hammock and its waterproof cover, the roll of solar cells that would power her world, and the camera and other equipment that would allow her to communicate her environmental message to the outside.

Given her youth, physical fitness, and mountaineering experience, ascending the half-built tower had been easy in the extreme, even in the semi-darkness. The hauling up of the plank had been relatively simple. She wished it could have been timber – using advantageously lightweight aluminium as the basis for her temporary roost was not the most environmentally friendly choice she could have made, and someone picky from the media, when and if they turned up, could trouble her with questions about that. It was inherently hypocritical given the environmental cost of digging up and refining the stuff.

Strapping the plank to the frame of the tower had been slightly more testing, and she had employed a safety rope and harness, reminding herself to keep it on at all times given the angles the plank had ended up at. It was quite slippery in the rain and mist.

The solar cells were easy to deploy. She just unrolled them and tied them north-facing to a strut. The live streaming camera and its relay were no problem either, with gaffer tape the universal fix. Similarly her hammock, the one she used for mountain climbing, was readily suspended from the available metal skeleton that surrounded her. At least, she reflected, gravity would ensure that she would not have to sleep at a weird angle, and it came with a waterproof cover. She also carefully secured her backpack with her supplies to an available piece of angle iron – well, galvanised steel. In summary she felt pleased enough with her physical situation, and as soon as she had finished setting up camp she turned the live stream on.

It was mid-morning before anyone came to talk with her about her activities, and it was one of the workmen whom she could see around the place planting trees. He had seen her anomalous presence from 150 metres away and walked over to see what she was doing. He immediately reported the situation to Christine, who attended the bottom of the tower and engaged in a shouted exchange with Angelique – that was until Angelique could advise Christine of her phone number, after which the conversational environment became more civilised as well as more practical.

Christine recognised three aspects to the problem. She contacted Security to deal with security, and Peter Main to deal with public relations. The situation was just a bit beyond her remit. She did not know where Peter was when she found him, but he did not sound very happy. Safety issues were her responsibility, and while waiting for management support she made sure Angelique understood the risks of what she was doing and tried to check that she had taken appropriate steps to deal with those risks. She also noted that Angelique was above the reach of any cherry picker readily available at short notice, and if she needed helping down, or dragging down for that matter, climbers would have to get up to her.

Angelique was surprised. She had expected anger from the people who represented the company, not someone who appeared to be in authority being concerned for her immediate safety and welfare. After the shouting stopped to be replaced by telephone contact, the woman on the other phone sounded most reasonable; someone she thought she would like to have met under different circumstances.

This was due to two factors. Firstly, Christine was a nice person as a person; and secondly, in her professional capacity, she saw no reason to provoke their visitor, because it would not help dealing with her – and in these days of modern communications she had no idea where and how broadly the trespasser might be able and prepared to record and broadcast any exchange they might have. Caution was dictated on many levels.

After the woman – Christine? – went away, Angelique decided

to have some food. She was getting thoroughly bored by the time she had finished an early sandwich lunch. She could last several days without further supplies, but the sandwiches were relatively fresh and therefore a priority for consumption. She would have to eke out what she had brought with her in the way of food and drink, and while her supplies could be called sustaining, they were somewhat less than delicious.

That's unless the pricks do keep their promise and do a resupply run; or I get some action going in the meantime.

Moreover, unlike when out tramping or climbing, she was not equipped halfway up an unfinished galvanised transmission tower to do any cooking or make a hot drink. The coffee in her flask was still warm but only just palatable, and climbing down surreptitiously could end up being the road to a fast interruption of her protest.

They'll talk to me nicely and then jump me if I climb down. Where are all the people anyway?

She was concerned that the media had not arrived.

There had been time since her protest had been observed by the Hot Rocks people, and her live stream was going out and would be suitably viral if her people were doing their job. The police hadn't arrived either, which was strange. She had power and so her phone allowed her unlimited access to the internet. She did not have to worry about conserving its charge. However, there was nothing that she wanted to watch, and she had dealt with all the messages of support she had received from her own group. There was no novelty there and the inevitable boredom was settling in.

About half an hour after the woman had arrived and spoken with her and she had eaten her sandwich and drunk her tepid coffee, a car pulled up nearby. She saw it had the company name, its logo and the word 'Security' written on its side.

Here we go. Here come the heavies.

There were two men in the car and following a look around, and at her, they removed some equipment from it. She watched as they set up a tripod with sandbags around its legs and placed what looked like a camera on it. One of them then set up a solar cell and what she took for a substantial battery, and when everything was connected, pointed the camera at her – well at the tower, although it felt personal. They then left. So, while she was broadcasting her one-woman protest, presumably they were now electronically observing and recording her.

Boredom set in again until about fifty minutes later when the woman came back with another man in a different company car. This time there was no 'Security' written on the door. The woman and the man got out of the car, and he produced a mobile phone. Then her phone rang – or at least it played 'Für Elise' to attract her attention.

'Yes,' she said into it.

'Angelique, Angelique Deloraine I believe,' a male voice said. 'My name is Peter Main. I am a director of Lucifer Hot Rocks. Welcome to Mordbury. I trust you are not too uncomfortable. Christine tells me that you are safety conscious and that you say you have immediate supplies. While I can't say you are a welcome guest, we take our duty of care seriously around here.'

That was not what she had expected to hear – on several grounds. Firstly, someone had obviously been doing some research and hearing Peter Main using her first and second name was a little confronting at this stage of her protest. However, she supposed once she had told Christine her first name it would not have been too hard to get the web to cough up the likely suspects for the kind of action she was taking. The woman knew how to do her research. Secondly the man was not coming across angry, and that was annoying. Getting the opposition angry was part of what she aimed to do, Angry people stop thinking and make mistakes. They also make good publicity, but not for themselves. She studied her own annoyance and tried to deal with it. Getting the company angry and then angry enough to do something stupid was what she had been hoping for, and that wasn't happening.

'Just to let you know, Angelique, I am having our conversation recorded and while you are with us you will be monitored by our security people, who will be recording what they see and hear too. Do you understand that?'

'Yes.' She found she could not keep the annoyance out of her reply. There was something about the voice she recognised too but she could not immediately place it.

Settle down and play the game.

'Now, Angelique, we obviously don't want to be seen to be inhospitable, but I think the rules of the game are self-evident. Sooner or later we will want to work on the tower you are in, and sooner rather than later we would like to not have to waste our time and other resources looking out for you. How long do you plan to be with us?'

'As long as it takes,' she said firmly.

'What takes, Angelique?'

'You stop building this transmission line and put it underground and agree to restore the forest.'

Peter Main held onto his own anger.

Settle down and play the game.

'Well, that is not going to happen, Angelique. Just to let you know, the police have been advised of your presence, but we are treating it as a civil trespass and have not asked them to get involved. The media have been invited to take our security feed of your sit-in when and if they want to, although I know you are putting a picture out on the web. We are not going to let them or any of your mates onto the property either. Now, I am going to formally ask you to come down, join my wife and me for dinner at my house and discuss your concerns; and then I will arrange transport off our property for you. If you don't accept that offer you will be trespasser and liable to everything that that implies legally. Do you understand?'

'Yes.'

Smart bastard. If he's putting out their live feed he can't be accused of anything underhanded. Playing the nothing to see here card!

'Will you join me for dinner, Angelique?'

'Get stuffed.'

'Will you leave our property voluntarily Angelique, even if you don't like the idea of my company or my food?'

'No.'

'Very well. I advise you that you will be considered as a trespasser. While the police may be called in due course, at this stage I think we shall let you sleep on it and talk tomorrow. Oh, by the way I should tell you that the camera on you has a night vision capability.'

What's that all about?

'So?'

'So should you answer a call of nature at any time you might wish to do so discreetly.'

She did not reply. She could not think of a reply. This was not how these sorts of things were supposed to go. Destroyers of the environment that overwhelmed you with consideration were somewhat low in number in her experience.

After a couple of seconds' pause, Peter reeled off a phone number.

'That's the number of the security office here, Angelique – one of the direct lines. If you need assistance at any time, you can call that number. I can't guarantee we will be watching the video feed constantly. We have other things to do. Did you get that?'

'Yes,' she said, lying. She hadn't had a chance to write down the number, but she did not want to ask him to repeat it because it would signal that she might be prepared to use it, and that would show weakness.

'Very well, I wish you a good evening,' he said, and terminated the call. He and the woman got into the car and left.

This was not what was supposed to happen.

'I don't think that's what she expected to happen,' remarked Christine to her boss as they drove away.

'No, well fuck her,' Peter exclaimed, his control abandoned. 'We do not need this; I do not personally need this. We shall remain calm and controlled,' he said, reminding himself publicly. 'Let me know if I am not, please, Chris.'

'Seems a good tactic, I mean what can she do but sit there and stream pictures of the site and give a commentary.'

'And get wet and cold. It's supposed to clear by the morning, but the forecast is for rain tonight. Security have been told to make sure she's OK, but I'd be grateful if you would make a personal check on her first thing, please.'

'No problem.'

I need a drink, Peter thought. *I'm doing that a bit too much recently but now this is getting to the pointy end I need a little help.*

When he got home he found a message from his wife. She was stuck late at work and would not be driving up in the dark but staying with a colleague in Launceston. She seemed to be doing that quite a bit, he reflected, thinking that it might be appropriate for the company to buy a unit in town, or even that it would be a good personal investment. Time and time again Australian real estate had proven its long-term returns.

He put his business brain to one side and reflected again that he would have another night in a cold bed. *That's all I need*, he thought, feeling lonely and deserted in his hour of need for consultation and consolation. A bottle of red would have to suffice. He hoped Mrs Scott had prepared something worthwhile for dinner. The lamb shanks had been very good.

In reminding himself again of his good fortune in having her to look after him it did not occur to him that Mrs Scott might well have chosen to move to Mordbury with his brother for her own reasons.

Chapter 20

Back at Vision, the (Christian) Wellness Centre, Margaret had her computer turned on and was watching Angelique's internet vision stream from the tower. The camera was pointed to the northeast so there was nothing in the way of a sunset to see; although, depending on the weather, tomorrow's dawn might in due course prove to be spectacular. There was no audio. The protest group's commentators had flagged as the time had gone on, and there was now no more commentary to be heard. The whole idea of a lone protest like this fascinated Margaret.

On the television news the ABC were reporting about the gathering of a larger protest group at the other end of the transmission line route, and the apparent infiltration of some of them onto Crown land. Apparently, they apprehended an active protest the following day. Young and old, fit and infirm, sanitary and insanitary environmentalists were reportedly gathering, sleeping in tents and cars. The activity was attracting sightseers as well. In the meantime, the flow of traffic on the highway was becoming problematical for regular road users and tempers were already being lost. Police trying to deal with that issue were already caught up with the disobedience of some of the protesters. Out of a spirit of general youthful rebellion against authority, if nothing else, a number were being difficult if not downright obstructive.

The Minister for Police was not happy when his turn came to be interviewed by the studio anchor. He was annoyed at the diversion of resources from general police work – that was what he said to the camera; but he was also apprehensive about any physical confrontation that would lead to the inevitable allegations of police violence, bad publicity, and expensive legal and administrative outcomes. The Commissioner had told him that the man and woman power he could muster would focus on keeping the road clear and that there was no chance that he would have the resources to chase after protesters trespassing on Crown land.

In the small Tasmanian cabinet being Minister for Police always required being minister for other things as well, such as the ongoing disaster that was Corrective Services and Juvenile Justice. It was an unenviable job at the best of times. Things were underfinanced, and under-resourced, and subject to adverse commentary throughout the administration. Moreover, by their very nature his portfolios were the ones that seemed most often to generate bad surprises. Governments do not like bad surprises.

Like most of his predecessors, the Minister had absolutely no qualifications that fitted him for the role; no qualifications other than that he was, primarily, a reasonably able member of parliament. Unfortunately, he was insufficiently close to the Premier to secure a portfolio with fewer negative connotations. However, he was sufficiently ambitious to bear the strain in the short term in the hope of a better preferment. Running a successful coffee shop and serving a term on Hobart Council was a pathway to becoming an MP but it did not exactly fit a person with a Bachelor of Arts for managing the agencies responsible for the safety and good order of the community. Some legal training would have helped, but the only elected lawyers the government had available were firstly, the one who was clever enough, diligent enough, and loyal enough to be Attorney General; secondly, the one who was too inept to even survive as a junior suburban solicitor, which was why she had sought a career in politics in the first place; and thirdly, the one who was so far to the left of the party that his appointment to cabinet would have been courageous to say the least. He might even be numbered among the protesters. Indeed, if he were to take up their cause, the Minister and indeed the Premier would have to tread very carefully. The government had a majority of two.

Chapter 21

Angelique, in demonstrating her protester convictions, spent a night which was no more and no less comfortable than she had expected. While she could have descended and slept much more comfortably on the ground, she did not feel that was in the spirit of the protest she was trying to make; and after all, as a sports climber she was practised at sleeping suspended over precipitous places in the rain.

Moreover, given she was being monitored on the company's camera, she suspected that should she descend, she could find herself surprised in the middle of the night and bundled off the property without having the chance to summon assistance or draw attention to any manhandling she might have to cope with by the security arm of Lucifer Hot Rocks. While their boss seemed a very mild-mannered man, she was suspicious. He could have been putting on an act. Security people in her experience tended to be of a different type; and with no potential witnesses to any assault on her person she might claim to have occurred, she fancied she might indeed be rough handled. It was much better in the media spotlight with one's struggles and desperate cries for help being recorded as one was carried bodily off by apparently uncaring official thugs. Although she did recognise that most of the police were reasonably caring and some, whatever the protest concerned, were often philosophically on the protesters' side of the issue.

While she was prepared for it, the cold did start to make itself felt about 4 am when the clouds cleared. Waking, she added an audio report to the live video stream on the internet, just to make certain that the public and the media knew that the protest was real and she, at least, was prepared to physically back up her convictions whatever the weather. Just after 6 am, with the dawn rising, she was relieved to find that Fabian and Elizabeth were people who also kept their word.

She asked them to throw a handkerchief over the company's camera while she descended and took the opportunity, while they turned their backs, to answer a call of nature. They supplied her with two rather cold bacon rolls and a fresh thermos of coffee. She was back in the tower fifteen minutes later feeling far more comfortable and drinking the coffee. It was somewhat tepid, having been carried a long way since it was made, and what was worse, was over-sugared for her taste. It was indeed so cold and undrinkable after the first cupful that she emptied the remainder onto the ground below.

At her request, her loyal support team had not removed the handkerchief from the camera as they left. Given there was no one from Lucifer Hot Rocks yet responding to the absence of a picture, Angelique felt she should try to make as much of an annoyance of herself as possible by having them leave it there.

She presumed that the lack of a response from the company staff meant they had not even noticed what had occurred. She would persist, and she made herself as comfortable as possible while she waited for the inevitable attempt to talk her down, and the possible follow-up of an attempt at her physical removal. Presumably they would use a cherry picker of some sort, and she imagined she could make that very difficult for them, and make them have to do it in front of her own live streaming camera as well.

While Angelique was starting her day, Christine and Stephen were up early getting Alette and Eltje ready for a morning ride. Under the protection of the renovated roof of the now almost re-abandoned old mill, the horses were very comfortable, with both Chris and Stephen spending as much time as possible out of working hours constructing the stables and other amenities they would need to start their Friesian horse stud.

Alette and Eltje were going to be their foundation mares. They were both imports and had cost Christine a substantial amount of money in terms of their purchase, transport and quarantine. While they thought they might in due course buy local mares of the less-disputed local blood lines to fill out their breeding group, they were waiting and saving for a quality foundation stallion – which compared to the price of the mares was going to cost them a small fortune.

The two horses stood close to seventeen hands, big and bold with flowing manes and tails, but for all their size they also displayed all the friendly characteristics of their breed. They liked to be with you, and in the warmth of the stables they were welcoming.

Knowing the routine, they were ready to be out for an early ride before a feed and a day on the grass outside. With winter coats growing, they had only light stable rugs to be removed, and after an obligatory brush concentrating on the saddle and girth areas they were tacked up and ready to go. Stephen favoured Eltje and Chris, Alette. Alette was her usual playful self, having several tries at nibbling at Christine's black puffer coat when she wasn't watching. There was no malice in it, but the fabric showed a couple of places where it had necessarily been repaired due to her depredations during previous reciprocal grooming efforts.

With the aid of mounting blocks to allow their riders to reach the higher places with their brushes and then saddle up and mount, the horses were soon ready for the vagaries of the Tasmanian weather. Given their genetics and origin their riders had no concerns about going out, however they did find them keen to go in the brisk air.

'Do you mind if I combine work with pleasure?' Christine asked Stephen. 'I want to make a quick check on our protester, and if we go over the hill we can combine that with exercising these two.'

'No problem. Even if there's been rain overnight the ladies will have no problem on that track, and a bit of climbing won't do them any harm at all.'

So they set out, the horses decidedly frisky with their nostrils widening to take in the outdoor smells and their ears pricked. Their big strides and elevated action covered ground quickly, and Christine and Stephen, following one of the several wider bush tracks that bypassed the official access, soon found themselves at the top of the hill between the valleys near the water treatment plant. Then, helping the horses find their way through the staked plantings that were the responsibility of Christine's environmental team, they descended and traversed along the edge of the bush on the other side. They crossed the area where any horticultural activity might in due course be established, and pulled up sheltered by overhanging trees. From there they could observe the transmission tower, half built and skeletal against the early light just peeping over the horizon.

They were unseen dressed in black on their black horses. They saw Fabian and Elizabeth arrive, and Angelique descend from the tower and then ascend again, while they themselves were unobserved in the gloaming.

Margaret Pursehouse had initially spent the night working on her hobby. Being somewhat tired after her afternoon trek in the bush, she finished up an experiment she had been doing with drying a fungus in the microwave and then crushing it to a powder with mortar and pestle. She was always careful to wear a mask when she did that kind of work, having once lost consciousness after inhaling deeply while pounding, and woken on the floor wondering where she was. She cleaned up her laboratory, which she had converted from the kitchen at Number 13; and, padlocking the bolt she had put on the door, went to bed early next door at Number 15. She knew the result would be that she would wake early too – and that was exactly what happened.

Accepting that she would not get back to sleep at five in the morning, she rose and had breakfast while watching the ABC news channel. Angelique's protest was mentioned and the live stream from her tower camera was featured in the report, as was a weather forecast for the protester for the day. The weather was going to continue to be chilly to say the least, with clear skies for the start of the day but with rain anticipated later in the morning.

Now, while Margaret was in principle conservative and not inclined to be respectful of what any mass of disruptive protesters were doing, she did sympathise with a lady who had the courage of her convictions. She felt she could somewhat empathise with her given her own commitment to accepting the hostility of others when she was prepared to stand up for what she believed in. *It has saintly connotations,* she reflected as she said her morning prayer and included Angelique's safety and wellbeing as something special in her requests for the Lord's care. In doing so she was stimulated to consider a charitable act. She went to the stove, and then having made sure what she had prepared would stay hot in a thermos, she put on her hiking boots and hooded rainwear and set off on foot. She decided to take a short cut she knew through the bush.

A bit of what I call Warmth and Happiness will do her good.

Hence, just before 7 am, Angelique heard another voice calling to her from below. She didn't know who it was, but it was a lady proffering, if she heard what she shouted up to her correctly, a thermos of hot soup. Concerned it might be a company ploy even if her visitor was not wearing company high-vis, she did not climb down to speak with her but lowered a line with a bag attached and gratefully lifted the thermos up to her perch. She emptied the soup into her own thermos and lowered the now empty container back down. The lady did not seem concerned about the process. As she had transferred the soup it had smelled very chickeny and herbal and looked very creamy. It would probably be delicious. The lady removed her thermos from the bag and waved. Angelique waved back and thought she heard her say something about 'it's something special to keep you warm', and then her benefactor wasn't there anymore. Neither Margaret nor Angelique had noticed the two big black horses and their riders watching through the mist from the edge of the uncleared bush.

'Well, she's obviously OK, so let's go back. I have a feeling this is going to blow up today and I'll end up handling the phone calls,' Christine said to Stephen.

Neither of them had recognised the lone figure that had attended the protester after the earlier pair had made their visit, given the gloaming, the mist, and their nondescript dress.

'You have to admire her sticktoitiveness though, don't you?' remarked Stephen.

'True, but I would have liked her to have stuck to it somewhere fucking else,' Christine replied, 'not halfway up a bloody transmission tower!'

The horses had almost gone to sleep. Picking up their reins and getting their attention, they gently moved them off, turning back in their tracks to go over the hill.

Angelique had a decision to make, and she went for the soup.

The bacon rolls were on their way to being cold anyway and would keep for lunch when hopefully the weather would be warmer, and they would be fully cold. There was something about a tepid bacon roll that spoiled them. In her limited experience of dead pig on wholemeal she felt they were at their best hot with the bacon fat and real butter seeping into the bread – or fully cold with a sort of unity between the meat, the fats and the carbohydrate that made them more appetising. She needed something liquid anyway, having poured away the over-sugared coffee she hadn't drunk. She was starting to ache from sitting still and felt the need for some pain relief, and that meant taking a couple of tablets too.

I can never swallow tablets without having something to wash them down.

If she had been climbing, she would have packed up and worked out the stiffness, and indeed the cold, with activity; but she wasn't, and the pleasure of the physical and indeed mental efforts of conquering a rockface was not on offer. Looking towards the east, with the sun now almost halfway above the horizon, she remembered happier mornings on mountainsides with the sun's warmth on her back as she overcame her fears and met the climbing challenge of the day.

After her brief reflection, Angelique rummaged in her kit. She found what she was looking for – a couple of moderate-strength painkillers which also had a relaxant in their formulation – and then she settled down with a tumbler of what turned out to be most deliciously flavoursome hot chicken soup. Angelique swallowed her tablets and watched the sunrise, determined to do her duty despite her relative discomfort.

As the rays of the rising sun reached out and lit up the bush, the mist cleared and the dew on the grass glistened. The world began to appear a wonderful place, and the soup seemed to be warming her from the inside. She poured herself some more. It was excellent soup.
Very morish.

Meanwhile, as the mist began to lift, Christine and Stephen were already almost home. Alette and Eltje were allowed a pipe-opening canter on the flats near the old mill and were snorting and shaking their heads with the pleasure of it as they were reined in and more sedately steered towards the historic building, its warmth, and their morning feed.

On her perch in the half-built transmission tower, Angelique's stiffness had vanished; to her surprise she was no longer cold at all. Indeed, she was getting very warm – so warm that she took off her waterproof outer coat, and then her pullover. That didn't seem to help. She felt the world becoming a novel and expanding space into which she could feel her mind stretching, expanding, reaching out. It was by no means uncomfortable, even if the transition was a bit strange. As the sun rose more and more, she felt warmer and warmer again. In fact, the world began to turn kaleidoscopic and even hotter.

She felt she could see into the ground and even to the bottom of the pipes where the super-heated water was pushing upward to fire her as well as the nearby generators. The vision made her feel so hot and uplifted that she took off the rest of her clothing and let the welcome magical rays of the early morning sun light up her nakedness, perched halfway up the transmission tower's framework – and then, empowered by the glory of the beginning of the new day, the evident power of nature above, below and about her, and totally bereft of reasoning in her overwhelming gladness, she threw herself ecstatically into the arms of Aurora.

An angel had fallen.

Chapter 22

Detective Inspector Adam Michaels never even got to put a foot into the Launceston Police Station that morning. Years of shift work as a member of the lower orders meant his circadian rhythms were maladjusted and he could guarantee he would be awake by five if not earlier. It was one of the reasons that he and his wife slept in different bedrooms. That was also because they both accused each other of snoring, and the use of a pocket recorder had proved their mutual accusations to both be correct. Another one of those lessons in making a marriage work.

This day, like many others, he had risen in desperation at being unable to even snooze after answering the inevitable early call of nature, and had gone for a walk around the suburbs. While there had been a sprinkle of rain overnight and the streets, still artificially lit, were damp, the skies had cleared and the air was fresh and invigorating. Home and showered, he was dressed ready for an early start when he received the call to get himself to Mordbury and the outlines of the report of an unnatural death.

His initial reaction to the direction was to say to himself, *Where?* He then thought, *Why me?*

He was never happy about rush, particularly when he had been looking forward to a quiet day finalising a rather complex brief for the Public Prosecutor concerning the conduct of a local government stores officer who had found ways he thought he might favour his friends with inflated purchasing contracts in return for kickbacks. There were piles of paperwork involved, and Michaels anticipated the DPP would bounce the brief if he did not index everything thoroughly.

The detailed statements from the council employees who had made the numerous computer entries were, he hoped, now accurately cross-referenced with each of the offences the brief sought to detail. He had spent a week already with his sleep interrupted by dreams about the elements of the seventeen detected offences. Adam Michaels was a competent detail man when the case called for it; and he was aware that even while calling on his expertise, his colleagues were wont to regard him as somewhat obsessive, if usefully so.

General Duties officers were already on their way to secure the crime scene. Forensic officers had also been roused from their beds, as central to the matter was the naked corpse of a previously healthy young lady. He was also told that the matter was believed to involve a foreign national, and was related to green protests about some damned power line. It was therefore political as well.

Oh joy. I didn't think we had run out of detective sergeants.

Fortunately, he had left his car on charge all night even though he had been anticipating working in his office. It was a good habit to get into, he reflected as he entered the details of his destination into the car computer and found out where Mordbury was.

Given the distance, the nature of the possible crime and that it was now what passed for rush hour, he felt comfortable getting through the traffic and out of town expeditiously, but without unnecessary fuss. Dead was dead, and the corpse wasn't going anywhere however political the death might be. It might be rather wet though, if the clouds over the mountains rising in front of him were an accurate indicator of the weather to come.

It was just gone ten o'clock before he reached Mordbury, and another half-hour before he sorted out the geography of the place and found his way through the Lucifer Hot Rocks security cordon to the crime scene. In full accord with his apprehensions it was not just pouring with rain, it was belting down. The immediate problem was that he had to get out of the car without shelter to dress in his raincoat, which meant that in the process he got damp, damp to the skin. At least the officers preceding him had, between them and the forensic team, somehow obtained and erected in lieu of anything else a lightweight mini-marquee over the corpse. However, between their activity in doing so and the rain, it was clear there was little hope that much would be gained from looking closely at the ground immediately around the half-built transmission tower from which the deceased had fallen, or jumped, or been pushed.

We should do it though, and wider out, and straight away. Someone might have dropped something. That will make everyone thrilled in this weather.

He stood beside a forensic officer and three uniformed police, dripping in the rain while he read the writing on the side of the mini-marquee roof: Lucifer Hot Rocks Geothermal Generation and a smart company logo. Another bedraggled forensic officer beckoned him over to the body from beneath it.

'You got up here fast! I'd like to cover her up,' she said. 'Are you OK with that?'

She had obviously recognised him, although while her face seemed familiar, her name escaped him.

'Just a quick look,' he said.

Angelique Deloraine's body was as advised, naked and wet, but most noticeably wasn't lying straight at all. Almost face down, the head was at an impossible angle and the left shoulder was pushed backwards and downwards.

'Not too much doubt about what actually killed her,' he remarked, 'but why naked in this fucking climate?'

'And did she fall by accident, or was she pushed, or did she want to make a dramatic protest gesture and commit suicide?' said the forensics officer.

Michaels backed away from the body so he could look up at the tower without the obstruction of the tent. His face was immediately dripping with water.

'I can't see anyone committing suicide in the privacy of this place to protest the building of a transmission line. Surely no one is that fanatical,' he replied.

'At the request of Sergeant Kane over there' – she waved towards the other officers who were looking as miserably wet as the inspector felt – 'the company is organising a cherry picker for us so we can get up there. Their security man, Gerry Mason, says it's going to take them a while though. It looks from here as if she had set up a bit of a platform to camp on and suspended a hammock or something. Given she seems to have climbed up, I want to look for any marks on the structure, if there any, before we mess them up.'

'And the ability to climb half-built transmission towers in the pouring rain is not in your skill set?'

'Exactly. Moreover, I don't like heights, and I have a strong aversion to scrambling around on wet metal platforms in the pouring rain. I was not born with a prehensile tail or a climbing instinct.'

'Understood.' Michaels did not fancy the job either when he went through the evidence of his eyes, and examined what it would mean.

Not that fit these days anyway.

'Can I put a tarp over her now? The mortuary ambulance is supposedly on its way up to us.'

'Yes, by all means do that.' He nodded his consent. 'So, cause of death a fall from heights for reasons yet unknown. Time of death?'

'At a guess, given the weather conditions and the temperature of the body, I would say between six and eight this morning at this stage. I'll know more later. The company security had a camera running, by the way, and they're getting the footage for us. You can see it over there. It's linked to their security office, and they had the sense to leave it there. There was a handkerchief over the lens—'

'Bugger…'

'—And we have it to test for DNA. I got it packaged up ASAP given the, uh, liquid sunshine.' She gestured at the rain and flicked her right hand, causing a little shower of water to scatter off her rubber-gloved fingers. 'Lots of liquid sunshine this morning. Obviously, someone did not want anyone to see what went on.'

'OK.'

'There was also lots of clothing scattered around the ground at the bottom of the tower. Soaking wet of course but we've got all that too.'

'So, was it taken off her after she fell or up there?'

'Well, there are no rips in it and the body doesn't show signs anyone interfered with it after it hit the ground. It was pretty much dispersed as well. So, until I know more, I would say it came off up there. Now whether someone took it off her or she took it off herself I'll leave for DNA, or the absence of it, and for you to tell me.'

'Thanks for that!'

'I've talked to my people and Sergeant Kane and his mates, and they are resigned to the fact that you'll want a ground search as soon as. I don't think there's any hope of getting any help with that given where we are, that everyone is busy, and the need for speed given the conditions.'

'Alright, I'll go over there and do what I can to show gratitude in advance, then I'll be going back to the plant to see what their security people can tell me before we go trampling all over the place.'

A visit to the security office revealed that they had not only burned a disc copy of the whole of the vision on the security camera retrieved from their database, but also had the recording cued up to start playing it as soon as he might want to see it. The security man, Gerry, was being very cooperative and pointed out to him what he could see with his own eyes. The night vision was blurry and lacking in detail, but still watchable. From a distance he could see a larger figure and a smaller figure, bundled up in suitable clothing for the weather, approach the tower from the far side to the camera. That meant they probably came up the easement, he concluded. That made sense given the protesters seemed to be based on the coast. While one of the figures started unpacking things from the backpack they had put on the ground, the other, larger figure walked diagonally out of sight to the right and soon after, the screen went dark.

'That's where it ends until your people took the handkerchief off the lens,' explained Gerry.

'And your people didn't notice?'

'Sorry about that. It's an extra to our regular cameras you see. While we set up a monitor and glanced at it once in a while, we just left it on record as instructed by Mr Main and didn't pay it any real attention.'

'Hmm.'

'Well, these days now we're over the construction there are only two security people on at night, and they're mainly concerned with who comes and goes and with the occasional foot and vehicular patrol – and before you ask there wasn't any reason for anyone to go and have a look at the tower. We check for trespassers in secure areas and the security of the fencing, but bugger it, it's in the middle of fucking nowhere here.'

Fuck. Michaels wished for once things could be easy.

'Disc,' he said, holding out his hand.

Gerry took his time to remove it from the machine, holding it by the edges, and placed it carefully into a protective cover before handing it over.

'Ta,' said Michaels brusquely, and took possession of it, and left.

He immediately returned to the transmission tower area, not realising Gerry had more to tell him. Michaels and a very wet Sergeant Kane went over to the line of the transmission line easement in the rain and almost immediately found multiple footprints in the wet disturbed mud. The rain was not improving their definition.

'Two people, small and larger footprints, probably a man and a woman, hiking boots I reckon,' stated the sergeant. 'You want casts of what's left?'

'I agree, and yes. Find the best ones you can. Get one of the forensic people over here, will you?' He subsequently shouted at the sergeant's back. 'And bring some markers back too.'

Shortly after, the sergeant returned with the very bedraggled-looking forensics officers, with Gerry from Hot Rocks Security a few paces behind them. While the two officers spread a light plastic tarpaulin over the most immediately prominent footprints and placed markers on its corners to hold it down, Michaels left them to it and went over to Gerry and said, 'And what more can I do for you?'

'Well, if you'd waited in the office before rushing off, I could have told you that two of our managers were riding horses over here this morning, and one had instructions to check that the protester was OK. They saw the two people you have now got the footprints of and then they say they subsequently saw another person go to the tower.'

'How do you know all this?'

'The one who had been told to check on her logged it in her electronic work diary.'

'Diligent.'

'Yes, she is. Most of us are,' he added pointedly.

Michaels looked at Gerry and smiled. He realised he had made a bad start. 'So, what can they tell us about this other visitor?'

'Give us your phone number and I'll send you their draft statements.'

'You what?'

'Give us your phone number, and I'll send you their draft statements.'

'You smart arse bugger. OK.'

The company's security man had obviously had the opportunity to follow up and check on the company's knowledge of the matter, and had gone to the trouble of interviewing and documenting details of what the company people had seen.

Part of his own job I suppose. Point taken, lesson learned. Just because we're all getting soaked there's no need to be putting people offside.

He smiled, holding up his phone for Gerry to read his number. With the right buttons being pressed two messages duly appeared on the inspector's own phone. In the meantime Sergeant Kane joined them, and he and the security officer stood silently in the rain as Michaels scanned the attached statements.

'Can we go for a walk, and you can show Sergeant Kane and me the geography? I'd like us to head out carefully from here to wherever you can put the two managers. By the way, what the fuck were they doing riding bloody horses?' Michaels asked.

Gerry explained as the three walked slowly, carefully, line abreast and about a metre apart, towards the general area that Christine and Stephen's statements suggested they had been observing from. They found nothing underfoot until they reached the edge of the bush where the hoof prints of the horses were evident.

'So they say,' said Michaels, checking Christine's statement on his phone, 'they say somebody came out of the bush from over there' – he pointed to his left – 'and walked from there and over to the base of the tower.'

'That's it.'

'Alright. Let's see if they left any evidence of their passing.'

The three men set off, with the sergeant watching closely as they approached the line of possible intersection and calling out his estimate of how close they might be.

Gerry – still looking unimpressed and rolling his eyes at the sergeant's directions – was the first to see the track, well in fact the first of two tracks, although they weren't tracks as such but just native grasses lying flattened where someone had presumably walked over them going to the tower and back again. All three of the men took their phones out and took photographs, looked at each other and laughed.

'OK. Gerry, you come with me, and we'll walk towards the tower and see if we can find a print. Sergeant, would you please walk towards the bush and do the same. Here, give us a marker. Have you got one? Good.'

And they set off in opposite directions following the signs of the visitor's passage. Gerry and the inspector were unlucky, but when they turned to see how the sergeant was doing, they saw he was bent over, placing a marker on the ground. They headed over to him to find he was taking photographs of some footprints at a spot where the grasses gave way to bare ground and what looked like an animal track leading into the bush.

'Medium size, hiking-type boots again. Could be a small man or a woman. Not much of them left though. Castings?' asked Sergeant Kane.

'Please. And while you do that, I'll get Gerry to come with me and follow that path to see where it leads.'

'I wouldn't,' said Gerry, firmly and somewhat didactically, after the sergeant left them to organise the casting materials.

'You what?'

'Look. Those animal paths are all over this property. We might have compasses and GPS in our phones but neither you nor I are equipped to go just marching off into the bush. We could end up anywhere if we take the wrong turn and that's at any time, but particularly in this weather that's more than possible. Plus, I don't know how old you are, but I'm not fit enough for that sort of thing anymore.'

'Point taken – so what do we do?'

'You reckon that whoever this person was might have dropped something on the track, or that it doesn't divide and divide again and will lead us to somewhere where we can get an idea about who the person might be?'

'You read my mind,' said Michaels.

'Hope in Hades.'

'What do you mean?'

Gerry laughed. 'Look at the track. It's not bare earth and mud, it's covered in leaf fall. Any signs of disturbance of that might not be our visitor but devils, or echidnas or even birds on the ground. And as I say, these tracks go off in all directions.'

'So, what do we do?' Michaels looked off into the bush along the way the track led, wondering whether he was being a bit too keen.

'I'd cut my losses. You have a footprint cast from the person, although I can tell you from just looking at it, it's a popular brand of boot. You know that the person either came in from the coast or from Mordbury itself. Following the track, if you can and you don't get lost or literally side-tracked, won't tell you anything more.'

'I suppose anyone coming from the power plant would have come to the tower more directly.'

'And you can check for that by going over our CCTV and gate-keeping records if you want. But I have already done a check, and nobody did anything like that at what I think you think would be the relevant time.'

'You've convinced me. What did you do before this?'

'Lots of things, but I was an SP for a long while.'

'Fair enough. Let's go back to your shop and we'll have a look at the CCTV. Got any coffee?'

'Of course – and being that we're in private enterprise it's pod coffee. Three choices. The milk might not even be UHT.'

They walked back to their cars at the transmission tower and the inspector said to his newfound friend, 'And I'd like to speak with those horse-riding managers, the two horsemen of the apocalypse, too.'

'Of course you would,' said Gerry. 'They're expecting you. By the way one is a person who identifies as female.'

'OK, the horseman and horsewoman of the apocalypse then.' *Whatever. I do not really enjoy being told what I should not do and outguessed, especially when I'm cold and rather wet.* Michaels sighed. 'I should speak to whoever is in charge too.'

'That's Mr and Mrs Main. He's on the company tape and on his own voice recorder. He spoke with the girl when she was first found camping up in the tower yesterday and offered to give her dinner if she would come down. She refused.'

'OK, I'll look at those recordings first, see him first out of politeness if nothing else, and then the two managers.'

'If he's not in the plant Mr Main will be at Perdition.'

'You what?'

'It's the name of his house.'

'Well, I suppose you can name your house whatever you want.'

'Oh, he didn't name it. Way back in colonial times his ancestors named it. The original place was just a timber cottage. Hard times. It's a lot bigger and a lot more comfortable now.'

OK. So, I am going to Perdition. Sounds about fucking right. This rain is bloody purgatory.

As he approached his car the mortuary van pulled up to seek directions. He left it to Gerry to sort them out and struggled out of his wet weather gear as methodically as he was able. Quite surprising, he thought, that they'd managed to get here so quickly given the storm. He reminded himself about the political elements to the matter and that in the face of a strong suggestion from above, the crew had probably been persuaded. The corpse of Angelique Deloraine was about to begin its journey to the post-mortem table.

Chapter 23

In the event, Inspector Michaels found himself driving up the approach to Perdition early in the afternoon. He had taken the time to carefully review all the electronic records held by the company about the arrival and death of Angelique Deloraine. He checked he had disc copies of everything in his own possession, and then organised for the electronic transmission of the data to the Launceston Police Station and its secure servers.

Michaels was running later than he wanted, as he was not looking forward to driving back to Launceston and then back to Mordbury in the morning in the dark and the wet, but it looked like the rain was setting in for at least a couple of days. There was nothing he could do about the latitude of Tasmania – or the need to make sure that he exhausted the opportunities to gather as much information as possible while it was reasonably fresh. Needs must when the devil drives.

Peter and Lyn Main obviously had a motive for ensuring Angelique Deloraine's protest was short and ineffective, but having met both of them he quickly concluded, as they chatted in the luxury of their home office with its blackwood desk, leather furniture, and one wall covered in shelves filled to overflowing with books, that neither of them would be top of his list of potential suspects if indeed it turned out the girl had been murdered.

Peter Main's apparent stress was no more than Michaels would have expected, given where the power station project was apparently at. His wife Lyn lectured in philosophy at the university and seemed a bit more cold and calculating, but not unsympathetic. While that did not prevent her from being a malicious murderous bitch, she did not come across that way. In fact both of them seemed genuinely concerned about what had happened, and not just because it had happened on their land.

Furthermore, neither of them objected to his recording their conversation, and they accepted that he felt it necessary to refuse to have a cup of coffee with them. On the other hand, they took up his time asking this question and that question about what he knew so far, and how the investigation would proceed. They also made sure he understood that they wanted their condolences to be passed on to Ms Deloraine's family, and even asked him to invite them to contact either of them if they felt it would help.

The inspector's most amicable meeting with the Mains was nearing its end when his phone rang, and he excused himself to take the call. Peter and Lyn Main could only hear his side of the conversation of course, and they were hardly enlightened by it.

'Michaels …

'… Give me the good news first.

'… Oh excellent, where?

'… OK …

'…Georgetown, why Georgetown? … OK they live there …

'… I suppose so; so why didn't they just speak to the police on site?

'…You are kidding me!

'… So that's the bad news?

'… You are joking this time …

'… I'll see if I can do that. I am with the owners now.

'… Yes, I'll call you back.'

Michaels terminated the call and looked at the Mains.

'We have some problems. Firstly, just to let you know, two people have presented themselves at the Georgetown police station claiming to be two of the people who visited the protester this morning before she died. They are being interviewed and their statements taken. Apparently as soon as they heard the news they went home and got into clean clothes and went straight to their local police station. That helps; helps a lot.'

'Excellent,' agreed Peter.

'What doesn't help is that we are now at the centre of a pincer movement of greenies. About fifty are marching up the transmission line easement intent on besieging the plant, and another group are driving up from the south and coming in to demonstrate here at Mordbury.'

There was a pause while the Mains digested the news.

'Well, you can probably forget about the people coming up the transmission line, Inspector,' said Lyn.

'Why is that?'

'The few who are fit enough and equipped for the trek in this weather on that ground are going to be pretty ineffective when they get here, and they could not possibly get near the plant for some time. It's quite a hike. It'll be starting to get dark too. I think they will give up. I would be more concerned about people knocking on the front door.'

Michaels thought briefly about the range of his responsibilities and the resources he might muster. 'OK, so I recommend we use police resources to help the distressed coming from the north and get them back down. What's your assessment of the possible problems that anyone coming in the "front door", as you call it, might pose?'

'No physical security,' said Peter. 'You saw for yourself driving in, Inspector; and if you are thinking about some kind of barricade, forget it. There's lots of bush and open country and people could just walk around it.'

'Blocking the bridge might help,' said Lyn. 'It would mean they'd have to find a way to cross the river, which will be running quite deeply with this rain, but in a couple of hours anyone could walk upstream and to the plant in open country.'

'Then back down the road here if they wanted to make things uncomfortable for us and the other staff personally,' added Peter.

'So, what do you propose?' Michaels asked.

'Peter Main tactics,' said Lyn.

Her husband looked at her questioningly.

'We set up a display about the power plant here. We've done something like it before. Invite the protesters to have food and drink. Provide people for them to talk to about the plant and what we are doing. Even get the Vision Wellness Centre involved for those who misguidedly believe that stuff. Christine and Stephen might bring their horses to meet them.'

'A charm offensive.' Peter grinned. 'They can park on the forecourt, and we'll do it in the garage under the building. It's big enough. If we get some people to work with our housekeeper, we can bake cakes and stuff.'

After some quick planning the inspector started making phone calls, following Peter through the house as he rushed off to confer with Mrs Scott, while Lyn began organising the Hot Rocks staff from the comfort of the leather chair behind the desk in the study.

Chapter 24

So, what was planned to be an 'environmentalists versus the mean, murderous Mains' confrontation, to satisfy a hungry media, turned into what became known in green protest history as the Farce of Hot Rocks.

Selected officers of a generous nature were asked to volunteer to assist, with all the trials and tribulations involved, by using their police four-wheel drive vehicles on the transmission line easement to dog the heels of wet, tired, ill-equipped, and disenchanted protesters marching up the easement and persuade them to desist. They were given the offer of a free ride back to where they started. Less and gradually less determined to make a show of it in the exigencies of the Tasmanian climate, the protesters in the northern group faded away, just as Lyn Main had suggested they would.

Selected police, more hardheaded types with helmets, stab vests, carbon fibre armour and equipment belts, had been flown into the oval and were ready to hand, enjoying the luxury of the Mains' sitting room and its amenities. Mrs Scott, assisted at short notice by Mrs Aziz, saw that they were well catered for, exhausting her unprepared food stocks by providing a smorgasbord far superior to the sandwiches and cupcakes they baked and put on offer to those beneath their feet. Both ladies were exhausted after they had carried tray after tray of homemade goodies down the internal staircase, even with Christine drafted in to share in the work.

In the garage, the door to the staircase to the house above was protected by no more than a sign that said PRIVATE. All vehicles had been hastily removed to the safety of the plant. By late afternoon, fifty or so protesters who had arrived in a motorised column were sheltered from the elements in the garage and were being well catered for. In return they suffered for their trouble an unrelenting display of greenness by Lucifer Hot Rocks, led by Christine and her environmental staff. With an onslaught of Christian wellness featuring a proselytising Margaret Pursehouse selling herbal soaps, lotions and homemade remedies with the help of two of her more committed guests who just happened to have chosen to be resident at Vision that week, things went well. The visitors were more than pleased to assist, having been asked on the basis that the cost of their stay at Vision would now be subsidised by the company for their trouble.

Peter Main was a bit apprehensive about it, but pragmatically it added to the dimension of the whole thing at minimal cost, while giving their uninvited visitors something of a diversion. *Gives them more people to talk to about more and different things – a surfeit of goodness too.*

Two television crews had made a late morning journey to Mordbury to report on the death of Angelique Deloraine anyway, only to find quickly made but professional-looking signs displayed on the roadside, directing them and the protesters to Perdition for refreshments. Disappointed that the Mains had refused to give interviews on the grounds of the ongoing police investigation and the delicacy of the matter, they did get footage of them circulating after the mood of the crowd had been ascertained and no hazard to their personal safety was anticipated. If anyone did show an inclination to cause trouble backup was nearby, so Peter and Lyn Main circulated and discussed the sad outcome of the lady's protest and commiserated with those who had known her.

There were no pictures of confrontation to transmit on the evening news. Backgrounded with glimpses of a damp but bucolic environment populated by well-fed wallabies enjoying the green and freshly wetted grass or sheltering under both old and maturing trees with groups of discontented Tassie chooks, reporters said what they could in voice overs about the protesters, whom they had recorded as impotent in the face of the generosity of Lucifer Hot Rocks Pty Ltd. The event looked more like a community get-together than a demand for action. Of course, no one in the know told the visitors of the police standing by. They ended up being paid overtime to relax discussing tactics, watching television on the Mains' big screen, and exercising their limited social skills on each other.

As protests go it was a flop. As darkness began to fall the protesters began to drift away, keen to get down the mountain before it got too dark. They were full of sandwiches, fresh cupcakes with blue and pink icing, green PR, and Christian messages of peace and wellness. Their leaders were sullen. What had gone wrong?

As the supposedly militant crowd drifted off, Lyn Main found herself with Margaret Pursehouse and took time to thank her for her participation and have a look at the products she had been quietly marketing. Heretofore Lyn had not taken any interest in the detail of what went on at Vision. She had confined herself to the knowledge that Margaret was apparently adhering to the terms of her contract with Lucifer Hot Rocks, and that her clientele, confined to travelling on the corporate bus, had not invaded the peace and quiet of Mordbury either by arriving in their own vehicles or by any reportable unwanted interaction with the contractors, the staff or their families.

While Lyn picked her way through the soaps and lotions on offer, Margaret reciprocated her interest. She had not had any interaction with Lyn Main since the management meeting. Watching her dealing with the protesters she had seemed diplomatic but firm, a woman full of confidence in herself.

Well, she is a senior university lecturer. Margaret glanced at Lyn. Physically they were very different and that would have helped her too. Tall, straight, and big boned without too much filling out despite her age; that must give one added self-assurance.

Margaret did not understand that almost everyone, at least those who are rational, goes through life suffering self-doubt. However, those who are shorter and a little dumpy, and who have surrendered to religious guilt, are probably programmed for self-doubt to a greater extent.

'And how is our local wellness centre going, Margaret?' Lyn Main asked her, without any prejudice in her voice and choosing carefully what she called the business, given an apprehension that if she called it anything else she might deliver her enquiry with a sceptical tone. She did not want to do that, given Pursehouse's cooperation on the day and that it had been given at such short notice. She asked in the same tone as she would have approached a student with whom she had had previous contact if met again at a social event.

'Well enough thank you, Mrs Main,' Margaret replied, having taken a mental pause to decide whether to use her Christian name or not.

'Please, call me Lyn. Business good is it?'

'Good enough, and I make a bit with these things.' She passed a hand across her table of goodies. 'And I have to admit I still do some days at Omicron in Launceston to keep the money coming in.'

Lyn took a good look at Margaret. She seemed very buoyant, much different from the humble supplicant who had been at the management meeting months previously. In a way she seemed to Lyn quite – well a bit at least – *wired*.

'All locally made?'

'Well, not exactly. I make up the herbal extract concentrates, and I have someone who makes a lot of this stuff make the actual products. They do the labelling and packaging as well. I don't have the room to do it here.'

'And you still manage a profit?'

'Well, I get a sort of discount rate. They get an extra cut from internet sales you see.' She added without too much emphasis, 'And they are in the Church as well.'

'Ah, I hadn't thought of that.' Lyn held a cake of soap up to her nose and smelled the aroma through its wrapper, in the process noting the cross on its label. 'A minority market but one that's loyal I suppose. So, what does one do at a Christian wellness centre?' She suddenly felt a bit of a change in her mood. She sniffed the soap again and noted an immediate increase in her relaxation and confidence.

'Oh, all the usual things. We talk about diet and exercise and how to live a good life in tune with other people and with everything that the Lord has provided for us, including His sacrifice. We pray of course.'

Lyn resisted the temptation to engage on that last point. Lyn had seen her share of religious enthusiasm and put Margaret's newly discovered energy down to that cause. 'I suppose the fact that Mordbury is dry helps you?'

'Dry? Oh you mean no alcohol. Yes, sorry, I thought you were making a rather strange remark about the weather.'

They shared a smile.

'We try to give people confidence in themselves and one of our offerings includes some coaching on makeup and that sort of thing.'

'I suppose you make use of your nursing background.'

'Oh yes, skin care and all that; and I'm learning more and more – about herbs and that sort of thing,' Margaret enthused. 'It's all fascinating.'

'Yes, I can understand that. I know there's some serious work being done on what we used to think of as home remedies. Even the aroma of your soap seems to lift the spirits, well done.'

'Thank you. Please, keep the soap, as a trial.'

'Very kind. I have a colleague at the university who has just got a nice little grant from a pharmaceutical company to look at some Australian-specific stuff, Indigenous cures, and all that. Not my area of course but she seems very optimistic about getting one or two breakthroughs – oh shit!'

'What's up?'

'Well, a lady named Catherine Wheelwright who is a … significant greenie, shall we say, just went up the internal staircase. Excuse me …' She hurried off to find her husband.

Peter was easy for her to find among the dwindling numbers and the two directors of Lucifer Hot Rocks hastened up the stairs to their living room. Margaret looked for someone to give her a more detailed explanation and, with no one else around, was forced to call on Christine for an explanation for the urgency.

'What you don't know, and our visitors heretofore didn't know, is that sitting above us all this time have been half a dozen police officers fully equipped to deal with any need to forcefully protect life and property if duty called.'

Margaret was looking puzzled.

'The riot squad if you want a generic term, although I believe they have a more politically correct description for it these days.'

'Oh!'

'I think the best thing I can do is get the media away now, before we provide a platform for Ms Wheelwright to spout whatever bullshit she might want to spout about that.'

Over their heads in a large room, furnished in a minimalist style with furniture expertly manufactured from sustainable plantation timber, carpeted with what looked like an expensive dark blue pure wool broadloom and lit with sustainable energy, Catherine Wheelwright could not believe what she had walked into. She had hoped to be there to talk to Mr and Mrs Main after everyone had left and she could ask some serious questions, the sort of questions the police inspector was indeed asking; and make what she felt were some serious threats if the answers were not to her liking. Instead, she had walked into a riot squad picnic with two female officers going beyond the bounds of what might be considered conventional discipline on one of the couches.

Lyn and Peter Main came up behind Catherine and Peter asked, 'Anything I can do for you, Catherine? I hope this wasn't another attempt to plant a bug in my house.'

'No, no, no Peter, Mrs Main – I just wanted to make sure I could speak with you after—' she stuttered.

'After the rest of the mob found there was nothing to see and nothing to protest.'

'Well …'

'Well what?' asked Lyn.

'Well, what are the police doing here?'

'As Spike Milligan would have said, Catherine,' said Peter, "everybody gotta be somewhere". They're my guests just as you and your friends are.'

She did not appear to appreciate his sense of humour. 'You know what I mean.'

A patient Peter explained. 'The police felt that your troops might not respect my privacy and company security and might actually try to enter the power station and do damage. It was thought there might be a need to maintain the peace. We persuaded them to let us try a more subtle approach, but they felt it necessary to be available to meet the contingency if we failed.'

The assembled constabulary had ceased what they were previously doing and were standing about, or sitting down, or lying back on the couch on which they had been interrupted, taking in the conversation. Most of the officers were looking somewhat amused.

Lyn took over. 'Having them or their vehicles on display was only going to be provocative, so my housekeeper provided them with some lunch while we waited to see what might happen.'

Just then Chris and Stephen appeared up the stairs.

'All gone,' announced Stephen, 'media and all, and in the right direction.'

'I gave the TV crews some Christian Wellness soap,' Christine said somewhat cynically. 'We owe Margaret some money. By the way did anyone else have a chance to speak with her at length? She seemed a bit more 'thing' than usual to me, but I understand from rumour that seeing Stephen and me together might have exacerbated any previous ill feeling she had towards me.'

No one had a chance to answer Christine's question about Margaret.

'You paid them off!' stated Catherine Wheelwright.

'No, she gave them a token of thanks for their cooperation. I'm sure that if the gift had been given before the visit concluded and something had blown up the media would have been more than happy to report it,' said Lyn.

'So, no drama on TV tonight for you and yours, Catherine,' said Peter Main pointedly.

There was a pregnant pause.

'I want to know what role you and your company had in the death of Angelique Deloraine,' demanded Catherine Wheelwright, in pursuit of her original objective. No one was going to deny her the opportunity she had created for herself to confront the Mains.

'No, you don't!' corrected Lyn. 'You want to fuck off before I get very annoyed, clueless bitch. The police are investigating, the coroner will no doubt enquire, and the truth will probably come out. You are not going to grandstand and make political capital out of everyone's sadness about what has happened, or find cause to defame me, my husband or our people. I am certainly not going to give you a free quote you can use against me. Now go. Fuck off out of my house.'

Peter Main raised his eyebrows. His wife's tactics were not the ones he would have used, but he had not initially realised how Lyn was setting their visitor up. She had read her well, balanced the taunt, and of course their unwelcome visitor rose to the bait. She blew up in Lyn Main's face.

The police, who had been looking for something to do, predictably welcomed the opportunity to do it. It's not easy to frog-march someone safely down narrow stairs, but one of the officers from the couch, who was a part-time football referee in her spare time, and one of her male colleagues seemed to manage it with practised ease.

Their subsequent formal report explained that they had anticipated the possibility of an assault, and they had cautioned and removed the potential aggressor from the premises. It was uncontroversial – that was, to everyone but Catherine Wheelwright. Having been orally cautioned and placed in the driving seat of her car, she drove away from Mordbury with a sore wrist, a couple of minor bruises and absolutely no idea how she could capitalise on the situation, even with the friendliest of the greeniest journalists she cultivated.

Meanwhile, Christine, Stephen and Mrs Scott started the cleanup. Peter and Lyn retired to the study. As far as the directors of Hot Rocks were concerned, they wouldn't do it in front of Stephen and Chris, but they agreed they definitely deserved a drink.

Chapter 25

Christine and Stephen had come to a decision. Regularly sharing a king single bed in one of their single workers' rooms was not a way to advance their now committed relationship, and the logistics of sharing a motel-sized bathroom were aggravating in the short term, let alone the long term.

A couple of days after the initial controversy about the death of Angelique Deloraine, and following a debrief meeting at Perdition chaired by Peter with his wife with all the usual suspects present, they sought a private meeting with Peter and Lyn. They announced they were going to get married and sought permission to move into the old mill manager's house, even though it needed renovation. Given they were saving for a stallion, they offered to renovate the house in exchange for a substantial reduction of the market rent they thought they might be charged.

In due course and after congratulations had been given, Peter had his say.

'I don't like vague arrangements,' he stated. 'We would like you to both stay on the permanent staff of the power station as you probably already realise by now. You are both working well outside your current job descriptions – you do I'm sure realise that; while we're still finishing off the environmental stuff and workplace health and safety will always be an issue, Christine's job has included more and more PR, while Stephen's has become more of a trouble-shooting and a maintenance role. How about we put you onto contracts—'

'Which means that we can ask you to do anything pretty well as long as it's in your fields of expertise,' interjected Lyn, not unkindly, and with a smile.

'—And we will include the lease of the mill and the associated building as part of one of your remuneration packages,' went on Peter. 'The other one of you can have a company car to even things up. We'll make the conditions of the lease pretty loose. I think we can trust you to do things properly.'

The young lovers looked at each other and nodded.

'Thank you,' said Christine.

'That brilliant,' said Stephen.

'There is just one thing,' said Christine.

'And what's that?' asked Lyn.

'Water,' said Christine. 'The horses are currently drinking water from the village mains that we haul up there in a tank we fill from a standpipe carried on the back of a ute. Also we can't use the old rainwater tank water up there because I tested it and it's full of heavy metals, primarily lead of course from the old paint on the roof, but other stuff as well.'

Stephen gave the rest of the pitch.

'We need to run a line from the treatment plant down to the house. The gravity feed is enough but it's quite a run of pressure pipe, and the trenching should be well underground to protect it. Can you help us with that?'

'Or at least give us permission to do it,' sought Christine, hoping Stephen had not asked too much.

Peter looked at his wife. 'Wedding present from the company?'

'Why not?' agreed Lyn. 'Stephen, please make sure it finds its way onto the list of final projects for early completion. The plumbing contractors can do it before they finish up. We'll leave it to you to rough out the design for them. It will keep some of them busy while we keep them around and then switch completely to maintenance.'

'Where and when is the wedding going to be?' asked Lyn.

'We thought we'd do it at the Eskbend Hotel,' said Stephen. 'There's a couple of people from Lonnie we would like to be there, and of course it's dry here …'

'It will only be small,' stated Christine, 'and there's a few people who might get a bit 'thing' about it won't be around to give us a hard time. We both like the place and they've just got a new chef too which helps. I'm a bit over what they called *bistronomy*.'

'Did that reach here? Pretentious French con in my opinion. We had it in the hotels,' said Peter.

'Anyway, we'll do it in the garden if it's fine, or in the lounge if it's not,' said Stephen, a little frustrated by the diversion. 'They've said they would do an early dinner in the function area of the restaurant for us. People can stay over if they want to or come back here. When was dependent on what you said about the house. I'll use whatever influence I have with the plumbers now you've given your OK for that and we'd be looking at about three months I reckon.'

'You can borrow Anthony's Rolls-Royce if you like. Who is giving you away?' asked Peter. 'That's if you are doing the old-fashioned thing?'

'I'll volunteer him,' said Lyn, nodding at Peter.

'Well actually someone else has already agreed to do that,' explained Christine. 'One of the doctors from the Omicron team, Dr Tan. He has sort of helped me through some of this. I met him when he first came up here and your brother had his accident …'

She paused, not wanting to open old wounds.

'Anyway, Lachlan Tan has become my GP. I go down to Lonnie to see him there now he's not here. He's not a psych but he's been helpful. Practical. Straightforward. And he finds time for me … working through things.'

Peter was looking confused. Lyn was obviously more across the story. 'For fuck's sake Peter, I know we have never talked about it but surely …'

'What the hell are you all talking about? And stop looking at me as if I'm a dummy.'

Christine explained. 'Peter, I thought you probably knew, and anyway if you didn't then it really didn't matter; you've never shown me any kind of prejudice.'

'Prejudice about what?'

Lyn administered the coup de grace. 'Oh, for fuck's sake Peter,' she said gently, 'you silly naïve power-plant-building hotelier. Chris did not start off life as a female.'

'Really?'

'Yes really.' Christine assured him. 'And I am not going to get into some sort of silly discussion about what words are appropriate to use to describe my gender status.'

'Oh.' Peter just shook his head. 'By the way, how did you go with the police?'

'Inspector Adam Michaels – fine,' said Christine. 'You just have to tell the truth. I presume we will all have to go to the inquest and give evidence – at least all of us who were involved.'

'Probably.'

Stephen interrupted. 'We think we *might* know who the third visitor to the protester was, but even now we can't be sure. They were wearing a hoodie and it was pretty dark, and we were some distance away. So, we just said there was a couple and then there was another person, and what we could see. The protester came down from the tower to talk to the first two visitors but didn't come down for the third person. We talked it over and decided it was not going to do anyone any good if we made a guess …'

'Even if the guess we came up with might have given me some personal satisfaction,' added Christine.

'What do you mean?' asked Lyn.

'Well, it *could* have been that woman Margaret, from the Wellness Centre,' stated Stephen to Peter and Lyn's surprise.

'But much as I would have liked it to have been her or cause her trouble we didn't know for sure, well not even probably, so we didn't say,' said Christine a little self-righteously. 'We have history,' she added.

'Do we need to know?' asked Lyn.

'I don't think so,' said Christine. 'It's got nothing to do with what goes on here.' She was defensive.

'Look,' said Stephen, before Christine was forced into an explanation. 'She's a religious nutter who thinks Chris is an abomination before God.'

'Really,' said Lyn. 'Well, I suppose there are a few around who might share that view but really. Really? In this day and age?'

''Fraid so,' said Christine. 'If I *have* to speak with her about something I do, and we are civil. I usually send one of my team if something comes up. If I've spoken with her half a dozen times since she started with Omicron, then that would be the limit of our dealings. All I know is she roams around the place a bit looking for plants for her remedies. She's big on God and herbs.'

'I have met her on one of her rambles,' agreed Peter. 'She said something about notebooks she and Dr Tan found at the old dispensary when they first came up here. If she and Lachlan found them there then they really belong to me, and Lyn …'

'Anyway,' Christine continued, 'the inspector asked us the same question at separate interviews – could we identify the people we saw visiting the protester at the transmission tower – and we both said "no". That's what's in our written statements too. I understand the couple that we saw arrive first owned up straight away. They brought her some breakfast. The third person is still unidentified apparently.'

'And how do you know all this about the case?' asked Lyn.

'Oh, just ask Gerry what you want to know,' said Stephen. 'He's buddied up to the inspector and seems to have the whole story.'

'Really!' exclaimed Lyn.

'I wouldn't get too excited,' said Peter. 'I asked him to do that, not that he wasn't nosy enough anyway. I asked him to let me know about anything he heard that could be of concern, and he hasn't – so I presume all is well.'

Chapter 26

The wedding of Christine Reynolds and Stephen Banbury was not a large affair, with just close friends and work mates present.

Lachlan Tan drove up from Launceston the day before and took Anthony Main's Silver Cloud out for a test drive from Perdition to the power plant bollards and back, several times, before pronouncing himself competent enough not to kill the bride and groom on their trip down the mountain.

'Or better still,' he said to Peter, 'not to damage the thing in the Launceston traffic. It's certainly a different drive to a modern car, albeit a most pleasant one when you get used to it.'

'There's enough fuel in it to get you into town, but you had better fill up on the way back.'

'What does she do?'

'Twelve to the gallon. My brother carried five litres in a container in the boot. He always said it was just enough to get you to somewhere you could safely pull off the road if you ran out,' he joked.

So the next morning Lachlan, in a suit and tie, presented himself in Anthony Main's proper motor car at the single workers' accommodation and picked up both the bride and groom already dressed for the ceremony. For such a big car he was surprised that the boot had a relatively limited capacity. The suitcases the couple had packed for just a couple of days away from work after the ceremony fitted in on top of each other, just.

Lachlan cast a fresh eye over Christine, seeing her for the first time in something other than jeans, and was more than ever objectively taken with her appearance. Stephen, like himself, was in suit and tie. Christine, who he had half expected to find in a pant suit, had gone for a frock. By the look of it she had not worried over the cost.

Class act, classic statement.

She saw him looking.

'Sends the message?' she asked rhetorically.

'Certainly does. It looks very well.'

He reflected on the progress of the couple's relationship since he had known them, particularly Christine, and sometimes offered counsel over the months. All three of them had learned from the experience and he could not avoid seeing himself in something more of the role of a parent rather than just their GP. They got in the car and onto the road before Lachlan stopped and turned around to ask, 'We do have the rings and whatever do we, before we depart this place?'

'No rings,' said Stephen. 'We don't do that kind of symbolism, either of us.'

'OK, but nothing else forgotten?'

The happy couple looked at each other but could not recall anything.

'Drive on, Lachlan,' said the bride to be. 'Drive on … I'll be in the back here smiling and waving at the plebs.'

They set off down the mountain. The weather was fine and they were, of course, early.

While they were in the car Christine broached the subject of the notebooks.

'Lachlan. Peter Main has spoken to me about notebooks that were in the things that I took away from the old dispensary, you know, the bottles and stuff, after the accident when you first arrived. Do you remember them? I don't, but we were sort of distracted.'

'He's already spoken to me about them,' Lachlan replied. 'There were two'. He looked into the small rear view mirror mounted less than strategically on the top of the dashboard and momentarily caught her eye. 'I do remember them but apparently Margaret has told him that she has them, and is making profitable use of them.'

'I think he wants them back.'

'I'm sure he does. I believe he's having thoughts about what he might do after the project is completed. I don't think he sees running the plant in his future. Frankly after all he's had to do I can't blame him.'

'He's certainly a bit wound up at times these days.'

'Well, my advice would be for you guys to get on with your lives and stay away from any issue between the Mains and Margaret Pursehouse.'

'Sounds reasonable,' stated Stephen.

'Working on starting a family,' said Chris.

'What, kids?' said Lachlan, more than a little surprised, again taking his eyes off the road.

'No, foals!' Christine giggled.

'Ah. OK funny girl, I'll accept you got me there. By the way, we are very early. Do you mind if I stop and fill this thing up before you get hitched? Or I may not get back up the mountain and it's easier now rather than later.'

'Permission granted, James,' she said. 'We shall leave the management of the motor to you.'

'Just don't start practising the royal wave on the general population, smart arse,' commanded Stephen.

The civil ceremony was held in the garden, as had been hoped, and was as simple and straightforward as it could legally be. Lachlan and Lyn Main were the witnesses. The couple eschewed all extra ceremonial, sticking to the bare necessities, although Lyn had persuaded Christine to carry a small bouquet which she had thoughtfully provided.

'It gives you something to do with your hands,' she advised.

The writings of Kahlil Gibran were avoided, and the bouquet was not thrown over the bride's shoulder.

After a bistronomy-free late lunch in celebration, everyone went their own way. Lyn was staying in town and keeping the Skoda for her own transport. Consequently Lachlan found himself with Peter Main as a passenger back to Mordbury, and Peter had a guest of his own who had appeared from nowhere after the wedding.

'Dr Tan, this is Benedict Tarleton, he'll be coming back with us. He's staying with us at Perdition for a couple of days.'

Lachlan extended his hand, and the man shook it. 'Nice to meet you, Dr Tan.' *American*, thought Lachlan. And not short of a dollar. Those jeans and leather jacket did not come cheap. Even the long sleeved collarless cotton T-shirt looked fashionable and expensive.

Benedict Tarleton had packed light, and his bag was soon resting in the boot of the car for the trip back to Mordbury. What Lachlan had not initially realised was that while he was concentrating on the road, he was being deliberately involved in a serious conversation with the two men riding in the back seat. It was a conversation that could change quite a few futures, at several levels. It became apparent that Peter had arranged everything so that the three of them could talk in confidence about the death of Angelique Deloraine, and other things – like notebooks on mycology and their possible value in for the pharmaceutical industry. Lachlan found himself going over what had happened when he had first taken control of the surgery at Mordbury, and giving opinions about a range of medical issues he knew little about. He was coming up with thoughts about how he might change the direction of his life.

At Perdition, Mrs Scott had prepared a light dinner and two spare bedrooms. The three men talked late into the night, enjoying Tasmanian liqueur whiskies and mapping out possibilities for the future, their different ambitions and the application of a range of technologies. In the kitchen Mrs Scott filled the dishwasher, and the classic Rolls-Royce cooled off in the garage below, sticking with tradition by leaking fluids onto the pristine floor.

Chapter 27

The coroner was reasonably kind to Inspector Michaels and the police team at the inquest, even if Mr Corbett, the Senior Counsel representing Angelique's parents, was not. Mr Corbett had been instructed to clear, as far as he could, his clients' daughter's name and reputation. He knew he had a difficult job to do given what he had seen in the extensive police report and the witness statements.

Notwithstanding the introduction of the police report to the coroner into evidence, several people were required to relate their story in the coroner's court. Christine had to appear to tell how she had become aware of Angelique's presence, the steps she had taken to alert the company, and what she did to protect the protester's safety. Peter was called as a witness for himself and on behalf of Lucifer Hot Rocks Pty Ltd. Everyone except Mr Corbett seemed quite happy about his conduct and the steps he and his team had taken in the matter. Mr Corbett had only one question for him.

'Mr Main. Prior to all of this happening did you ever meet Ms Deloraine?'

Peter's response was a quick 'No'.

'Are you sure?'

Peter felt that he might be falling into a trap and gave a qualified answer.

'Well not that I can recall.'

'My information is that she was employed at one of the hotels you managed in North America, The Rocky Peaks Hotel … as a tour guide.'

'Really?'

'I don't make things up, Mr Main.'

'I'm not suggesting you do.'

'Well?'

'Well, if she was there at the same time I was, I may have met her, but she would have been working under a junior manager so I wouldn't have had cause to deal directly with her. It was a big place, and a busy one.'

Most of my days there were spent dealing with whingeing Floridians, but I'm not going to volunteer that.

'She told her parents she enjoyed her time there.'

That's not a question so I am not offering anything. 'It's more than likely that she was a temporary employee hired for the summer season. I do not remember her.'

Mr Corbett had no further to go with his line of questioning. There was no hint from his research of any acrimony or indeed the reverse between his clients' daughter and Peter Main; but he felt it was worth asking. One never knew what one might provoke.

'Very well, Mr Main.'

At a nod from the coroner Peter resumed his chair at the back of the room. He was a bit shaken.

The forensics officer was on routine ground when it came to explaining her examination of the site. She produced the notes and relevant photographs made of the things found and secured on the day and the custody and control of those things, and showed pictures of the casts made of the rain affected footprints that suggested there had been four people active on the site that morning, Angelique and her three visitors. She explained that the rain had made the taking of the prints difficult and what they had been able to identify had been of common brands.

It was also within her competence to give the police evidence on what was found by the rescue squad members who had gone up the tower with her to note the conditions up there and retrieve Angelique's possessions. Yes, it would have been precarious for the average person, but the evidence was that she was an experienced mountaineer; yes, she had set up a safety line and the body harness for it was found attached to it; it had been discarded rather than just unclipped – see the photograph, Exhibit 38. They had also found various things that they presumed to be the possessions of the deceased including sandwich wrappers, two cold bacon rolls and a thermos that contained the apparent remains of soup, and these had been forwarded to the government forensic chemist for analysis. Why? Because people don't usually strip down naked in inclement weather and fall or jump from building structures – and the officer, without any evidence of someone having pushed the deceased from her perch, or evidence she had been shot or had other injuries to suggest outside physical interference, had been suspicious that she might have consumed something that had made her do it.

Mr Corbett had no cause to query any of that evidence. It was routine police work and it would seem that it had been done by the book. The photographs were available in hard copy prints signed by the officers who took them with the time, date and place particulars, as well as being shown on the large video screen on the wall of the courtroom. Whatever the implications of the evidence might be, and while the inference the officers had made from what they had found were obviously not palatable for his clients, counsel assisting the coroner had a perfect right to ask what the police motivations had been for the avenues of inquiry they had followed up.

Mr Corbett turned around in his chair and looked at Mr and Mrs Deloraine and gave them a half smile and a conciliatory nod.

They were not happy, but he had warned them that it would be coming.

In their turn Elizabeth and Fabian told their story and identified two of the boot castings as the same as theirs. Fabian admitted to putting his handkerchief over the Hot Rocks camera and then leaving it there at Angelique's request.

'She came down to have a shit and wanted the camera covered while she did, and then asked us to leave it there to be as much of a nuisance as she could be,' he explained somewhat ungraciously.

Mr Corbett was keen to pursue what the two of them knew about the personal habits of his clients' daughter, particularly as to any knowledge they had of any drugs that she might have taken, but neither Elizabeth nor Fabian knew her well and both of them turned out to be clean living, hardworking young people.

'As soon as we heard what had happened we went straight to the police station,' Elizabeth testified. 'She was a bit of a hero to many of us.' She gave a sniffle. 'She didn't deserve to die like that.'

Inspector Michaels, when his turn in the witness box came, forgave Mr Corbett because he was used to being in the witness box and knew that picking away at things was the barrister's job. He also recognised the police report was somewhat startling in its own way, with an unidentified visitor to the transmission tower being untraceable. The casts of the boot prints that had been taken had revealed no new information. Due to the rain they were not very good, and they were of common brands anyway.

He had to explain the rationale for not following the tracks of the person into the bush on the day. On reflection he was still glad he had followed the security officer's advice, but it took some explaining. Whoever had been the third person they would have had to have known the tracks and trails thoroughly, and the police had been unable to locate a contender even with door-to-door enquiries in

Mordbury. Nobody had admitted to knowing anything, and indeed the residents had all seemed focussed on their daily lives rather than what a greenie protester had been doing up a half-built transmission tower. Except for the lady at the Christian Wellness Centre who expressed, as perhaps might have been expected, more sympathy for the deceased, the matter was not of great interest.

Given all the circumstances I would guess it was another greenie, but we don't put guesses in reports to the coroner.

Peter, who had decided to attend the hearing for the days after he had testified, because it was interesting and a process he hadn't seen before, pricked up his ears at that evidence. He could think of a different contender. So could Christine, whom he had given permission to stay if she wanted to. However, Christine was firm with Peter in the lunch break when they discussed it. She was not going to volunteer her suspicions of whom she and Stephen had seen.

The evidence provided by the post-mortem pathologist from the Coroner's Office was straightforward. Angelique Deloraine had several injuries that could had been the cause of her death including burst fractures in vertebrae of her cervical spine, intracranial bleeding and a ruptured spleen. She had suffered other fractures as well including a broken shoulder. There was no controversy about the fact that she had died from a fall from a height.

Why she had fallen was of concern, however, and the forensic chemist from the government laboratory who followed the pathologist into the witness box was unused to rough treatment.

He did not come off so well.

The government chemist found himself being questioned not only on what they had found and identified in the blood of Angelique Deloraine, but also what they had found and couldn't really identify. The evidence concentrated on the flask containing the remainder of the soup, and the contents of Angelique's backpack. There was nothing of concern with the bacon rolls save for their potential long-term health effects if eaten regularly. The chemist, who thought he could try that piece of humour, found it fell on stony ground. It was bad start from which he never recovered.

The painkillers were easy, although perhaps his reeling off the chemical formula $C_8H_9NO_2$ for the medication, and only identifying it by its common name of paracetamol when asked, annoyed the court even more after his earlier attempt at levity.

Mr Corbett felt a need to intervene in the evidence being led by counsel assisting, and counsel assisting was pleased to give him the floor. After all, Corbett was getting paid a great deal more than he was to be there. Mr Corbett rose and rebuked the witness in the only way he indirectly could early in his evidence.

'Your Honour, strangely enough neither I, nor I suspect the court, can understand chemical formulae. I would be grateful if the witness could be instructed to keep his answers out of the more rarefied atmosphere of his higher levels of pharmaceutical knowledge.'

The coroner intervened, as the forensic chemist was looking very miffed. 'Yes, Mr Corbett,' she said in repressive tones, and then to the chemist, 'I too would be grateful if you would keep your evidence at a level that can be readily understood by all of us here. I realise you want to be exact but common names will do unless you are asked otherwise. Go on, Mr Corbett.'

'Did you find anything else that was remarkable,' Mr Corbett asked, hastily adding 'and relevant?'

'Three things, and they were psilocybin, that's 3 bracket 2 dimethylaminoethyl close brackets indol 4OL; and something like psilocin, which is a tryptamine alkaloid' – the coroner and counsel assisting Mr Corbett were looking daggers at him – 'but wasn't; and something else we couldn't hang a name on – anyway they were hallucinogens and probably came from mushrooms.'

The chemist had run down into simplicity and waited for the next question, given the looks he was getting. It was all in his written report anyway. His answer begged further examination, but Mr Corbett let the conclusion drawn by the witness pass. The last thing he needed was evidence that the chemicals had possibly been manufactured by human hand and all that that would imply for the reputation of his client's daughter. If the coroner wanted to go there in due course, then it would be up to her and counsel assisting. He would get at the evidence that he wanted in another way.

'Are the chemicals dangerous, and please, can we avoid the detailed chemistry?'

'Well certainly, psilocybin and psilocin are found in Australian fungi but the combination of what we found with some of the other chemicals present is very like, but not exactly the same as what you would expect to find in a certain mushroom native to Europe.'

'But not found here?'

'Well not to my knowledge after some detailed research; but you never know given there was no biosecurity in colonial days; there could be a location where it would grow in Tasmania – or it could even be a native species not previously identified.'

'Would the Mordbury area be suitable?'

'I am told so.'

'You are told so?'

'Well yes, it's not my field and I had to do research with colleagues overseas to track it down. It could grow, or something like it could grow, in several places in Australia, although more likely the trees it would like to grow on would be found in wetter parts of Tasmania.'

'What is it called?'

'Well, I don't want to say.'

'Why not?'

'Because this is a public inquest, and, with respect I don't want to encourage people to go out looking for it. It's recognisable by its common name which is descriptive of what the fruiting body looks like. It's potentially a killer even in very small quantities.'

'Hmm.' The barrister took another tack. 'I'll leave that and may come back to it, Your Honour, if I think it may be material. So, when you say psilocybin, you mean what we all know as the stuff that's in the so-called magic mushrooms?'

'If you want to put it that way, yes.'

'And psilocin, that's well known too?'

'Oh yes, there's been a lot of terrific research going on into these chemicals recently, they could be adapted to help people with depression and anxiety. Although it wasn't actually psilocin. Bits of it were but a bit of it wasn't.'

'Can you explain that in simple terms; what was the difference?'

'No.'

'No what?'

'No, I can't explain it in the simple terms you obviously want. I can give you what looks like its formula, I can draw you a diagram of what its structure probably looks like, and some of the alternative arrangements of the molecule—'

'But it would act like psilocin?'

'Probably.'

'Probably?'

'Well yes, you see that's down to the third chemical present. We had to send samples to several labs, and they came back with a range of answers because … well, because …'

'Well?'

'It seems to jump around a bit.'

'It does what?'

'It adapts itself.'

'You mean it's alive?'

'No, no, no. This is the problem when you oversimplify. It's a very flexible biochemical molecule. It's got all sorts of ... bits hanging off it, and these bits are unstable and can grab hold of other chemicals in all sorts of places. Put it with one chemical and it will link up in possibly two or three different ways, even change arrangements while you watch. It can change shape, form linkages, lock in or not. It's very novel.'

The forensic chemist was obviously much taken with his subject. He was starting to enthuse.

'And you couldn't work it out?'

'Not yet, and neither could three other labs we sent it to, including one in the USA. We were, are fascinated by it. They are fascinated by it. One of the labs we sent it to is doing some of the pharmaceutical work I spoke about earlier and they are trying to analyse it even now. I'm not ashamed about my lab not being able to nail it down. You need comparative molecules, and we don't have them. What's more we just don't have the equipment and they do, and even they are still a bit baffled.'

Mr Corbett seemed to sigh. 'So, given you are the government expert, what do you say was in this biochemical cocktail?'

'I would say psilocybin and psilocin, but the psilocin could have been altered by a third chemical.'

'Alright let's leave that there. What would have been the effect of these chemicals?'

'In the quantity we found in the deceased's blood, I would say that she would have undergone hallucinations at a minimum. With the painkillers in the mix as well she most probably would have suffered acute neuropathy.'

'Neuropathy?'

'Well in relation to this case you can get muscle weakness, cramps, the twitches, numbness so you might not feel the cold, loss of sensation or feeling in body parts, loss of balance or other functions' – he took a breath – 'emotional disturbances, confusion, inability to sweat properly leading to heat intolerance, dizziness, light-headedness or fainting because of a loss of control over blood pressure, and difficulty breathing or irregular heartbeat.'

The chemist ran out of breath. He had seen that obvious question coming and had rehearsed his answer.

'Could she have gone on what is commonly called a trip? Could she have tripped out?'

'Yes. I'd put it down as more than likely.'

'How long would such a trip have lasted? Would have just been for half an hour say, or would it have gone on for hours?'

'Given what she ingested I think she would have died from the drugs anyway, even if she hadn't fallen. If she had managed to survive the drugs in her system, and I don't think she would have although to be fair all the evidence is that she was in generally in good health with a good level of fitness, I have no doubt she would have been permanently impaired psychiatrically and physically.'

'What does that mean?'

'Well to keep it simple for you,' the chemist responded somewhat gratuitously, 'I believe that she would have been a cabbage with no control over her bodily functions.'

With the government having called Fabian and Elizabeth to explain what they had done on the day and the background to Angelique's protest, Mr Corbett called three more of Angelique's fellow protesters; all claimed that they had never seen Angelique Deloraine taking illegal drugs. He also called one of her fellow mountain climbers to give evidence over the internet, from Nevada, about her capacities as a skilled mountaineer.

It was a good try, but Angelique's parents knew the mud would stick. They were downhearted because, while their barrister had gone on to argue that their daughter had no history of drug taking and that the coroner should find that she had been administered the drugs by a third party either at the tower on the day, or by putting them in something she had with her, and that she had inadvertently consumed them; their child would go down in history as a drugged hippie greenie, and not as the intelligent, respectable and respected environmental protester they lovingly knew her to have been.

The media didn't help. You can't legally defame the dead and they had a field day with the evidence – naked women jumping or falling out of transmission line towers not being run of the mill – and they benefitted twice because environmental protesters of all stripes besieged the court not just for the public hearings, but also on the day when the coroner brought in her verdict. Some of them did look like drug-taking hippie greenies.

In due course Her Honour Melania Ives found that Angelique Deloraine died an accidental death while under the influence of narcotic substances, apparently commonly found in mushrooms, mixed with a dose of a common painkiller. How the mixture of drugs came to be in her system Her Honour could not formally determine, although she accepted the evidence of Elizabeth and Fabian that they had not been the suppliers, and that of Christine and Stephen that there had been a third visitor to the tower whom the police had subsequently been unable to identify.

She complimented Lucifer Hot Rocks for their cooperation in the investigation and apportioned no blame to them for a situation that had been very much out of their control. She noted that the company had now placed barbed wire around the legs of their transmission towers to reduce the chance of anyone climbing them, even at this late stage when the company was now producing the green power everyone needed on the mainland. In respect of the drug Angelique had consumed she remarked that given its novelty and obvious capacity to injure if not kill, young people should refrain from experimentation – that being a small hint that she felt a suspicion in her own mind that Angelique may have known what she was doing all the time.

The police, in the meantime, had found no problem with obtaining multiple search warrants and kicking down the door of every possible drug lab, distributor, and user their extensive knowledge of the drug scene brought to mind – and then some. The Minister for Police, who had suffered at the hands of the media and especially from the pictures of Angelique's distressed parents, was overjoyed that he had an excuse for what he regarded as positive policing. As a result, road patrols were limited, and domestic violence calls went unanswered, as the men and women of the force filled the courts with many unfortunate minor drug users who had a health rather than a drug problem, and a few more major drug offenders, those who actually made money out of misery.

Chapter 28

Soon after his commitments to the coronial investigation of the death of Angelique Deloraine, Peter made a trip to New Zealand. He gave himself two days to recover from his trip. It had been a tedious if necessary inconvenience, being strictly a business trip and not a simple one. Taking an early morning Friday commuter flight from Taupo to catch a midday from Hamilton to Melbourne, and the last flight out to Launceston to be driven to Perdition in the dark, had knocked him around, and he needed to be in the best shape he could be for what he had to do next.

'I can do it if you want,' offered Lyn, but both of them knew it was his job to do. It was his name on Anthony's will, and in his name that he had fought for Anthony's wishes in court. Moreover, it was to him that Margaret Pursehouse had personally admitted that she had taken it upon herself to appropriate the two notebooks that had been left in the former dispensary.

'No, I'll do it, and without sounding sexist or full of my own self-importance I rather fancy she'll accept me as an authority figure and do what I ask.'

'Well if you wait until Monday or Tuesday she's possibly going to have a new batch of guests, so she won't be wanting to put on a turn in public,' suggested Lyn.

'Monday's out because I have to meet with Gabriel, and I'm doing that here and then going up to the plant so I can catch up with anything that came up in the last week.'

'I can assure you that we managed quite satisfactorily while you were away. Your phone was silent because I was in control, and nothing happened. We're pushing power out at eighty percent of full capacity. Consistently. Nothing broke. Oh, I suppose the only thing you should know is that the Minister rang on Wednesday.'

'Oh God, what did that dickhead want?'

'He actually wanted to say how pleased he was. I allowed him to tell me that and accepted on behalf of everyone the metaphorical pat on the head. So, it will be Tuesday?'

Peter heaved a sigh. 'It will be Tuesday.'

His Monday went off perfectly and Gabriel had everything he wanted in hand, and he was on his way back to Launceston straight after lunch – a very satisfying one too because Mrs Scott had known Gabriel before he did, in the Anthony Main days, and she liked to look after him.

'He's BP,' she said. 'Like me.'

'What?'

'Before Peter.'

Just as his wife had said, the plant was running fine. Demand was a little variable but not bad and there was room in the batteries to allow them to run things at a consistent output.

All in all, Peter Main, you don't build a bad power station.

He made a quick check with the bus driver on Tuesday morning and found that there had indeed been some customers for Vision come up, and he took the time to frame the words he was going to use before walking down the drive and up the road to Number 13. On his way out he patted the entrance wall on his left at the bottom of the drive and sent an unspoken thought to his brother.

We did it, Anthony, we did it.

Number 13 was quite a hive of activity, with what appeared to be a yoga class of sorts in progress under the guidance of a man he had never met. Half a dozen people were on the floor in a variety of casual clothing trying to achieve the impossible to Peter's eyes. Margaret Pursehouse was nowhere in sight so he went next door to Number 15, where he found her with a couple of women of more robust build than those next door. She was talking about diet. He respectfully waited in plain view until Margaret could avoid him no longer and gave her group a break.

'The problems caused by alcohol are next,' she said and impertinently added, 'You can stay if you like.'

I shall be nice. Firm but nice.

'I've come to pick up my notebooks, the ones from the old dispensary, Margaret. The ones that never found their way back to me after Lachlan Tan went through the old stuff left there.'

She looked him in the eyes and he thought she was going to argue as he had anticipated but, to his surprise, that was not what happened.

'OK, I'll get them for you,' and she went into one of the rooms that he knew had once been bedrooms, and probably still were. As he waited, he noticed for the first time that there was a large picture of the current Pope on the wall.

His distraction was interrupted.

'There you are,' she said. 'Undamaged. Very interesting. Thank you for letting me have them for a while.'

She put two ancient leather-bound notebooks into his hands. 'Was that all?'

'Yes …thank you … I see you have some clients in so I won't stay. Thank you again.' He left and started his walk back to Perdition.

Behind him, Margaret watched him go. She was a little annoyed because she had grown rather fond of the notebooks and had felt a certain empathy with their author, not because she needed the books in terms of the information in them. She had long since copied out everything page by page, as close as she could possibly get to the originals.

Chapter 29

Most of the faces around the table at the management meeting Margaret Pursehouse would have recognised. A very few of them were new – or at least new to the forum, and two of them were new to the company. Peter Main called the meeting to order.

'I am going to do a lot of the talking, at least at first, for which I apologise but needs must when the devil drives,' he announced. 'For those of you new to the table, the amazing Mrs Scott has once again provided a sideboard laden with refreshments and there is no rule that stops you getting up and getting what you want – even if Mrs Main or I are speaking. The other rule at this table is that no suggestion or comment on the business of the day is considered stupid. Nobody, least of all me, is an expert on anything except their own area and some of us have done novel things in the past and may have useful insights foreign to the rest of us.'

There were grunts of acknowledgement around the table.

'For reasons that will become apparent, this will be the last power plant management meeting here at Perdition. All future meetings will be held at the power plant. In the meantime – agenda item one – I'll ask Gabriel to report on our search for someone to use our waste heat. Gabriel …'

'We have advertised for four months and all of us that have relevant contacts have used them. No one seemed interested in giving us a viable proposition. However, we got a suggestion informally at

Chris and Stephen's wedding which we have pursued and hence we have a new face at the table. Lucifer Hot Rocks Proprietary Limited now has a related company called Little Lucifer Proprietary Limited. It also has another related company called Devilish Consulting. I'll let Mr Main go from there.'

Peter took up the going.

'The other reason we have another new face at the table is that we have formally terminated what we might call the construction phase. As most of you know everything seems to be working, and working well. We don't have any major contractors left on site, and we've all been to the farewells of some of our colleagues who have moved on, with their experience here hopefully fattening their CVs. That's where Devilish Consulting comes in. The government is happy with us and offered Lucifer Hot Rocks the opportunity to build another geothermal station to the south of here. At this stage the location is a bit of a secret for obvious reasons … one of them being that it's on Crown land with old-growth forest on it' – there were murmurs around the table – 'but after much consideration Lyn and I decided it's not something we want to do. Enough is enough, and as most of you know even our being here was not planned. If my brother had not managed to drive into a truck and incinerate himself, he would be sitting here not me. I would still be running hotels, and Lyn would have been trying to imbue an understanding of philosophy into North Americans. So, we have agreed to act in a consultancy capacity only. All care and no responsibility.'

'Frankly, we need a rest,' interjected Lyn. 'That's what it comes down to.'

'Little Lucifer,' Peter continued, 'will be establishing its own enterprise to consume our excess heat. For those who have not met him previously I would like to introduce you to Dr Lachlan Tan. Lachlan is currently a general practitioner and one or two of you may have been treated by him in earlier days when Omicron had a surgery here, or even may be seeing him at their surgery in Lonnie. He is going to be continuing as a locum for them, but he has decided he would like to pursue something new. Lachlan …'

Lachlan cleared his throat. 'Thank you, Peter. It's nice to see some old friends around the table and meet some new ones. Briefly, I want something more exciting to do before old age catches up with me. Yes, it's a mid-life crisis,' he joked.

Some around the table nodded and smiled back.

'Before I went on to do medicine I had a general interest in science, and with some overseas experience with the forces I had the chance to observe food insecurity at its worst. We are therefore going to build a hydroponic fruit and vegetable growing facility. Everything needed is here. We have unlimited energy, almost unlimited water, and a stable government. There's a growing market both here and on the big island, as well as overseas. Just quickly, we will be building some greenhouses but also growing selected crops in completely controlled environments.'

'For those who don't know, Lachlan has qualifications in economics as well as a Bachelor of Science and his medical degree, and until recently was an officer in the Army Reserve,' Lyn announced. 'As of next week, Lachlan will be living at the old doctor's surgery when he's here. We'll be upgrading the place a bit for him, and I suppose that brings me logically to Elias.'

She nodded in the man's direction. 'Elias has been with us for a while in a senior role in the maintenance area and will from now on be in charge of the general maintenance of the whole of the power plant as others are moving on. Just to keep his team busy, we're retaining a number of tradespeople in various areas, and they will not only be looking after the plant but also be constructing the hydroponics facility.'

'With the help of contractors,' interjected Elias. 'I'll be project managing.'

'Christine has agreed to move into a more general role reporting directly to me, well me and Peter, while Stephen will still be looking after our low voltage installations. Which inevitably leads me on to the lady who has been patiently sitting here, and whom many of you have seen visiting the plant with Peter from time to time over the last month: Anne Clare. Anne has agreed to leave her current position with Business, Innovation and Employment in New Zealand, who if you don't know run their geothermal plants over there, and is going to come and run ours.'

'Hello everybody,' said a rather quiet voice with a pronounced Kiwi accent.

'Anne is an engineer, has two kids, and she and her husband will be moving into Number 24 up the road. Her husband will be taking up the responsibilities that Chris had for our environmental concerns and outdoor maintenance, but not health and safety.'

'He's a gardener,' announced Anne. 'With all the qualifications that seem to be flying around I don't think he will mind me telling you that he has a trade qualification. However, if there were a God, he would have been born green on the outside as well as the inside. Heavens knows I am a fully qualified engineer and can therefore kill anything vegetable. Sylvester seems to be able to make anything grow. Oh, just a warning, please don't call him Sly. Makes him stroppy.'

'You have a nickname though, don't you?' asked Lyn with a smile.

The new plant manager smiled back at her.

'Oh yes, and for those of you who would be minded to research me you would come across it, so I thought you should know what it was up front, and that I don't mind you using it. My middle name is Bernadette. Clare's my married name. I had a minister who gave me the nickname ABC. It stuck. I don't hate it. My kids love it.'

'Alright, we might formally break for coffee in a minute, but there is one more change in the staffing, and I'll let Anne announce it as it's now in her purview,' said Lyn.

The metaphorical handover of responsibility was nicely managed, and Anne Clare was ready and prepared. 'As my first decision I have decided to restructure our Security section. I think everyone knows Gerry, and from what I can see he is the most appropriate person we have to take over the responsibility for security. Some of you will have known him for a while and he seems to have proven himself capable in both theory and practice. He will also manage the village bus service and, instead of all and sundry from various departments driving it, his security people will.'

'Coffee,' stated Lyn and stood up, temporarily adjourning the meeting.

Fifteen minutes later she called out 'Back to the table', and she, Peter, Chris and Gabriel adjourned to Peter's study with Lachlan, while Anne Clare took her seat as chair.

'OK, people,' she announced, 'get your laptops open and operating and have a look at your emails. You'll find one from Lyn and Peter which sets out the new management structure which we referred to earlier. Lyn and Peter have sent it to everyone. You'll also find one there from me headed up Risk Management. It's also gone to everyone, from the highest to the lowest and it's what we are going to work on for the next three months alongside the day-to-day stuff.'

She paused to make sure everyone had their computers open and working.

'Now, from what I have observed in the last few days we seem to know how to operate every bit of our brand-new plant, and we know how to deal with breakdowns – piece of equipment by piece of equipment. What we don't know is what our risks are, and we haven't estimated their potential frequency or gravity. That's everything from blowing a high-pressure seal on the water feed to people invading our land and jumping off transmission towers. Once we know that, we need to know what the knock-on effects will be across the range of possible outcomes, from going offline, closing a turbine down, or calling the police; and we don't have any plans for disaster recovery especially on a grand scale …'

'Like what?' someone interjected with a note of cynicism in their voice.

'Like an earthquake,' said Anne, not rising to the tone of the question. *At least one of you is going to have to learn that I am running things around here from now on.* 'Or even everyone catching Covid at the same time; or we have a battery leakage or fire. Now this is how I plan to do this …'

The meeting in Peter's study had nothing to do with a novel geothermal power plant. It concerned what had taken place when Lachlan had cleaned out the old dispensary, what he had found, and what Christine had taken away in a cardboard box after the truck driver had been treated, now so many months ago. How there appeared to be a discrepancy of two notebooks, as apparently confirmed by Margaret Pursehouse when she had met Peter in the bush on one of his rare days off, and how Peter had resolved that discrepancy. The implications as to what those notebooks contained and to what end those contents were already being put by Margaret were also discussed.

'I think various people want to comment on that,' said Peter, 'just between friends.'

'Well just sniffing her soap can made your head spin,' stated Lyn.

Christine was next. 'We never said anything about it because we weren't sure, but Stephen and I both felt that she might have been the mystery person that was never found in connection with Angelique Deloraine's demise.'

'And no one lets her make them a cup of tea at Omicron. There's nothing certain, but there have been some stories from both patients and staff about some strange things going on with people when she has been around, and people getting what looks like withdrawal symptoms when she's not,' advised Lachlan. 'There's no proof and we're so decentralised and use locums from all over, so it took a while for things to get noticed, but we try not to use her much anymore.'

'But no one has actually died, have they?' Lyn asked jokingly.

'Well, I can't actually guarantee that,' said Lachlan gravely. 'I for one have my suspicions, but they were old, or quite sick or both so nothing was overly surprising at the time, and with a lack of continuity of care …well … One of the other doctors and I have had a look at a couple of things.'

'She did tell me she tried things out on cats,' said Peter.

'Really?' said Lachlan. 'Personally, and this is only a personal opinion, mind, I think she moved her experiments up the evolutionary scale some time ago. A couple of the other nurses say she takes some of her own stuff. She carries it around and puts it in her tea apparently. By the way, you see her up here, have you noticed any change in her behaviour?'

'Well, I for one stay away from her,' said Chris, and everyone else nodded in agreement. 'But I have my own reasons.'

'You would seem to be the one with the most contact with her, Lachlan, working with her even if it's now less than before, but she was fine with me when I went to get the notebooks from her,' said Peter. 'Very calm.'

'Too calm perhaps. Well just to let you know, the nurses she works with in Launceston, and that's the only place she works with us now, reckon she's losing it. She's a bit erratic. They say they don't know which of several Margarets they are going to be working with on any individual day, and the religious fervour has gotten worse. That's what is being said for what it's worth … well … but it's all anecdotal of course and we all have our good days and our bad days.'

'OK', said Lyn, 'enough of Margaret for a bit. Peter got the notebooks back and had them digitised, which took a while and cost a bit, but we sent the copies off to a friend of Peter and Lachlan's in the pharmaceutical game.'

'Its early days,' said Peter, 'but—'

'Perdition could be sitting on a goldmine.'

Chapter 30

While the power plant management meeting was proceeding under the new General Manager and the select group around Lyn and Peter were looking towards their futures, the newly minted Security Manager was giving the customary orientation and induction tour to Sylvester Clare. Like Christine, Gerry had long since forgotten to count how many times he had done it, but of course over the years it had progressively changed as the plant had been built, Peter Main had taken over from his brother, and battles had been fought and won. The tour was constantly changing to bring things up to the present.

Sylvester seemed a rather gentle soul, although on first appearances some might have found his presence a little threatening. For Gerry, with his military background, it was not new to meet men who were larger than he was, but even so, Sylvester Clare was an impressive figure. He wasn't over tall, but he wasn't short either. He obviously had some Māori blood but there was something else in the mix. His hands betrayed the fact that they had seen heavy physical work, and the way his body filled his working clothes suggested that, as the saying went, he was built like a brick shithouse.

He has presence.

It always made sense to start the tour in the customary manner, so Gerry drove them out to the entrance to the valley, did a U-turn, and pulled over to the side of the road. For once it wasn't raining and the valley looked its most attractive. After the usual commentary about the vertical windmills, the river turbines, who owned what, and how Peter and Lyn Main came to be running things, he slowly motored down the hill to the bridge and pointed out Perdition and where Anthony Main had been killed, the Christian Wellness Centre, the single workers' quarters, and in due course the old mill with the water treatment plant just visible on the hill behind it.

After negotiating the security barrier, he diverted to the left onto one of the tracks and parked on the hillside looking back towards the power plant. Spread out immediately in front of them were the open areas with their network of piping. Behind that were the curved roofs of the plant itself with their rows and rows of solar cells shading the meadow grasses that covered them. The battery park was just visible behind those. To their left they could see the first transmission tower, so recently the subject of the coroner's inquest, which marked the direction the power lines ran.

They had company. Surveyors were at work in the area.

'This is where greenhouses will be going,' explained Gerry. 'It wasn't in the original plans but apparently the plant produces a lot of excess heat and rather than just ventilate it into the air they are going to use something called sand batteries to store it in and use it to grow food crops. I don't quite get the technology of it all but according to Dr Tan we'll be growing tropical fruit like paw paws as well as other stuff. Clever man Dr Tan.'

A short history of Omicron's involvement with Mordbury was called for, and after explaining about Lachlan Tan, Gerry mentioned Margaret Pursehouse and explained how the Christian Wellness Centre came into being.

Sylvester Clare was just trying to take it all in, but he asked, 'And what does this Pursehouse woman do at the Wellness Centre?'

'From what I understand it's all about God and herbal remedies, the gifts of the good Lord. People come up and spend a few days there presumably drinking herbal teas and praying. Not my thing but she seems to do a bit of trade. She also makes soaps and ointments and things. Sells a bit on the internet they tell me. Anyway, they're pretty quiet. We bring the clients up in the company bus, so there is no extra traffic above and beyond what comes and goes to the plant and the cars that residents drive. We police the speed limit a bit, but you had better warn your kids. With all the electric vehicles you can't hear the things coming, and as you will have observed there are no fences around the houses.'

'Well, she can keep anything religious away from me and mine!'

There was a pause while Gerry wondered whether he should ask, and Sylvester wondered whether he should give more. Given its significance and his ongoing need to talk about it even now, Sylvester explained.

'I grew up as an orphan in a so-called Christian children's home.' There was a note of despondency and a tinge of anger in his voice.

'This lady is Catholic. Did you have to put up with the priests and nuns?'

Sylvester grimaced. 'Yep. Not a happy time. Being of mixed race didn't help. But given what went on nothing really helped at all.'

'I can't say anything bad about my childhood, although I can't say there was a lot of what you might call love,' said Gerry. 'I found a home in the forces.'

'I ran away when I was fourteen and went bush. I was a big kid and could pass as older, and I could do a day's work. Learned to love growing things and put up with being called Sly. Actually, named after Sylvester the cat I believe, not Stallone. Got teased a lot about that. Anyway, growing things seemed to like me.'

'So how did you meet your wife?'

'I got a government gardening job after I went to college. Seemed like a good secure option at the time. You know, start at the bottom and work up. I literally ran into Anne, or she ran into me, in Taupo. We still haven't decided who was a fault. My government tractor came into contact with her government Toyota. After that it was pure lust.'

'Fair enough.'

'She gets on with engineering and managing things, I get on with growing things and of course the kids. Always wanted kids. Anyway, she has a big career, so I took them on.'

'So, you grow kids as well as plants.'

Sylvester laughed. 'Oh, I don't say that Anne doesn't do her bit, and after all she's always earned the big money which has allowed us freedom to choose what we want to do and where we want to go. We just come together around family. Something I never had as a kid.'

'How old are they?'

'Ten and eleven-and-a-half. It's going to be good for them here as they get older because they can go to boarding school in Launceston during the week and be home at weekends.'

'And what do they like to do?'

'Wondering if they are going to give you cause for concern?'

'No, just wondering if they are going to need an eye kept on them. It's a small place and we tend to look out for each other.'

'Wouldn't have a clue. They both love the outdoors but neither of them plays sport. Not team players, either of them. Isaac is into science a bit. Follows his mother's talents in that direction. Marie, well who knows. She's fascinated by the big black horses she's seen being ridden around but.'

'Ah, they belong to Chris and Stephen. You've met Chris of course. Stephen just became in charge of our low voltage electrical department. They live up at the old mill manager's house and use the old mill as stables.' Gerry put the company ute in gear. 'Look, I have to go and check on something up at the water treatment plant sometime today and that's not far away from the mill. If it's OK by you I'll take you back that way.'

So, Gerry and Sylvester bumped their way across country to the water treatment plant. While Sylvester had a look around the small fully automated facility, Gerry changed the rusty and almost inoperable lock on the door. He also swapped over the padlock that was rusting on the chain that secured the gate. Sylvester, having shown himself around the first mini reverse osmosis treatment plant he had ever seen and roughly sorted out in his own mind how the thing worked, queried Gerry on why he was personally fixing the locks.

'Quite simple really. It's one of those low priority jobs that has been put off for ages and I saw the stuff still lying around in the security office this morning. So I decided I'd do it myself rather than badger the maintenance people again. The padlock on the gate is the standard padlock we have around here, coded G for green, which is not the same key as you need to open the door lock. We have a single key system with a hierarchy of key levels. This,' he said, waving one of the keys among a number he was carrying on a ring, 'is marked yellow, and when we get back to the office, I'll issue you with one just like it. Yellow will get you into the treatment plant shed and will get you through a green lock too.'

'You've got it all worked out.'

'Well, no one gets a key to a higher level than they need to do their job. There are five levels. The keys are all coded and numbered, and I know who has what key from the register. If you find a key lying around, bring it to me and I'll be able to trace who hasn't been looking after it.'

He took the key and held it out so Sylvester could see it was stamped with a Y and a 2.

'Level four is R for red. It will get you almost everywhere. Managers have those. Top of the tree is purple. They go to the people who work in really specialist or dangerous areas. Red will get you into the high voltage yard for example. While your crew will be working weeding the battery park and use a green to get in, accessing one of the battery pods can't be done without a purple. Your wife won't get a purple and Mr Main doesn't have one either.'

'So, what does he have?'

'Well, as of this afternoon with the new organisation chart he'll be surrendering his red for a green. He'll have no need for anything higher, not that he has needed to use his red much at all anyway. It's all about function you see, not hierarchy. You don't start off with a green and graduate to a purple.' He laughed. 'Which is good because I can give Mr Main's red to Dr Tan. His house has a company lock, and he may need access to other places if someone has a medical issue and he's here at the time. Lyn Main's red can go to your wife.'

'Speaking of medical, what happens if we have an issue?'

'Margaret Pursehouse at the Christian Wellness Centre. For the time being she still has access to the medical centre, although that may change with Dr Tan moving in there. She's a bit of a pain in the arse but she's here and qualified in an emergency. You'll need to find your family a GP in Launceston.'

'And you said she's a Catholic?'

'Yup – rabid, and getting worse they tell me.'

'Fuck. They're everywhere.'

'And she tries to get everyone on board. I told you she was a bit of a pain in the arse.'

'That's all I need. Will I have much to do with her?'

'No, and even less if you follow what Chris did and get someone in your team to go and see her if she wants something.'

'Didn't get on?'

'No, but there's history there which I won't go into – if Chris wants to tell you she will. Town services is all she will want – you know like getting the grass mowed or the garbage emptied. If Margaret rang Chris she was always somehow committed elsewhere and, as I said, sent one of her people. But I try not to have anything to do with her if I don't have to.'

'Lots to know.'

'My advice is you let people come to you rather the reverse. It's a complicated set-up with the Mains owning the land. Lots of wheels within wheels. If you have any problems with anyone, I'd leave your wife out of it and look up Chris. She's reporting directly to Peter and Lyn as of today. She's been around almost from the start and knows who's who.'

'Sound like the way to go.'

'Just trying to stop trouble before it starts. Anyway, speaking of Chris, she'll probably be looking for you to get rid of her current responsibilities, so we won't dawdle anymore.'

Chapter 31

It was quite a while since Damian (Ned) Stavropoulos had been to Mordbury, and for one week he was back. He was not hauling pipes, he was hauling sand, and then only for four days.

This time with a big truck and a big trailer he was carrying loads of sand to the site of what he understood to be something called sand batteries which were going to store heat for greenhouses; and each successive day he made his delivery he could see the project was progressing at some speed because the prefabricated steel parts for what he called the silos were being put together remarkably quickly. The contractors doing the job said it was all going to be built in just three weeks.

His days were long and started early, driving from the truck depot in Lonnie to Devonport; loading, which took no time at all; then driving back to Lonnie for lunch; and then up to Mordbury in the afternoon. However, all the roads involved were good these days with the Bass Highway finally fixed and the road to Mordbury totally different from when he had been hauling pipes to and fro in the early days of the power station project. The Mordbury road, although nothing like the highway, was now fully tarmacked and two good lanes all the way. It still wound its way around the hillsides, but it was almost a casual drive in the country, especially since traffic was minimal.

Coming over the hill into the first valley was always something that took him back to the day of the big crash when he had killed the owner of the place. He always thought of it that way, and Mordbury had not changed in the sense that the first valley and the village looked as it had always done, just to bring it all back. His absolution by the authorities for his part in the crash had not changed the feeling of responsibility he had for what had happened. It continued to haunt him.

However, he had come to terms with it; just as he had come to terms with the residual stiffness and occasional pain in his leg that represented the permanent physical effects of the crash that would be with him for the rest of his life.

While this was the last day he would be doing this, every time he came into Mordbury he would register what was going on and take extra care. It looked like work on the old medical centre. Maybe someone was finally moving in, he thought, noting the brand-new all-electric Subaru parked in the carport.

Sexy little bugger of a car.

The medical centre sign had gone. He was sure it had been there yesterday, but two blokes with a ladder were putting something different up – but no time to stop and read it.

The odd solitary insomniac wallaby wandering about – or were the bigger ones kangaroos? – still seemed to want to commit suicide. He had to use his horn to scare one out of the road as he got down to the bridge; he knew it would be heard all over the valley and annoy the residents, but there was nothing he could do about that. At least in the early afternoon there was no chance of devils being about, and the occasional active echidna or wombat seemed to have learned where the tunnels under the road were.

He took extra care when turning right across the bridge and then left towards the power plant, making sure he did not cross onto the wrong side of the road, even with the length of the combination he was driving. The new wall on the right-hand side of the gateway to the big house was looking more weathered, he noticed, as he gently turned the wheel and let it straighten up of its own accord, the electric power steering doing all the work for him. A quick check in the left-hand mirror showed the trailer had not tried to take its own shortcut on the turn; and with contentment about his judgement of the curve, Ned eased the truck up the slope through the village, taking the utmost care to note any pedestrian traffic.

With the power plant construction being for all intents and purposes done and dusted, the workforce had become fewer and more permanent, with families and kids more evident. It was school holidays too. As he passed Number 24 on his right, a boy and a girl waved to him, and he waved back.

School holidays and a lovely safe place to grow up. Nice.

As he continued up the rise, he made sure to check either side of the road and noted the two big black horses were out playing in a timber-fenced paddock adjacent to the old mill building.

That fencing wasn't there in the early days, that would have cost a bit; and some more work has been done on the building.

Having been passed through over the intercom and negotiated the bollard barrier at the top of the rise, he turned the rig left onto what was now a well-made gravel track and made his way to the temporary dump to tip his load. The contractors were starting to connect a network of pipes to the big barrel-like structures, and a new crew had started work assembling a transportable hopper and conveyor. There was a backhoe hard at work digging a trench towards the power station and the big orange plastic pipe stacked next to it suggested a power supply was being put in. He didn't bother getting out of the truck but just jack-knifed it around the back of the growing pile of sand heaped from his earlier visits and dumped from the trailer and the truck.

Retracing his route, he negotiated the bollards again and started his descent into the valley. With a caution engrained after his earlier accident he was always doubly careful going down to the bridge; this turned out to be a good thing, as standing in the middle of the road were two middle-aged women having an argument – and it was a good one by the look of it. While he couldn't hear the actual words being said with his window up, the conversation looked pretty full on.

So, do I give them a couple of blasts with the airhorns, or do I stop until it's sorted?

Gently applying the brakes, he pulled up about forty metres away. The argument was so good and the truck so quiet they hadn't heard him so, deciding not to use the horns, he put the truck into park mode, put on the parking brake, and climbed down to ask them to move.

I know one of these women, he said to himself. She was thinner than the nurse he remembered from the day of his accident and night under her care, but he was sure it was her. She looked a bit strange he thought – a bit sort of wild.

Perhaps it's just the heat of the argument.

🐈

Mrs Scott was having a bad day anyway, and the last thing she had wanted to do was to run into Margaret Pursehouse. She had run out of milk, and a visit to the shop only provided her with UHT. She knew that Lyn Main could and would spot the difference. While she was not concerned about any comment from Mrs Main, she was displeased with herself for underestimating her weekly shop, and for not finding out her error earlier when she could have nipped into town and remedied it without anyone being the wiser – not that she considered herself obsessive at all.

I just like to get it right.

In her view the trouble of having to do that extra trip to town would have been an appropriate and sufficient punishment for her mistake. Mrs Scott considered herself a professional at what she did and relished her status in both the Main household and the village.

I won't lower my dignity by doing the rounds trying to borrow some real milk. UHT will just have to do.

Josephine Scott might have been a fixture in the village and respected for her knowledge of the comings and goings, but Josephine Scott had always kept the secrets of Peter and Lyn Main, and indeed those of Anthony Main before them. She did not gossip about them or company business. She had regarded Hughey Main as a likeable rogue, but a rogue for all that until he mended his ways. She was a strong woman underneath her comfortable exterior. The exigencies of life had made her so. The position of the job as housekeeper, firstly to Hughey in Melbourne and then in Mordbury, followed by Peter and Lyn, she considered very valuable.

It's my refuge.

Now she had to take a dose of Margaret Pursehouse, who frankly seemed high on something; not that Mrs Scott would have known what someone on a high would have looked like. Moreover, Margaret bloody Pursehouse was in one of her proselytising moods. She was becoming an annoyance to everyone in the village this woman was, even to those with a residual religious inclination. She carried a bloody bible around with her a lot too.

Pushed beyond her limits on a bad day when nothing seemed to be going her way, Mrs Scott resorted to language she had long since been motivated to use. The bloody woman had her book with her and had jumped on her out of nowhere in the middle of the road and as quoting scripture to her!

'Look, it's right here in the Bible, in John: "Jesus said to her, 'I am the resurrection and the life. Those who believe in me, even though they die, will live.'"'

Mrs Scott tried to walk away from her but found herself being followed down the middle of the road.

'"Those who believe in him are not condemned; but those who do not believe are condemned already, because they have not believed."'

What is the woman on?

'You need to read your Bible, Mrs Scott!'

She stopped walking and turned to look at Margaret, and fixing her eyes firmly with hers, she let herself go.

'I have read the fucking thing Margaret, and you can stick your nasty, violent, immoral book up your virgin cunt where no one will ever again find it, and please take your God somewhere where he won't do any more damage to the course of human history.'

As they stood there barely a pace apart, neither could believe what had happened. Mrs Scott was more than just disappointed in herself. It had been a long time, in fact she could not now remember it, since she had been even tempted to use such language. Margaret was stunned. She had never been so blatantly and rudely told where to go. People generally had an underlying respect for those holding a religious belief.

Ned, who overheard the end of the conversation as he reached them, was not shocked by the language or indeed by the sentiments expressed; just by the people who had used it.

'That's enough of that, people. End of round three. Fight over. Now if you will go to your corners and get out of the road I can get on with my job, and the people watching you from their homes, and hearing the language I might add, can go back to their normal lives.'

Mrs Scott looked around and saw her position, and was doubly disappointed with herself. *I should not let myself get provoked.*

While she knew why she had been angered, she did not like

herself for it. People like Margaret Pursehouse should not in her view be pushing the grace of God line at any time, but as a person who had lost a young husband to testicular cancer diagnosed too late, Mrs Scott was never going to tolerate the view that everything some mythical being had supposedly created was great and good.

'Stay out of my fucking face woman,' she commanded Margaret, followed by a 'Sorry about that' to Ned. Having had the last word, she pulled back her shoulders and, grasping her shopping bag securely, marched off down the hill.

Ned looked down at Margaret. 'I think you should go home, don't you?'

'I know you, don't I?'

'If you were the nurse who helped the doctor strap my ankle when I ran into a Range Rover a couple of years ago, then yes.'

'Oh yes, of course. Your hair is greyer.'

'Everyone gets older. You're looking a bit strung out. I didn't recognise you at first. Home and a nice cup of tea,' he advised as he led her to the side of the road. 'Where do you live?'

'Just down there. Number 15. I run Vision, the wellness centre – the Christian Wellness Centre.'

'OK. So, are *you* going to be OK?'

'I'll get over it.'

Ned nodded and walked back to his truck. Necessarily sounding the horn, as the truck was almost silent, he put it back into motion. As he slowed and carefully turned back over the bridge, making doubly sure there was no traffic coming over it, he had almost forgotten the incident with the two women, and as he left the valley it was but a memory. *Yesterday's news*, he said to himself, looking forward to his weekend.

In the meantime, Margaret continued her walk around the town. Not the most careful of formulating amateur chemists, and ignorant of the real toxicity of some of the things she was playing with, Margaret had over the months inhaled both dry ingredients and the vapours of variable concentrations of different potions and tinctures. The wear and tear on her body was beginning to become visible, and Ned was not the only one who had noticed that some days she was a different person to the one they were used to. Between that and her religious fervour, even those Mordbury residents who had some belief, or looked to her for help with the odd accident or ailment, were now tending to avoid her.

Mrs Scott found Lyn Main was in her kitchen when she got home to Perdition. She was making a cup of tea and was looking for milk. Mrs Scott somewhat meekly proffered the UHT she had just bought, and seeing the disappointed look on Lyn's face made her burst out into tears.

A great deal tumbled out over that cup of tea, with Mrs Scott sharing for the first time in many years. Lyn was astonished, because she realised that between university, the company and Peter, she had not really taken time to actually talk to the person who facilitated everything around her living arrangements. Mrs Scott was someone valued greatly for her willing service, but Lyn had inherited her just as she had inherited the rest of the Main family's history.

I suppose I've spoken with her often enough, but I haven't really listened.

Mrs Scott had a great deal to tell her that she hadn't even imagined she didn't know. Because Mrs Scott had been a fixture from the days of Hughey Main's occupancy, everyone coming to the village had sought her advice and counsel. She was a mine of information and she needed to unburden herself of not only her personal trials and tribulations, but also the secrets she had kept over the years.

Everybody seems to have leant on her.

'There's things I could tell you,' she said, 'but I have confidences to keep even to those who are no longer with us. For example I think almost everyone knows about Christine Reynolds, good luck to her I say, but none of us gossip. It's none of our business anyway.'

'Indeed. So you keep people's confidences? What about those of Mr Main?'

'You mean Anthony Main?'

'Yes, sorry.' Lyn smiled. 'I believe you keep mine and my husband's.'

'Hughey especially. Did you know we used to call him that, behind his back of course?'

'I had heard. God-like was he?'

'Not like that, but I didn't know him in his very early years in business. He had a reputation for being a bit of a crook back then. He underwent a change in his later years, especially after his divorce, and among other things started Hot Rocks. He did seem to make things happen though.'

'And you worked for him in Melbourne.'

'Sure did. A part-time job as a cleaner. My husband was the main breadwinner. But if you came in to buy a Range Rover, I was the one who was responsible for making sure you could see your face in the tiles on the floor – and the rest of the place was spotless as well of course.'

'So, can I ask what happened?'

'My husband got sick, and died, pretty quickly, and Hughey looked after me. He gave me more work when I was living hand to mouth with what seemed like a mountain of bills. Later I moved in to run his house when he learned I could cook. Then when he was moving down here, he asked me to come with him and I jumped at the chance. I love this place. Except for people like that stupid religious bitch Pursehouse.'

'So are you alone in this.'

'No way. She was bad enough right from the start, but she is turning into a religious nutter – and she won't take no for an answer. Everyone's started to avoid her like the plague.'

Mrs Scott brough Lyn up to date with the detail her latest encounter, blow by blow, and the message was clear. The woman was not only a religious nutter but was also out of control.

Having concluded it was probably down to her not only to do something, but to be seen to do something, Lyn Main made a promise to Mrs Scott that she would go and talk to the person in question about her behaviour. Moreover, with a sense of duty and moved by Mrs Scott's distress, she promised to do it *right now*.

So as Mrs Scott dried her tears, gathered her wits about her, and applied herself to the preparation of dinner, Lyn went to the study to arm herself with a weapon to counter Margaret Pursehouse's religious fervour. Used to dealing with academics, students and higher-level company employees, she believed that she could discuss things rationally.

She ran her eyes over Hughey's books, which had now sat unread for years. She was looking for the references she had given him when he was on his moral quest, hoping to find he had indeed bought what she had suggested. She found he had, and having rejected the work of several authors, she settled on Dawkins. The book's title, *The God Delusion*, might be challenging in the first instance but, more used to people with at least an enquiring mind if not a fully open one, she felt it would spell things out simply, directly and completely.

After all, she has a background in science. She's a nurse. The least the woman can do is to read the book and see why other people don't see the world as she does and how they could resent her attitude.

So, armed with one of the most significant works of, in her opinion, one of the planet's most readable proselytising atheists, she put on a coat, grabbed an umbrella and set out for Number 15. She had a firm belief that she could sensibly resolve the problem. Admittedly she didn't think she was going to induce a conversion, well at least not at once, but time would tell.

Half an hour later she was back, and she and Mrs Scott were sharing a bottle of Prosecco and some smoked salmon sandwiches to help her over the experience she had just had.

'You were right,' Lyn said. 'That woman is an absolute religious lunatic.'

'I told you so.'

'Biggest case of confirmation bias I have ever seen. Wouldn't even agree to read the book I took for her. Threw it in my face.'

'Actually?'

'Well, no, not actually, but close to it. She told me to stop pushing my anti-religious beliefs onto her. Would you credit it?'

'And her always pushing her religious ones onto everyone else!'

'I said words to that effect to her. She wanted to know why unbelievers were always so hostile to faith. I thought I'd deflect that with some history about what believers had done over the years in their God's name, colonialism and all that. I even brought up the Taliban.'

'Didn't work.'

'Wrong God apparently. Fill up my glass. You know there's about 3,000 gods available in the history of religion as we know it and she has rejected 2,999, and she can't understand why most of us these days can't find enough evidence to believe in the remaining one she's chosen either.'

'Well at least you tried,' said Mrs Scott, sharing out the rest of the Prosecco in equal measure.

Chapter 32

It got worse the next day.

Lyn Main was having a bad day anyway. Peter had gone into Devonport to speak to the people he and Lachlan had been talking with on and off since the inquest into Angelique Deloraine's death, and had left her in charge for the day. He seemed to be more relaxed about doing that now, since he had Mrs Clare in the day-to-day management chair. Lyn was marking assignments. In the study with a closed door, she had told Mrs Scott that she did not want to be disturbed if at all possible.

It was something of a trial because young university students had mostly had so little life experience. She could understand the cultural background of her Chinese students who she knew presumed, possibly rightly, that they might receive messages to the effect that their relatively privileged and wealthy parents had received a visit from authorities back home should an incorrect opinion be expressed. They had quoted references ad infinitum to show they had done some work, or at least Professor Google had, but expressed no views of their own, controversial or otherwise, on the writings of John Locke.

Getting them to open up and argue in tutorials was impossible too. Too many spies in the camp, probably; even friends you don't think you would be able to trust.

You'd think they might think assignments were safer. Perhaps it's too much to ask of them, given the potential political context.

It was hard to design assignments that challenged their understanding of the history of the great philosophers if they thought their own views might find their way back to their country's political masters, only one, and the current philosophy at that, being allowed.

She had dutifully managed her way through the majority of the work, and was just thinking about lunch, when a very angry newly minted Environmental Services Manager burst into the room, followed by a troubled Mrs Scott, who had been unable to stop him.

'If that woman comes near me of my kids ever again, I shall not be responsible for my actions,' Sylvester Clare stated forcibly. 'She is a menace. The way I bring up my children is my business. I have a good mind to call the police and have her charged with assault.'

'Who, and what assault, Mr Clare?' Lyn asked, remaining calm. 'Please sit down and tell me.'

'That Christian Wellness Centre woman.'

'Oh, Margaret Pursehouse. What has she done now?'

'She baptised his kids,' said Mrs Scott.

'She what?'

'She baptised my kids.'

'She ran into them playing down by the river,' explained Mrs Scott.

'She didn't dunk them or anything? That water is freezing anyway, not to mention fast moving,' Lyn said, astonished. She had a sudden vision of Margaret Pursehouse standing in the river and enticing the kids in, holding their noses and immersing them.

'No, she just dipped her finger in and baptised them, according to what they told me,' said Mr Clare. 'Talked to them about God and asked if they went to church, and when they told her they didn't she asked them their names and baptised them by dipping her finger into the water and crossing their fucking foreheads with it. In the name of the father and the son and all that bullshit …'

'Well, we knew she was a bit loony that way,' said Lyn, 'but really?'

'Can you do that – I mean if you're not a priest?' asked Mrs Scott.

'I understand so,' replied Lyn. 'Anyone who is among the faithful can baptise anyone into the faith if need be.'

'Shit,' said Mrs Scott. 'Sorry, Mr Clare.'

'Fortunately, the kids won't be too damaged by the whole thing, and I'll explain to them later what it all meant. Isaac is probably old enough to understand. He might even have a laugh. Marie might be different. I'll have to have the conversation about letting you get old enough to make your own choices with her.'

'Where are they now?' asked Lyn.

'Chris has taken them home for me. She was with me in the ute, and I was taking her to our place to have a coffee. We were finalising the handover. Save going through security into the plant and then back out again … I want something done.'

Mrs Scott was looking at her quite pointedly, her face asking the unsaid question.

'So, what are you going to do?' demanded Sylvester Clare, asking it.

'Well, I'm going to ring Gabriel, our Administration Manager – you've met him – and give him an hour to get me a letter warning her that we might terminate her lease. I don't know if she had read her lease, but we put quite a bit of general conduct stuff in it. I can print the letter out here and sign it. I'll get one of our security team to come with me and I'll serve it on her straight away.'

'I want a written apology.'

'Well, I can ask for it, but I don't think I can make her.'

'Do that.' Mr Clare rose from his chair and headed for the door. 'I understand that all this is your private property, it belongs to you and your husband, and you can have whoever you want on your private property. But if that woman comes near me or mine in the future you can enjoy her company not that of me and Anne.'

It was a long while since Lyn Main had anyone point an angry finger at her, let alone deliver a threat and then march out of her presence.

'Angry man,' remarked Mrs Scott.

'With some reason,' replied Lyn, reaching for the phone. She had several calls to make.

By the time she had finished a very long call to her husband, Lyn had changed her mind. Or at least she had had it changed, and she gave different instructions. Gabriel was put to work on a draft of a letter terminating the lease Margaret Pursehouse's company had on numbers 13 and 15, Mordbury Road (Extended), Mordbury. When it came through in her email, she made some minor changes and printed it out and signed it. Gabriel had found three breaches of the lease with little difficulty, and on the basis of the limited knowledge Lyn had of contract law she felt that it would stand up to any legal challenge.

She contemplated ringing the security office direct, but then realised she was no longer, administratively speaking, really entitled to do that, and as a matter of courtesy rang Anne Clare instead, to borrow a security officer for half an hour. Fully understanding her purpose, and informed and angry herself about the interference with her children, Anne agreed with alacrity.

Shortly thereafter, Gerry presented himself at Perdition for the mission. He and Lyn drove down to the Wellness Centre and found their target at Number 13.

Margaret, who was hard at work distilling what she called Warmth and Happiness concentrate in the kitchen-turned-laboratory, was filled with warmth and happiness herself. She had to deliver more concentrate to her soap manufacturers urgently. It was turning into her best seller. Manufacturing two litres of concentrate at short notice had not been in her plans.

She was filled with warmth and happiness for three reasons. Firstly, she was pleased her soap was selling so well; secondly, besides being a good advertisement for what she believed was her mission, it was making her money; and thirdly, she was somewhat euphoric because she was a little high on Warmth and Happiness through her careless handling of the potent ingredients in the small room in which she was working.

Hearing her name called by a visitor, she came out of the kitchen into what had been an open plan lounge room but was now a work and prayer space, to see who was there. She left the door open behind her and was followed by a strong wave of the odour of Warmth and Happiness. She was wearing a white full-fronted apron with the slogan WALK WITH GOD and a cross printed on its chest in gold and red. Her hair was uncontrolled, to put it politely. Lyn was astonished by the apparition.

Looks like a fucking witch. Double double toil and trouble, fire burn and cauldron bubble.

She and Gerry found it difficult to focus on their task in the face of the wave of herbal perfume, the apparition that was its maker, and the semi-industrial scene that they could glimpse through the open doorway behind her. Pulling herself together and watching Margaret's eyes with their somewhat out-of-focus look, Lyn stated her purpose, and thrust the letter directly into Margaret's hands.

'Read it. You have three months to close down, pack up and go,' she said, determined not to enter into discussion. She turned on her heel and left with Gerry in tow. They both took several deep breaths when they had gotten outside and looked at each other in a moment of speechlessness.

'What was that?' asked Gerry.

'I don't really know,' replied Lyn. 'I don't think she really understood what I was saying, but she's got it in writing. Perhaps when she comes down from whatever she is on then it might hit her.'

'She has been served. I can witness that.'

'Thanks for that. Look, I think I'll walk home and get some fresh air into my lungs.'

As she strolled back to her home in the evening light, she breathed deeply and found most pleasant the natural scents that surrounded her. Some of the wallabies were still resting under their favourite trees, but the majority were about, alone or in small mobs, nibbling away on the green grass. There was only a faint breeze and for once it wasn't raining. She stopped on the drive up to the house to watch a large mother wombat and her smaller joey wander across in front of her. As she waited for them to take right of way, somewhere in the distance she heard devils debating their proprietorial status over a prospective supper.

The screams used to scare her, as they no doubt scared the original colonists, but now Lyn, like Mrs Scott, was very comfortable at Perdition.

Chapter 33

Not so comfortable was Margaret Pursehouse at Number 15, with her head clearing, an overwhelming thirst for a good cup of tea, and an eviction notice to study. It took her several cups of tea to grasp its import. She searched her own papers, kept for security in her own bedroom, and finally found her own copy of the lease she had signed so many months ago.

She had to admit she hadn't really studied it back then, when she had signed it in the throes of gratitude for getting what she had wanted. She had left the detail for her solicitor to finalise, and she hadn't realised that he had allowed through several general clauses that may have seemed reasonable and innocuous at the time but were now being used to evict her – well technically, legally her company, but that really meant she was being thrown out.

She sat on the bed and read the document. The devil was in the detail.

She was forbidden to engage in retail trade. Well, she was selling to the people who came and stayed. They bought their share of skin care products.

She was forbidden to engage in any form of commercial manufacturing. Well, she was making various concoctions, and if she had stuck to experimentation, she would probably have gotten away with that, but she was certainly making what could be seen as commercial quantities of some stuff. After all, she had just made two litres of Warmth and Happiness.

She, as a director of the company, and any employees of it, and any guests at her wellness centre, were to avoid any behaviour that would upset any other residents at Mordbury.

It doesn't say how many people I need to have upset!

She reflected on recent days and had to admit that lately she had not been at her best when it came to getting on with people. It was also true, she realised, that she seemed to be being avoided by the locals.

If Mrs Scott and that new man with the children have both complained, then perhaps that has prompted Mrs Main to act so ungratefully. After all, I helped out with those protesters; and I always pay the lease on time. I'm being persecuted just for my religious beliefs! Well, it's my Christian duty to fight back.

She went across to the wall and momentarily touched the crucifix that went with her wherever she laid her head, taking strength. Obviously, she needed to have everyone want her to stay, and that meant that anyone who had complained about her, however many that might have been, would have to withdraw their complaints. The selling of stuff to her guests was a minor matter, she realised that; so was the manufacturing when she came to think about it. Margaret could see through what was happening.

They're just excuses to get rid of me that they have added in because a few people have complained.

But what to do about it? It took just a moment to get people offside but a long time to regain trust.

What if I could speed that up?

Margaret thought she had a plan.

Divine inspiration.

While Margaret was calculating how she was going to turn around the hearts and minds of the other residents of Mordbury, and especially the hearts and minds of Lyn and Peter Main, Christine and Stephen were bedding down the two big black horses for the night. With the need for only one rug each, Eltje and Alette were now very comfortable in two of four 6-metre-by-6-metre stables that Stephen had constructed under the cover of the old mill roof. It was a large area, dotted with posts that provided useful supports for the walls of the stables, while the abandoned hardwood lying around had given them a useful free supply of construction material. It had meant they had to buy only a limited number of new boards. Fittings had been another matter, but the savings they had made on timber had allowed them to buy the sturdiest of bolts and hinges. They had splashed out on horse-activated watering bowls for the stables too when the water had been connected. Stephen had fudged the project scope when he wrote it up for the plumbing contractors and had not just ordered piped water to the house. He had it run to the old mill as well, and only after he had done it had he told Christine.

'I think even if we are found out we can say that what was decided at the meeting was a bit vague and I did what I thought I had permission to do – and we did pay for the extra fixtures and fittings. If we hadn't have done that it might have looked a bit more suspicious.'

Christine had agreed. 'No more fucking hauling water and no more bloody cleaning rotting hay out of big dirty troughs. I can cope with that.'

They stood somewhat contentedly together, reflecting on their own situation, and watched as Alette left her hay net and wandered over to the corner of the stable and pushed her muzzle down onto the spring-loaded flap, that in turn operated the tap that allowed a stream of water to fill the bowl of the waterer. She drank and then returned to the hay net and started tugging at its contents again.

'They learned how to do it quickly enough,' remarked Stephen.

'You do not know how many hours I spent teaching them,' grumbled Christine. 'Standing there waiting for them to be thirsty, then operating the bloody things until they got the message. Then I got the message myself and put a dob of molasses on the flap.'

'So that's how it's done.'

They stood together with Stephen's arm around Christine's waist and watched the two big horses as they munched at mouthfuls of hay, and the horses in turn calmly watched them back.

'OK,' said Christine. 'Another big day tomorrow. I've got a meeting first thing with Peter and someone he's been talking to about a new project.'

'What is it?'

'I'll find out tomorrow. All I know is that he's from a pharmaceutical company. Apparently, Peter met his boss at a hotel in America. He's kept it very much to himself so far although he's been up here. It seems he met up with Peter after our wedding and got driven back up here by Lachlan Tan. There were discussions into the night – it's all a bit mysterious.'

Stephen turned out the lights as they left for the house. He made certain the kettle and the coffee pod machine were full and the makings were laid out so they could grab a quick breakfast in the morning. He was going to be busy too. He was working on designing the power supply for the greenhouses. All they had there at the moment was a builder's pole. They would need more than that, a lot more. He looked out of the kitchen window over the sink as he filled the kettle.

It's bloody dark out there tonight.

Chapter 34

Dark it was as Margaret Pursehouse, encumbered as she was by a plastic bottle containing two litres of newly distilled Warmth and Happiness clutched to her chest, clumped her way through the long grass. She was wearing rubber boots as a precaution against snakes, and they made the going harder than it would otherwise have been. Moreover her puffer jacket was proving more than warm due to the exercise. She felt her mind was clear and did not resent the physical task she had set herself. However, if Lachlan Tan had been asked to examine her, as she tramped breathless on her climb up the gentle slope past the old mill, he would have been troubled by her state of physical health as well as the rationality of her thoughts. She didn't realise she was sweating, and that her temperature was elevated.

Her pace slowed as the pitch of the ground increased on the approach to the top of the rise. She topped the hill and paused to take a breath and to work out exactly where she was. Finding her bearings, she discovered her goal was to her left, and she resumed her trek to cover the thirty metres or so between her location and the gate in the chain link fence that surrounded the water treatment plant.

The medical centre key she had been trusted with opened the gate padlock, but as she removed the key from it she discovered she couldn't remove the padlock without putting down the Warmth and Happiness.

Bother. I need two hands.

She put the container down at her feet and was careful to remove the key and put it in her pocket before fumbling to remove the padlock from the chain. It fell somewhere into the grass.

Well, it can just stay there for the time being.

She opened the gate and went to the door of the shed that contained the water treatment machinery. The key happily worked on the deadlock there too, and she went into the building to find the equipment inside doing its job autonomously. The LEDs on the control panel and the computer rack behind it provided adequate lighting given her eyes were accommodated for the almost pitch blackness outside.

Margaret looked for a point where she could introduce Warmth and Happiness into the system, but was defeated as much by the complexity of the plumbing as her capacity to understand it. Standing back to take stock, she discovered she was leaning on a substantial stainless steel tank, and moreover that the tank had an inspection cover. Undoing the large T-shaped screw clamp that held the cover shut, she flipped it back on its hinge to reveal the tank's still and murky contents. The vapour rising from the water inside gave off a faint but characteristic swimming pool smell. She guessed, quite correctly, that this was the holding tank from which cleaned and chlorinated water flowed, with the help of gravity, to the power plant to the north, and the village to the south.

I suppose it doesn't have to be huge given the size of the place.

On the other hand, it was big enough and, with some regret about the thought of having to make another batch for the soap manufacturers the next day, she emptied the whole of the two-litre bottle of Warmth and Happiness into the tank and then closed and secured its lid. The strange molecules that made up the concentrate began to dissolve almost evenly into the water, responsive only to the pull of a small eddy caused by someone up late calling on the supply.

There were only three people and two horses drawing water from the system at that hour. It was going to take some time for Warmth and Happiness to make its way down to the security office and the two duty security officers, and to the meal room in the power plant and the three rostered technicians. It was a much shorter run to the house and stables at the old mill, to the two big black horses that had recently been trained to use their new waterers, and who at that moment were keenly and contentedly finishing off their evening ration of dry hay.

Margaret closed and screwed shut the lid on the tank. Having completed the task she had set for herself, she was satisfied she had done all she could. That ought to make Lyn Main receptive to her submission the next day, and perhaps change the mind of anyone who had complained about her.

As she left the shed she closed the door behind her and made sure she locked the deadlock.

Perhaps it's not tomorrow. It's probably today already.

Suddenly feeling tired, she was faced with having to secure the gates. Having kicked around the grass fruitlessly trying to find the padlock, she gave up and just looped the chain around them. Squaring her shoulders, she set off down the hill towards her home at Number 15, taking care where she put her feet lest she stumble on a tussock and fall over in the dark.

Chapter 35

There was no CCTV in the water treatment plant shed, nor on the outside covering the gates to it either. In the rush to install the plant years before at the start of the project, Anthony Main had not thought of it; securely fencing it appeared to be all that was needed, the remoteness of its position seeming reasonable security in itself.

Besides, there were so many other things to be done, and the set-and-forget nature of its operation was such that no one paid any mind to it. It was easy enough to visit the shed on a regular basis and download the readings from the computer to make sure it was doing what it was supposed to, and to top up the chlorine supply if required. No one had thought to link up the systems to the power plant control room either. Not that the control room at the power plant, or even the plant itself, had been built when the water treatment plant had been commissioned.

Christine did, however, have her own personal CCTV looking over the stables. She liked to be able to check on the horses from time to time, and to do so without leaving the comfort of the house. When she was the first to rise at five, she casually pulled up the app on her phone to check on the horses as she made two cups of coffee. The pod machine did its job, and she swallowed a mouthful of hers as she made Stephen's. With an expectation that nothing would be amiss, she casually glanced at the picture from the stables as she was preparing to go back to bed with what was left in her cup, and the full one for Stephen.

Oh fuck, fuck, FARK!

She gulped down the rest of her coffee, rushed back to the bedroom, woke Stephen and thrust the phone in front of his face.

'Get some clothes on, now!'

There was over a half a million dollars-worth of horseflesh thrashing around on the floor of the stables.

It looked a lot worse when they got there and tried to decide what to do. The horses were lying down, they were breathing, but irregularly, and taking huge gulps of air when they did. Their eyes were rolling, and their necks were covered in sweat. Every so often they threw themselves around, frequently striking the sides of the stables with their hooves. Going in with them to try to calm them down seemed out of the question.

'Hay bales,' shouted Stephen and rushed off to the pile at the end of the stables. Christine saw what he was going to do and joined him in a frenzy of activity. Every time a horse went still, they rushed into her stable and dropped a hay bale around her where there was space they could safely access. Christine then frantically googled the symptoms, although from experience she guessed one or two possibilities.

They've eaten something I bet.

The various websites she found all suggested that or snakebite as the most likely.

Both horses are down so it's unlikely to be snakebite. Too much of a coincidence.

'It's got to be poisoning,' she stated firmly.

'But all they had last night was their usual evening feed and then hay. We've been using the same feed for a week now and this has only just happened. The hay we have had for months. It's not that,' said Stephen somewhat didactically. 'Check the CCTV and see if anyone's been in here.'

'That will take hours.'

'Flip through it. Look, give it to me.' He grabbed the phone from her.

Smart arse.

Stephen took several minutes to fast play the CCTV while Christine waited, spending her time worrying, and crying, and trying to imagine what had happened. Every so often one of the mares would be subject to some kind of seizure and thrash around again, although Christine had to admit the duration of each bout seemed to be shortening and the time between them getting longer.

'No one I can see,' pronounced Stephen. 'They seem to have gone down about an hour ago.'

'What can we do?'

'Buggered if I know. You're the horsewoman.'

'Gee thanks.'

They stood back and watched and after a while the horses did seem calmer. Eltje raised her head from the floor and seemed to be trying to get up. Christine went and got a lead rope and by the time she got back the mare seemed doing better again.

She went into the stable and clipped the lead rope onto the horse's head collar. Giving her lots of encouragement, and by standing in front of her and pulling on both sides of the headcollar, she managed to get her to organise her front feet under her. A quick retreat to the end of the lead rope resulted in no more progress, but there was no way Christine was going to stand closer. The big horse could try to get up only to lose her balance and come crashing down again. However, after a few minutes sitting down, Eltje managed to get her hind legs organised and struggled to her feet.

'I'm going to try and walk her,' announced Christine.

She gave the rope a tug and Eltje took a starting step towards her and then pulled towards the waterer.

Understandable. She's covered in sweat. Must be quite dehydrated.

'Stop her!' Stephen half shouted. 'It's the fucking water. It's not something they ate. It's gotta be the water.'

'You are kidding me.'

'No, I'm not. What else could it be?' He reached for his phone and started making a call.

'Hey, what are you doing, get a rope and see if you can get Allie up.'

'Second priority. If it is the water the horse can wait a couple of minutes. Think who else might have drunk it or who might be about to.'

In the event Stephen's good guess and quick action saved a good many people from taking a trip they had not been planning to take that morning.

Chapter 36

Once Stephen had gotten the word out, the cleanup, although urgent, was reasonably easy, with Gerry, his people, and the power plant maintenance team roused from their beds doing the work.

Gerry was first to the water treatment plant and found the gate unlocked, the padlock lying in the grass. Neither it nor the lock on the shed were damaged, so he concluded whoever had done the presumed deed had a company key. Moreover, that the padlock had been removed seemed to confirm Stephen's conclusion that someone had tampered with the water supply, and that was what had poisoned the horses.

Canaries in the coalmine. Lucky.

The maintenance man with him turned off the two distribution valves that supplied water to the plant and the village, and opened the dump valve that released the water in the tank to allow it to surge down the hill. It was presumed that it would be sufficiently diluted or absorbed into the ground before it seeped into the river, and whatever was in it would not have any further effect on anything, or more importantly anybody. It would not be closed until the tank was empty and flushed. In the meantime, every company phone was rung and then every door in the village doorknocked. The lowest tap in every building was turned full on.

Down by the bridge a search found a service valve long since forgotten, and this was opened to drain the system at its lowest point.

In the meantime, a meeting was convened at Perdition.

Chapter 37

Peter, Lyn, Gerry, Stephen and Christine were eating an ad hoc breakfast, with an interested Mrs Scott for once listening in to what was going on.

Everyone congratulated Stephen and Christine for taking action in time, and for their horses' escape.

'I have a surprise for you,' announced Christine, holding up a paper bag. 'Before the pipes were opened I went home and grabbed a cup and ladled some of the water into a plastic container.'

She extracted it from the paper bag and placed it onto the table between them all, but then put it back in the bag.

'My knowledge of chemistry is basic, but I do know that light can affect chemicals, so I suggest it stays in the bag until we can get it somewhere that can tell us what's in it.'

'Better still,' said Mrs Scott from the sideboard, 'I'll get a clean thermos. I don't know if temperature would affect it, but it can be in something more secure than that.' She nursed the sample out to the kitchen and brought it back decanted into a little black thermos flask.

'So, Chris, environmental expert and former paramedic, who do we send it to?' asked Lyn.

'I can answer that,' said Peter, 'and I think Chris who was at the Deloraine inquest with me will back me up. No lab that's generally available, even to the police, at least at short notice. It may have to go overseas.'

'True,' confirmed Christine. 'If you are thinking what I'm thinking.'

'I'll make a call. You lot keep going. By the way you guys, quick thinking both of you. We're all in your debt. You realise you may have saved lives this morning, don't you?'

Stephen explained that one of their shared domestic duties was to make the morning coffee and, in anticipation of his waking first, he had filled both their electric kettle and their pod machine the night before. 'I do both because the pod machine can play up,' he said. 'Some days we have to have instant. The pod machine has to be flushed regularly or it blocks up the little tubes on the delivery side of the pod.'

While the explanation from Stephen about Christine and his domestic arrangements was clear, and the table did seem to feel that it was somewhat irrelevant, it did give them some time to think over Peter's remark and consider just how much risk there might have been lying wait for them in the water supply that morning.

'Well thank you for that, Stephen,' said Lyn. 'Very informative.'

Gerry reported factually what he had found, and no one argued about who to blame. While the evidence was circumstantial, there was a lot of it.

Christine and Stephen spoke openly of their suspicions about the death of Angelique Deloraine for the first time. Gerry was quizzed about the availability of a company key to the prime suspect. The key in question on issue was apparently coded O for orange, which explained why it could have been used to go through both the gate and the door.

While he was talking, Anne Clare joined them.

'Why did she still have a key?' she demanded to know.

'Well not only did she need a company key to access the houses used by Vision, but we let her keep an orange one so she could render first aid at the medical centre if necessary,' replied Lyn. 'An error in retrospect but who was to even guess?'

Gerry was dispatched to retrieve the key with the message for its holder that she should not leave her house, for her own safety because a lot of people were very angry, and that whether the police were to be called was still under debate.

Christine reported that the horses seemed to be recovering, albeit slowly.

'I filled buckets for them from the river,' she said. 'We'll keep that up until we get the all clear.'

Peter was off his mobile. 'Sorry for the delay, but things are being organised for that sample to be picked up. I know someone in the pharmaceutical industry.'

'So how long before we know what's in it?' asked Lyn. 'A couple of weeks?'

'I hate to tell you this, but my best guess would be two months if they can do it locally, or six if it's got to go to the US.'

'Jesus!'

'You should have heard the evidence at the inquest,' said Christine. 'It's not that easy with some of these things.'

'Complex organic molecules,' added Peter, suddenly sounding authoritative. 'We are into the realms of infrared spectroscopy, mass spectrometry, and nuclear magnetic resonance spectroscopy.' He laughed. 'Sorry about that. The inquest got me interested.' He waved his hand breezily. 'Just basic stuff.'

'Stephen,' asked Lyn, 'would you go for a walk around the place and talk to the maintenance people and see what the situation is and come back and let us know please? Start at the plant will you. I'm asking you since you can access all areas there pretty well. Then come back through town and see what's happening.'

'Sure. You OK?' he asked Christine.

'No problem,' she said, and he gathered up his phone and left.

'My understanding would be that thanks to the early warning, we can assume that unless someone else was out and about early there is less likelihood of stuff in the house systems, or even in the plant drinking supply,' said Lyn somewhat hopefully.

'There's always the early morning visit to the loo,' Christine reminded her.

'But even that would only have brought it into the mains surely.'

Peter's phone rang again. He answered it. 'Yes Anne. OK … and you are happy with that advice? … I see. Have you told them to do that then? … Good, thank you. Let us know what's happening, will you?'

He reported back to the table. 'As you know, we have some serious water guys on the staff in the plant and they pulled out the plans for the reticulation and did some calculations. Erring well on the side of caution, they suggest we should flush the mains twice from the treatment plant and then do a house-by-house. She's got them writing up instructions for each householder for distribution and the maintenance people have been told what to do.'

'How long is that going to take?' asked Lyn.

'Haven't a clue,' said Peter. 'I suppose Stephen can give us some feedback from the field when he comes back.'

Mrs Scott appeared with a tray of tea and coffee, and Lyn looked at her.

Seriously?

'Don't get your knickers in a twist, people,' she said cheerfully. 'We'll be out of mineral water and soda water by lunchtime, but this stuff is straight out of the bottle. I've got cakes and biscuits on their way, and they were made in the last couple of days.'

A few minutes later they were tucking in when Gerry reappeared.

He threw a key onto the table and headed for the coffee. No one saw any urgency in getting his story once they knew he had retrieved the key. His explanation could wait for five minutes.

Hot blueberry muffins appeared in the magical hands of Mrs Scott.

'I have a reserve in the freezer. They're microwaved. Sorry about that.'

'Don't be sorry, Mrs Scott, please,' said Lyn. 'Now Gerry, what's the story?

'I know a liar when I see one and that woman is lying. I've been lied to by some of the best in my time and she is no expert. Her eyes won't meet yours when she speaks to you.'

'So she denied putting whatever it was into the water?' asked Peter.

'Sure did. Didn't know anything about anything until she got the text this morning and then one of Chris's maintenance crew came to the door and told her what to do.'

'And she gave up the key without any trouble?'

'No problem at all, Mr Main. No trouble at all. But she was seeing her guests off on the morning bus. Given the situation I think she sent them home, or they had decided to leave of their own accord. It would have been embarrassing if she had put up a fight. I did tell her I would get her a key for the houses in front of them, no choice.'

'That's OK. You had to do that.'

'She is frightened though. She knows we know, whether she wants to admit to it or not.'

'Alright,' said Peter. 'We'll have to do some thinking. Thanks Gerry, we'll let you know if we need you again.'

Just as Gerry left to go, the front doorbell rang and Peter called after him. 'I'll come down with you and get that. I'm expecting someone.'

After they had left the room the meeting moved into a working lunch. For once Mrs Scott joined them, at Lyn's invitation.

'Look', said Christine, 'I know most of you know Margaret and I have some history, but fuck it, Stephen and I live closer to the treatment plant than even the horses. It's just sheer bloody luck he and I were not dead before the horses even drank the water. They've got a lot more body weight than us too.'

As she was making her statement Peter came back in with Benedict Tarleton in tow.

'Morning, people. I'm here to pick up your mysterious sample,' he announced. 'I got here as quick as I could. We all know that speed signs and white lines down the middle of the road are optional for Tasmanians.' He grinned. 'I brought the other stuff you wanted on mushrooms by the way, Peter. So, are you going to call the cops?'

'I think we need to talk about that,' said Peter. 'Our Margaret Pursehouse has to go, but the question is how.'

'Food first,' suggested Mrs Scott, and the meeting broke up while everyone adjourned to the kitchen to lend her a hand. With food on the table, in their hand, and then in their mouths people moved around and options were put up, knocked down, argued over and a consensus developed. No one put forward the whole of the parts, but each had their input into what became a plan.

'Morally we'll be doing what is best for the greatest number of people,' remarked Lyn. 'I don't think we could stop her otherwise. She probably wouldn't stop what she's doing even if we move her on. To allow her to do that would be inconceivable.'

'Biblical solution,' said Christine, well satisfied.

'More Kant and/or Utilitarianism,' responded Lyn. 'I can lend you some reading.'

'I'll skip the philosophy, I think,' replied Christine. *Let the punishment fit the crimes.*

Peter rang Gerry. 'Have you given Margaret her new key yet? … No, well, good. Tell her she is required at a meeting here at the house at 11 am tomorrow when you do. It's not a request. Her presence is commanded.'

'I'd better get going,' said Tarleton. 'I'll just make a couple calls and get things organised and come straight back. See you later tonight.'

'I'll have your bed made up,' said a cheerful Mrs Scott. It was all working out rather well. Given all the circumstances, she had no qualms about seeing the back of Margaret Pursehouse.

Chapter 38

Margaret wished she had driven the short distance from the Wellness Centre to Perdition.

The rain started sheeting down as she got to the bottom of the drive, and it was a long walk up the slope in the downpour. Typically, it looked like it was going to set in for the rest of the day. She had thought to get her fears about what was going to happen out of her system with the exercise. Of course she was apprehensive, although to her all the actions she had taken were fully justified.

For he makes his sun rise on the evil and on the good, and sends rain on the righteous and on the unrighteous. Matthew Chapter 5.

Lyn Main opened the door to her and was friendly enough as she helped her take off her shoulder bag and then her coat. There was nothing she could appropriately do with her wet hair, so she followed Lyn in something of a bedraggled state with her shoulder bag held under her armpit into the big open plan living/dining room and sat in the chair offered to her.

Peter Main and another man were already seated. That pseudo-woman Christine was also at the table. Margaret noted Peter Main had the courtesy to stand as she came to the table. *I must look like a drowned rat.* The other man didn't rise, he just watched her. She looked at his face and into his eyes and could detect a hardness but also a disinterest. There would be no sympathy from that quarter – no sympathy at all. *He might be police.*

Apart from a computer in front of him, another in front of Lyn, and a couple of sheets of paper and a pen in front of Peter, the only other things on the table were a teapot in a cosy and the makings for a convenient cup. Peter, it seemed, had just finished playing mother for the others at the table.

'Make yourself a cup, Margaret, warm yourself up. The water is bottled water,' said Lyn. 'Peter says you take sugar so help yourself how you prefer it.'

As an act of defiance as much as from a need for warm refreshment, she did so. Given the purpose of the meeting she put two spoonsful of sugar in what was a relatively small teacup. Peter opened the meeting with a statement.

'Margaret, this is what is going to happen,' he said. 'Mr Tarleton here is going to buy your lease to the two houses that make up the Wellness Centre and his occupancy will start immediately. He, and the people who will be waiting to take over when you get back down there, will allow you time to pack your personal things and leave – for good. I don't want to see you back at Mordbury – ever.'

'But don't I get a chance to say something?'

'No! You can leave or we can call the police; and before you say it the evidence is indeed circumstantial at this stage. But Chris and Stephen might suddenly be motivated to firm up their view that you were the third person to visit Angelique Deloraine in the early morning on what soon after turned out to be her last day. Your colleague Lachlan Tan might start some official enquiries about what you have been doing at work. Christine might accuse you of almost killing her two valuable horses this morning, I might accuse you of trespass at the water treatment plant, and I'm sure there's an offence somewhere about deliberately polluting a public water supply, and there's certainly something about attempted mass poisoning. Then there's the theft of the notebooks that you stole when you first came here and anything else you might have done with the information in them.'

'We kept a sample of what was in the water, Margaret. It's being analysed. I think you'll be locked up for ever, don't you?' said Lyn. 'Don't bother answering, it's a rhetorical question.'

'But—'

'Stop saying 'but' please, Margaret,' said Peter. 'In return for the purchase of the lease, Mr Tarleton will immediately give you the sum of two hundred and fifty thousand dollars in cash. If you bank it, it's your problem. You may risk not doing so. His company will show the amount as a purchase of the lease so you should pay tax on it, but that's down to your advisers to work out.'

He slid a piece of paper over to her with the pen he had next to him.

'Sign this and Lyn will make a copy of it for you. There is nothing in it—'

'Like a confession to a murder and the attempted poisoning of a community,' interrupted Christine, only to be frowned at into silence by Lyn.

'—To cause you concern. It simply says you have sold the lease to Mr Tarleton's company.'

'Which is?' Margaret asked.

'It's there on the paper, Margaret: Arcadia Pharmaceuticals.'

'Proudly from the great state of California,' Mr Tarleton interjected in his soft American burr.

'They are going to make money out of my work, aren't they?'

'Well not exactly,' said Lyn. 'We all are with any luck.'

'You may hear more of a company in due course called Arcadia and Lucifer Proprietary Limited,' said Christine. 'I have a ten percent shareholding in it.'

'A payoff for keeping quiet about what you think you know,' grumbled Margaret.

'If you want to put it that way, yes,' spat out Christine. 'From where we stand you are a killer and a terrorist, and after the way to treated me you should be grateful it's not actually costing you more. If I had my say—'

'Now ladies,' interrupted Peter, 'back to your corners. Chris, you promised.'

Lyn pointed at Christine, waggled her finger at her, and looked at her sternly from underneath her eyebrows.

All around the table they watched as Margaret read the paper in front of her and apparently could find nothing that especially disturbed her. There was nothing for her to find. It was simple, just a receipt for the money for the sale of the lease. She finished her tea and signed the paper. Lyn took it from her, inspected her signature and left the table, returning shortly with a copy of it and a wad of cash. She handed both over.

'Count it if you like, it's all there.'

Margaret retained her dignity by not counting the money, and put it and the copy of the receipt into her bag.

'So that's it?'

'That's it,' said Peter. 'Go today. If you are still on the property at noon tomorrow, we will have you removed.'

Christine was surprisingly conciliatory.

'Look,' she said, 'you can't walk back in this rain, why don't you let me drive you back. I've got a company ute down below and I can take you. It's on my way.' And she actually smiled as if all was now forgiven.

Margaret, suddenly tired in defeat, agreed; and Christine led her down the internal staircase into the capacious garage below the house. She found she was feeling even more tired, bordering on exhaustion, when they neared the ute with its company logos on the side.

I must be stressed out emotionally.

Christine opened the passenger side door, which Margaret thought very courteous before she staggered one step backwards and everything went black.

Christine checked for a pulse and found none at Margaret's wrist. She double-checked and could find no carotid pulse either.

That was a bit quicker than expected. Nothing like a dose of your own medicine.

The fungal extract provided by Benedict Tarleton had been in the sugar.

She stripped the body of all its clothing where it lay on the concrete floor. She reflected that it had been a long time since she had seen more than just a photograph of a totally naked woman in the flesh, and she could not resist comparing what she knew of her own conformation with what was in front of her. She felt she had nothing to complain about and found that gratifying especially as prejudice told her that Margaret was probably a virgin.

She undid the tonneau cover on the back of the ute to reveal it half-full of chipped pine from the company stock of mulching material, and she put on the work gloves she had left on top of the pile. The chipped pine would be subsequently distributed around the site and would limit the amount of Margaret Pursehouse DNA from contact with or leaking fluids in the ute, which would be thoroughly washed anyway.

She had rehearsed her next moves several times in her mind.

She unceremoniously lifted Margaret's corpse from behind firstly to lean front-facing against the side of the utility back, its arms over the lip and breasts drooping unsupported, and then quickly grabbed the ankles of her erstwhile tormentor. She lifted the bottom half of the body and swung it around as she moved to the back of the vehicle, letting gravity roll it fully in. She then put the gloves back in after it and secured the tonneau.

As she did so Lyn appeared from the bottom of the stairs.

'All done?' she asked as she retrieved Margaret's bag and the cash that was in it.

'Yes. Are you right with the clothing and the bag?'

'Fine. Mrs Scott is doing the washing up by hand and then again in the dishwasher.' She smiled. 'We wouldn't want anything to hurt anyone else, would we?'

'So, the clothing …?'

'We'll pack up the houses tomorrow morning and the stuff we don't burn will be an after-hours anonymous donation to Vinnies. I'm sure that would have been in line with Margaret's wishes.'

Christine laughed.

'Benedict will take her car away tonight.'

'OK. I'm going to drive this up to the mill and Stephen will take over from there.'

'As per the plan.'

'As per the plan!'

Chapter 39

It was evening and Stephen Banbury was slowly negotiating his way up the hill on the back track past the water treatment plant to the greenhouse site in a company ute with a body in it.

Driving carefully was taking up only half his concentration even though he had no lights on, and he was mulling over what had put him in the position he was now in. He had the driver's side window open, and the sounds and smells of the night pervaded the cab. The screams of at least a pair of devils arguing over carrion punctuated the overall calm, and he mused that leaving what was in the back of the vehicle to their tender mercies was an option that had been considered, but the choice had fallen for a more secure, certain and complete method of disposal.

The vehicle itself was almost silent, being electric, but its wheels cracked the odd twig and its suspension wheezed as it absorbed the unevenness of the track. Stephen was reminded of the old American joke: A friend won't tell the cops about the murder you committed; a very good friend will help you dispose of the body. So, he had gone from a young electrical engineer to the partner of a trans woman and embryonic horse stud owner, to an accomplice to a murder, all in three short years. His mind looked for sense in it and could find no logic. In a way things had just followed one after the other.

Shit happens.

He had occasionally worked on the greenhouse site, although the principal activity had been structural rather than electrical engineering, and he was more than just familiar with the layout. Once he had the utility on the flat, he drove a little faster and reached the piles of sand that were destined for loading into the giant silo-like cylinders that rose six metres above him.

He had come up with the idea and had suggested it because he was a fan of Tom Sharpe novels, and the idea of making use of a sand battery that would remain sealed for years resonated with the experience of Henry Wilt and his drunken efforts to bury a blow-up sex doll in a pile hole. However, Stephen was cold sober and a lot more skilled than a drunk Henry Wilt in the use of machinery. He knew the Number 2 battery was half full. He knew the loading hopper was full. He had personally checked on the switch gear that afternoon on the pretext of a routine inspection. Peter had assured him that he had been unable to hear the electric conveyor system working in the security office when he had casually called in earlier. There was no way it could be heard in the plant itself.

Stephen was young and strong and had no difficulty getting Margaret's corpse out of the ute, although getting her onto the bottom of the conveyor belt around the hopper feed was a little more tricky. However, with the remains and the gloves his wife had used in place, he started the conveyor and watched as the body, nestled in the concave profile of the belt, steadily rose and then flipped over the end into the internals of the battery to find a resting place somewhere between the heat exchanger pipes therein. Allowing the conveyor to continue to run, he opened the hopper feed, and sand filled the belt at the required speed to fall, in its turn, into the void. He let it run for a good fifteen minutes to make sure that even if someone did inspect the internals of the battery in the morning, nothing would look out of place.

Rest in peace, Margaret Pursehouse.

The only possible anomaly the construction crew might spot was the half-empty hopper, but they would probably put that down to someone wanting to quit the worksite before seeing it full the previous afternoon, or that it had settled. There was no doubt in his mind that in decades to come when the battery might be dismantled, even though it was not a high-temperature installation, the mortal remains of Margaret Pursehouse would have been toasted, dehydrated and fragmented to the point where their components would be almost integrated into the sand that surrounded them.

As he got back into the ute and drove away, he looked at the battery in the mirror and gave their victim some last instructions. *If you were right and we are wrong Margaret, when you reach the afterlife, please ask to speak with whoever is in charge of all of this and have a firm word with them about the human condition.*

Margaret was the one who was wrong, as everyone had reasoned. So, having passed through perdition, her mortal remains continued into a type of immortality as all of us will do, her structure toasting and her cells degrading, the atoms from which she was once assembled becoming available once again for reprocessing in the ongoing cycles that are the trammelling gyre of space time.

About the Author

Paul Frisby was born in England and grew up in Australia. After what he describes as a misspent youth doing everything from working in television to teaching horse riding, working in casinos in the UK, and advertising copywriting, he found a home in the public sector, principally in compliance and performance management related roles. He was a long-serving senior volunteer in the NSW State Emergency Service and a Justice of the Peace in NSW and Queensland. He now lives in Queenstown, Tasmania. Among other vehicles he drives a 1981 Rolls-Royce Silver Spur.